BUTTER WOULDN'T MELT

'So it is true,' he said. 'Well I never.'

'What do you mean?' I asked.

'Never you mind what I mean,' he said, 'just you get those little knickers off, and your skirt. I think I'll have you work bare bottom today. In fact, I think I'll have you work bare bottom every day. Just let me lock the door.'

I hesitated, wondering if I could negotiate, perhaps agreeing to go bare if he promised not to touch me too intimately, or whether I'd only succeed in revealing my darkest fears and encourage him to take advantage. He locked the door twisting a huge iron key in a lock that looked as if it had been in place since the building was first put up.

'Come along, let's have you bare,' he said as he turned again, his tone of voice suggesting he was talking to a not very intelligent child, or a dog.

Again I wondered if I should try to bargain, but decided against it. Struggling not to make faces, I reached up beneath my office skirt, took hold of my knickers and levered them down. He watched, his little piggy eyes bright with pleasure, as I removed my panties and hung them on a peg by the door, alongside his musty old overcoat.

Why not visit Penny's website at
www.pennybirch.com

By the same author:

A TASTE OF AMBER
BAD PENNY
BARE BEHIND
BRAT
DIRTY LAUNDRY
FIT TO BE TIED
IN DISGRACE
IN FOR A PENNY
JODHPURS AND JEANS
NAUGHTY NAUGHTY
NURSE'S ORDERS
KNICKERS AND BOOTS
PEACH
PENNY IN HARNESS
PENNY PIECES
PETTING GIRLS
PLAYTHING
REGIME
TEMPER TANTRUMS
TICKLE TORTURE
TIGHT WHITE COTTON
UNIFORM DOLL
WHEN SHE WAS BAD
TIE AND TEASE
WHAT HAPPENS TO BAD GIRLS
BRUSH STROKES
SLIPPERY WHEN WET

THE INDIGNITIES OF ISABELLE
THE INDISCRETIONS OF ISABELLE
THE INDECENCIES OF ISABELLE
(Writing as Cruella)

BUTTER
WOULDN'T MELT

Penny Birch

This book is a work of fiction.
In real life, make sure you practise safe, sane and consensual sex.

First published in 2007
Nexus
Thames Wharf Studios
Rainville Rd
London W6 9HA

A catalogue record for this book is available from the British Library.
www.nexus-books.com

Typeset by TW Typesetting, Plymouth, Devon

Printed in the UK by CPI Bookmarque, Croydon

The paper used in this book is a natural, recyclable product made from wood grown in sustainable forests. The manufacturing process conforms to the regulations of the country of origin.

ISBN 978 0 352 34120 4

Distributed in the USA by Holtzbrinck Publishers, LLC, 175 Fifth Avenue, New York, NY 10010, USA

nexus Symbols key

 Corporal Punishment

 Female Domination

 Institution

 Medical

 Period Setting

 Restraint/Bondage

 Rubber/Leather

 Spanking

 Transvestism

 Underwear

 Uniforms

One

'So what's it like being spanked, Pippa?'

It's not the sort of question you expect from your little sister, and it took me a moment before I could answer at all.

'How should I know?' I demanded, but I'd already started to blush.

'I know you get it,' she insisted.

I threw a pillow at her, but she dodged it easily and folded her arms across her chest, looking down at me with that stubborn look she always uses when she wants something. She wasn't going to go away until I'd answered her, but I still didn't want to admit it.

'What makes you think so?' I asked, hoping she was only guessing.

'I saw AJ make you bend over her bike when you came home last night,' she answered.

Now my cheeks were really burning, and I was wishing I had something a lot harder than a pillow to throw at her. The little witch had been peeping at me, but I knew I should really be angry with myself and not her. I'd been teasing AJ, and not surprisingly she'd punished me, but I could easily have refused, or at least put it off. Oh no, not me, I'd done as I was told, bending over the bike and sticking my bum out, in full view of the house.

She'd told me to get bare, and like an idiot I'd done it, turning my skirt up and wriggling down my knickers to show my bum to the night so that she could plant a dozen firm smacks across my meat. It had felt good, so good I'd left my knickers down while I'd kissed her good night, confident that at two in the morning everybody would be asleep in bed. I'd been wrong.

'Well?' Jemima demanded.

'It . . . it's just something we do,' I blustered. 'A game.'

'A punishment game?' she asked, all interest. 'Like, when one of you is naughty the other one smacks her bottom?'

'Sort of,' I admitted, fighting down the dreadful compulsion to tell her the truth.

'So what's it like?' she went on.

'Stingy,' I told her, but I knew I couldn't hold it in, not any longer.

I'd wanted to tell her, right from the start really, but I'd always persuaded myself not to. All our lives she'd followed where I'd led, and I'd always liked my role of confident, protective big sister, but now it was different. I'd grown up to be a little pervert, but that's my nature, not hers, and I didn't want to risk corrupting her. Now she knew anyway, and I could only hope she was old enough to make her own decisions, because I wanted to tell her, badly.

'Stingy,' I repeated, 'stingy but nice. AJ's my girlfriend, and she spanks me for fun . . . for pleasure.'

'I thought so,' Jemima answered, thoroughly smug. 'You never really liked boys, did you?'

I just shrugged, unable even to begin to explain my feelings; on other girls, on men, on the whole confusing mess of my sexuality. Jemima came to sit on the end of my bed and began to toy with a string of her hair, her voice soft and sympathetic as she spoke again.

'Are you going to tell Mum and Dad?'

'No.'

'But they're bound to find out.'

Again I could only shrug in response. It wasn't a subject I wanted to talk about, or even think about. Jemima continued to play with her hair, curling the long brown strands around her finger.

'I'd already guessed you were a lesbian,' she said after a pause, 'but I never imagined you'd like to be spanked.'

I gave another embarrassed shrug.

'So, last night,' she went on, 'what did you do to get it?'

'I was teasing her,' I explained.

'To make her spank you?'

'Yes. It's better if I feel I'm being made to give in to it. Only I get it.'

'That's not very fair.'

I couldn't even look at her for embarrassment as I began to explain, but I still felt the most wonderful sense of relief.

'That's just the way it works. I like to be spanked, and she likes to do the spanking, so we make a good couple. It feels right for her to spank me too, because she's so tall and strong, and because she's older than me.'

'She's scary.'

'She turns me on.'

'But ... doesn't it feel bad, being made to take your knickers down like that? Doesn't it make you feel small?'

'Sort of, yes, small and stupid, but being made to feel that way is part of the pleasure, especially when

3

I'm made to show my bare bum. Normally, when she spanks me, she holds me down across her knee and takes my knickers down herself. I feel so helpless, and it's hard to explain why I like it, because it ought to feel awful, but it's so nice, just to be completely under her control, to be bare and know she's going to spank my bottom and that she won't stop until she's done with me, and . . .'

I realised I was babbling and went quiet, my face hot with blushes for my confession, but Jemima merely gave a solemn nod. Maybe she even understood, a little, because I'd expected her to laugh at me. Some of my confidence had begun to return as she spoke again.

'She always gets your bum bare then?'

'Always. It's part of the ritual, for any girl who's going to be spanked to have her knickers taken down. Everybody does it.'

'Everybody?'

I realised my mistake immediately, grimacing as I tried to cover up.

'You know, everybody who's into it. I go on net forums and that sort of thing.'

Again she nodded, apparently accepting my explanation. After all, it was supposed to be the truth, that only AJ got to spank me, and there was no way on earth I was admitting to who had introduced me to my secret pleasure, and still did me occasionally, as I did her.

'Tell me more about what you do with AJ,' Jemima demanded.

I found myself colouring again, but I wanted to tell her.

'Usually it's just like last night,' I told her, 'mainly play really, but special too, something to confirm how we feel for each other, like a kiss. Then there are punishments, which are a lot harder, and longer.'

4

'You let her punish you? What, for real?'

'Yes. It feels right, and it's what I want. It's cathartic too, that means . . .'

'I know what cathartic means, Pippa. I suppose that makes sense, to feel better after a punishment, so long as you've done something wrong. What does she spank you for?'

'Anything she likes. You see, I've given her the right to discipline me as she sees fit, so it might be anything. She's quite strict, and sometimes I know it's just because she wants to do it, but it's always best when I've actually been naughty.'

Jemima giggled, bringing the colour to my cheeks once more, but I went on.

'Last week she spanked me for scuffing her boots – which is a big dyke thing – and she put me over her knee in the kitchen and spanked me with a wooden spoon, bare bottom of course. It hurt like anything, but I felt so good afterwards, even though my bum was red hot . . . no, because my bum was red hot . . .'

Jemima was smiling, the same mischievous little smirk I knew so well. I stopped, blushing again even before she spoke.

'I wish I'd seen that. You must have looked so funny!'

She laughed as she finished and dodged for the door, reaching safety an instant before my hand closed on my second pillow, which was the only missile within easy reach. Her laughter trailed off as she fled down the stairs, no doubt expecting me to follow, but I stayed on my bed, my thoughts as confused as ever. I was glad she'd found out, in a way, because it had hurt to keep a secret from her, and yet I knew there would be drawbacks. She would tease me mercilessly, but I could cope with that. What I couldn't cope with was the thought of her trying to imitate me.

5

I rolled over onto my front, listening to the familiar morning sounds, with which I was no longer involved. It felt strange, after following the same routine for so long, and I even got an involuntary flush of panic as I heard the sound of the bus, worried I'd miss it and be late for school. That set me smiling. There was no more school, never again. I was free, with over a year in front of me before I went up to university, a year to discover myself.

Not that I intended to waste my time. With any luck I would manage to find a work placement with a law firm, allowing me to get ahead of my colleagues before I even arrived at uni. That would mean I'd be earning enough to fulfil my other ambition and buy a motorbike, although that was going to mean facing up to the parents. They didn't like me riding pillion with AJ, despite having no idea about our true relationship, and it wasn't just the danger. To Mum in particular a motorbike represented everything she disliked, and which they'd done their best to keep me away from. Buying my own was not going to be popular.

Fortunately they couldn't stop me, not once I was earning my own money, although it was tempting to keep it at AJ's for the sake of peace and quiet. Then again, AJ would laugh at me, the way she always did when she felt I wasn't standing up to my parents. Possibly she'd even spank me, for being weak, or even something worse, a thought which sent a delicious shiver right through me.

I began to daydream, imagining the conversation, how I would explain what I wanted to AJ. Her mouth would move gradually into a knowing sneer as I spoke, and I'd know what was coming long before she told me I deserved a punishment, filling me with that wonderful sense of utter hopelessness that only comes when I know I'm going to be spanked and there is nothing whatsoever I can do to get out of it. It was always best that way, as a proper punishment. I like teasing her to make her do it, but I far prefer finding myself in trouble and no way out.

My mind began to dwell on the possibilities. Maybe it would be in her room and she'd put me over her knee on the bed, take down my knickers and smack my bottom until I was well and truly contrite, after which she'd put me on my knees and make me lick her pussy. Then again, if we'd been talking motorbikes it might be in her garage, in which case she'd probably put me over the seat of her big black machine for my punishment. Perhaps she'd even make me mount it, after having me strip from the waist down, or nude. Either way my bottom would be fully open to her, with my bumhole showing between my cheeks and my pussy all wet while she spanked me. Her hands would be dirty, making black handprints all over my skin, and when she'd finished she'd use the grease-gun to lubricate my bumhole so that she could slip a screwdriver handle up my bottom. She'd leave me like that too, to think about how ridiculous I looked, mounted on her bike in the nude with a screwdriver sticking out between my smacked cheeks.

I was going to have to play with myself. There was nobody else in the house anyway, so why not? I wanted to do it face down and imagine I'd been spanked, so I quickly lifted my hips to push down my knickers from underneath the old shirt I'd worn to bed before turning up the tail to leave myself bare behind. Just the feel of exposing myself was enough to send a powerful shiver through me, and I knew it wouldn't take long. Parting my knees and lifting my bottom a little more, I imagined myself in the same position over the seat of AJ's bike, legs spread and

7

vulnerable, hiding nothing as she worked my bottom over with her dirty hands.

Everything about it felt good, the cool air on my bare bottom, the tautness of my knickers around my thighs, the subtle feel of my upturned shirt tail on my back, all of it keeping my exposure firmly in mind. I slid a hand back to find pussy, already moist, my lips puffy and swollen, pouting out from between my thighs. My cheeks were open too, my bumhole on show, tempting me to reach back and tickle the tight little knot of flesh until it began to pulse and squirm.

I imagined how the screwdriver handle would feel up my bottom, hard, thick and round, and wondered if being sodomised with a tool counted as losing my anal virginity. It was such a delicious thought it made me squirm, wiggling my bottom as I eased the top joint of my finger into my hole. For a moment my mind slipped, as I wondered how it would feel to have a man insert his penis into the same tight orifice, or even in pussy, taking my true virginity as I posed spanked and spread before him. As always when I thought of men, distaste quickly pushed aside the thrill, and as I began to tease my clitoris my thoughts were back on track, or almost.

My mental image had shifted, to my kitchen spanking of the week before. It had hurt like anything, and left my cheeks marked with dull bruises, but the sense of utter helplessness under so much pain had been overwhelming. I normally take it quite well, fairly well anyway, but not then, not held firmly down across AJ's knee with my bottom stripped as she applied the big wooden spoon to my meat. She'd been mercilessly hard, and I'd wriggled and kicked and squirmed, going into what a certain somebody called a spanking tantrum. Jemima was right, it must have looked funny.

I was on the edge of orgasm, unable to stop myself as my fantasy slipped to where I desperately did not want it to go, imagining that Jemima had really been there, watching as my jeans were pulled down, giggling as my knickers followed and big sister's bottom came bare, laughing openly as the spanking began and I went into my helpless, agonised tantrum. A sob of deep shame escaped my lips, but I couldn't stop myself, and I couldn't get the image out of my head, spanked in front of my little sister . . . spanked bare bottom in front of my little sister . . . spanked bare bottom in front of my little sister and then made to masturbate with a finger up my bumhole, just as I was doing now.

My orgasm came and I cried out in a mixture of ecstasy and overwhelming shame, but I still couldn't stop myself, my mind fixed firmly on the image of my own well-spanked bum with my finger inserted into the little central hole as Jemima laughed at my plight. Not that it was the first time I'd got carried away with a fantasy, but I was left feeling sheepish and distinctly sorry for myself as I went slowly limp, and I stayed lying on the bed with my knickers still down behind for a long time, lost in thought.

I'd put a lot of effort into getting my work placement, writing to dozens of firms and constantly pestering Dad to use his business contacts. Unfortunately I wasn't the only aspiring law student with a clutch of A*s on my CV, and so far I'd had nothing but rejections. Now, as I finally managed to haul myself downstairs after playing with pussy and taking a leisurely bath I found that another two refusals had arrived in the post, which completely spoilt my mood.

There was nothing to do, and I spent the day mooching around the house, until Jemima got back from school, along with Mum, who'd spent the day at Granny's. They picked me up a little, but nothing like as much as when Dad got home. He was grinning from ear to ear as he threw a big white envelope down on the kitchen table.

'I think this might be what you're looking for, Pip,' he told me.

I'd already guessed what it would be, and was tearing the envelope open even as I kissed him in thanks. As I'd hoped, it was a letter from a firm of lawyers, and not just any old lawyers, but a firm in the City of London with a very grand and old-fashioned sounding title – Montague, Montague, Todmorden and Montague – arranged beneath an elaborate gold crest and a foundation date in the mid-nineteenth century.

'How did you manage it?' I asked.

'Contacts,' he replied casually. 'No, seriously, one of the Montagues is the lawyer for the firm who're developing Thames Vista Estate, and they owe me a favour. You have to get through an interview as well, so it's not a foregone conclusion.'

'Thanks anyway,' I answered, already scanning the letter.

They wanted me to come down the very next day, to an address in the Minories, EC3, which sounded very grand indeed. As I let my imagination run that evening I was imagining a stately old house nestled in among the smart office blocks and ancient institutions of the city, quiet and respectable, with only a polished brass plaque to announce their name – Montague, Montague, Todmorden and Montague – four words that were still going around and around in my head as I fell asleep.

Next morning I was up early and through the shower while Jemima was still yawning and dishev-

10

elled in her nightie. I was determined to make a good impression, and had a clear idea of what Montague, Montague, Todmorden and Montague would expect. They were an old firm, and old-fashioned too, so would expect me not only to be smartly turned out, but in a style that reflected their values.

I didn't have to be there until the afternoon, so I badgered Mum into driving me into Henley to buy some new clothes. For once we were largely in agreement on the sort of thing I'd need, and we quickly purchased a set of white blouses, smart black shoes with just an inch of heel, three packs of black stockings and, at her insistence, three packs of plain white knickers and bras to match. I tried to point out that the people who interviewed me weren't going to be seeing my knickers or bra, but got her lecture on dressing properly in return.

That left my suit, and while we both agreed it had to be black I couldn't resist a new style they were showing in Russell's, which not only had a tapered knee-length skirt and a tight-waisted jacket, but also a neat little waistcoat which I felt gave it a daring touch as well as making me look as if I had hips and a bust. Mum said I looked like a boy who'd dressed up in his sister's clothes.

Back at home and inspecting myself in the mirror, I had to admit she was right, but if I looked like a boy then it was a very pretty one. AJ was going to love it, but I brushed my hair out and tied it back in a curly black ponytail instead of the tight bun I'd been planning, which softened the look a little. It was going to have to do anyway as time was getting on and I needed to be at the station in less than half an hour.

I just made it, and spent the journey fidgeting with impatience and adjusting myself as I rehearsed what

I would say to either Todmorden or one of the Montagues. Only when I got to Paddington did I begin to lose a little enthusiasm. The tube was packed, and I found myself wedged in at armpit height among a group of German tourists who seemed to have spent the morning working out and not bothered to shower. The thought of having to repeat the same journey every morning in even thicker crowds was pretty depressing, until it occurred to me that I might be able to use the journey as an excuse to stay with AJ.

She lived in Kingsbury, and came in early every morning to her bike couriers, so I would be able to catch a lift as far as the West End of London and get to work with just a short tube journey. I'd spent the night with her a few times, but actually living in her house would be rather different, and opened up all sorts of exciting possibilities, which kept me smiling as I finished my journey.

I hadn't been to the City for years, but it was as I remembered, the modern mixed in with the ancient, and everything redolent of money. Everywhere I looked people were hurrying from place to place, all of them smartly dressed and about half of them talking into mobile phones. It was hard not to feel a little awed, but the way I'd planned my life I'd be doing the same soon enough, and hopefully earning as much as the best of them, perhaps even as a partner of Montague, Montague, Todmorden and Montague.

By the time I turned into the Minories I'd constructed a wonderful fantasy world, in which I would be a partner before I was out of my twenties, with an office in the top floor of their fine old building, only to have my dreams crumble around me as I searched for the address. The top of the road was much like those I'd already followed, but it quickly changed, first to great low concrete buildings like something from a council estate, and then to dirty red brick where a railway bridge crossed the road in a broad span, with a tiny shop built into the wall. Next to the bridge, and also made of red brick, although perhaps a fraction less dirty, were the offices of Montague, Montague, Todmorden and Montague.

The only part of my mental image that was at all accurate was that the office was old and surrounded by taller, newer structures, only not so much nestled in as loomed over, with a vast concrete and glass building casting the whole area in a somewhat dank shadow. Nor did it look particularly busy or efficient, with the huge black door firmly closed and the windows open against the July heat. A single buddleia had managed to insert itself into the corner beside the railway bridge, to send up long shoots tipped by deep purple flowers nodding lazily in the sun.

I tried to put my disappointment aside, telling myself that they would no doubt be handling all sorts of fascinating cases and that the experience would be far more valuable and interesting than anything I could gain from a firm dealing with financial matters. There was at least a brass plaque, although it looked as if it had last been polished around about the same date the firm had been founded – 1852. I rang the bell and waited, my hands folded in my lap and my face frozen in a smile, which had worn off long before the door opened to reveal a man who looked like a lizard.

'Yes?'

'I'm Philippa Bassington-Smyth,' I told him. 'I have an interview.'

'Come right in,' he said, his initial look of perplexity vanishing to be replaced by a toothy smile. 'I'm

Mark, by the way, Mark James. Anything you want to know around here, just come to me.'

'I have to be accepted first.'

'Oh you'll be accepted,' he assured me, pushing open a door. 'Maggie, this is Philippa Bassing . . . er, something double-barrelled, our new trainee.'

Maggie, or Miss Phelps as the sign on her desk read, looked as forbidding as Mark James had been welcoming. She was a thin, middle-aged woman, very precise in her crisp white blouse and with her dull blonde hair wound up in a bun. The look she gave me over the top of her glasses as she turned away from her computer wasn't exactly unfriendly, more irritated, as was the tone of her voice when she spoke.

'Your name is?'

'Philippa Bassington-Smyth.'

She moved back to her computer, frowning as she examined the screen and employed her mouse with brisk, exact motions.

'Catch you later, doll,' Mark James addressed me and he had left.

'You have an appointment at three-thirty,' Miss Phelps said after a while, her tone suggesting that by being twenty minutes early I was making a thorough nuisance of myself.

'I thought it best to arrive a little early,' I began but trailed off as she reached for the telephone on her desk.

I waited as she spoke into the receiver, and was surprised to see her irritable scowl suddenly soften as whoever was on the other end replied to her statement that I had arrived. When she put the phone down again she was positively beaming.

'Mr Montague and Mr Todmorden will see you now,' she said. 'if you would like to go up. Second floor, the front office.'

Thanking her, I quickly climbed the stairs, telling myself that the worn state of the ancient wine red carpet was a sign of reserve rather than merely slovenly. There was no mistaking the room she meant, with a set of double doors open on the second-floor landing and two men visible at a huge desk within. I knocked anyway, smiling as I quickly took in my surroundings.

The office was comfortably furnished, if a bit shabby, painted in foxy brown and magnolia with paintings and photographs decorating the walls, while a sign in the middle of the desk allowed me to identify Mr Montague, presumably the senior partner. He was tall, almost military in his bearing, and somehow managed to look stern and benevolent at the same time, for once absolutely in keeping with my original image. Mr Todmorden was very different, a squat, heavy-set man with a roll of reddish fat escaping from around his collar, while his smile of greeting was pretty much a leer. He was going bald, and had combed some strands of greasy-looking hair across the top of his head in a futile effort to hide the fact. Both rose to greet me, Mr Montague extending his hand.

'Ah, Philippa,' he said, 'a pleasure to meet you. We've heard a lot about you.'

'Nothing bad, I hope?' I joked, not at all sure why he would have heard anything about me at all, beyond my desire to spend my year off working as a trainee in a law firm.

'Not at all,' he chuckled. 'You come highly recommended. Indeed, I believe Morris is a little jealous.'

I had no idea who Morris was, but it didn't seem advisable to ask and risk making a fool of myself. There was a chair in front of the desk, to which Mr Todmorden was gesticulating, so I sat down on it, smiling and wishing every detail of what I'd learnt in the last two years hadn't abruptly left my head. I did at least have my CV, which I passed across. Mr Montague took it, but only gave the top sheet a cursory glance before speaking once again.

'Your qualifications are, of course, not in question. When can you start?'

'Immediately, if you like,' I answered, astonished at what seemed such ready acceptance.

'I don't think we need be quite that precipitant,' Mr Montague replied. 'Monday morning should do very well, don't you think, Lucius?'

Mr Todmorden nodded his agreement. I seemed to be in, without having to answer a single question, which just went to show that's it's not what you know, but who you know. Naturally I would have preferred to get in on my own merits, but if that was the way it worked then only an idiot would have protested.

'You'll be assigned to general duties at first,' Mr Montague was saying, 'filing and so forth, but I'll make sure you have plenty of opportunity for work experience. For the moment, I'll get somebody to show you around. Not one of us, of course.'

'Of course,' I answered hastily. 'I wouldn't dream of taking up your valuable time.'

'I mean to say, not one of us,' he repeated, now emphasising the final word.

'Um . . . no,' I managed, thoroughly confused.

'There are, in fact, only four of us,' he went on, 'Lucius and myself, my secretary, Helen Stevens, and Maggie, Miss Phelps that is, our clerk. From what Morris tells me you will find Maggie particularly gratifying.'

I nodded, now completely lost. He had pressed a button on his desk, and spoke briefly into a microphone. Before I could ask any questions a young woman had appeared.

'My secretary, Helen,' Mr Montague explained. 'Helen, this is Miss Bassington-Smyth, who'll be joining us as a trainee, if you would be so kind as to find somebody to show her around.'

'Certainly, Mr Montague,' she replied.

'Thank you,' I said, trying to address all three of them at once as I stood up.

'My pleasure, I assure you,' Mr Todmorden answered me. 'I look forward to seeing you on the Monday, unless of course you'll be there on Saturday night?'

'Um . . . no, I don't think so,' I answered.

'A pity,' he said, 'but another time, no doubt.'

The interview was obviously over, and I'd been accepted.

I was so astonished I barely heard what Helen Stevens was saying as she led me out onto the landing, and I had to make myself focus on her words.

'. . . you'll like it here,' she was saying. 'We're very informal, although of course you must dress the part for the sake of the clients. The partners' offices are on this floor, and my own. There's Mr Montague, and Mr Todmorden, and young Mr Montague, Mr Montague's nephew.'

'Aren't there three Montagues?' I asked.

'Oh no,' she said, smiling and nodding towards an open door as we approached it. 'Old Mr Montague, who was young Mr Montague's father, died several years ago. Mr Montague, meet Philippa Bassington-Smyth, our new trainee.'

There were altogether too many Mr Montagues for me, but the man she was introducing me to was obviously the young one. He was very much like his uncle, tall and straight with a handsome, clean-cut face, but with jet-black hair and a fresh, almost boyish look despite being maybe thirty-five or forty. My smile was returned with a knowing grin, and as soon as we were out of earshot Helen Stevens spoke again.

'Watch out for that one. He's a bit of a wolf.'

I'd already guessed, but thanked her for the warning. She was going to go down the stairs, but Mark James appeared coming up them, speaking immediately.

'Showing the new girl around, Helen? Let me do that. I'm sure you have something to type or whatever.'

Helen Stevens made no protest, but I was quickly hustled off, back up the stairs to the third floor, which was entirely occupied by a large, open-plan office in which half a dozen men and women of assorted ages were seated at their desks while the walls were lined with ceiling-high bookcases and ranks of files.

'Hi guys,' he greeted them. 'This is the new girl, Philippa Double-Barrel. Say hi to the Blockhouse, Philippa.'

'Call me Pippa, please,' I answered, trying not to blush as every head in the room turned to me.

'Pippa it is,' Mark James assured me and began to make the introductions.

Half-an-hour later I'd completed my tour and even knew where I was going to be working, a tiny cubby hole on the top floor which looked out over the railway with the Tower of London and the Thames beyond. Among the staff, old Mr Montague and Mr Todmorden apparently only worked for a few clients, while young Mr Montague, Richard, was the driving force behind the firm. Most of the actual work was done by the five men and two women in the big office known as the Blockhouse, including Mark James. The first floor was the domain of Miss Phelps and her two juniors, with the library and various utility rooms, while the ground floor contained her office, a big reception room for clients and the kitchen. Downstairs was a shadowy area in which the older records were kept, apparently under the watchful eye of an elderly custodian, Mr Prufrock, who was the only person I wasn't introduced to.

By the time I left my head was whirling with names and faces, while I was elated to have been accepted, and so easily. I immediately rang AJ, hoping she'd be in the office and not out on a job, as despite running her company she insisted on riding as well. She was there and invited me over, promising a congratulatory drink. I took the tube, now indifferent to the crowds although they were thicker than ever with the rush hour already picking up.

Getting out at Tottenham Court Road, I walked up to AJ's office, to find her in conversation on the phone and not looking too happy. I kissed her anyway, quite hard as there was nobody else about, then sat down to wait for her to finish her call. She did so almost immediately, throwing the phone down into its cradle as she spoke.

'Bastard! How dare he!'

'Who was it?' I asked, taken aback by her anger. She may be my girlfriend, but she stills scares me sometimes.

'Morris fucking Rathwell!' she swore. 'Do you know what the bastard wanted?'

'No,' I admitted.

'He wanted me to come to one of his parties,' she spat. 'Me! God I'd like to kick the little shit right in the balls.'

I didn't answer, because I knew who she was talking about, and a horrible suspicion dawned on

19

me. Morris Rathwell was a notorious pervert who ran spanking clubs for dirty old men, with girls provided for spanking and worse, and if he'd tried to invite AJ it explained why she was so angry. Mr Montague had also mentioned somebody called Morris, as if I should know him, although how the two could be connected I couldn't imagine. Yet Mr Todmorden had asked if I was going to the party on Saturday, and it was all too easy to imagine him getting off on spanking young girls, or any girls for that matter.

'Is the party on Saturday?' I asked.

'You keep well away from that party, Moppet,' she warned. 'I've told you about Rathwell.'

'I don't want to go,' I reassured her, 'but is it on Saturday?'

'Yes,' she answered, 'but there's some big club on too and he's short on girls, so he asked me, when he knows full well I would never go to play his dirty little games, the bastard. Come here, Moppet.'

'What are you going to do?' I asked, a little uncertain.

'Just come here,' she insisted.

I came, holding my arms out to hug her, which I hoped was what she needed, only to be snatched by the wrist and hauled across her knee, my raised bum towards the door as she began to fiddle with my skirt.

'AJ! Not here, someone might see!'

'Sorry, sweetness, I have to take it out on somebody.'

'Yes, AJ, but . . .'

My words broke off in a squeak of shock as my brand new skirt was jerked up over my bottom, exposing the seat of my knickers, on which she laid a single hard smack before hooking her thumb into my waistband. I knew my knickers were coming down. They always do, and I was helpless to prevent it, but that didn't stop me babbling pitifully as they were drawn slowly down over my cheeks.

'No, AJ, not bare, please, not in the office. What if somebody came in? Oh, please, no . . . no . . .'

It was too late. My knickers were down, inverted around my thighs to leave my bum showing bare behind me, so that anybody who walked through the door would get a prime view of my spanking. It would only be one of her riders, most of whom were hardcore dykes anyway and would only think it was funny, but that didn't do a great deal to quell my sense of embarrassment as AJ set to work on my bottom. She had me tight around the waist, holding me firmly in place as she spanked me, and she was laying on the smacks so hard that I was rapidly losing control of myself to the pain anyway, but that wasn't what made me so helpless. I can never resist her, however humiliating the circumstances, because just to be with her makes me go weak, never mind to be held down over her knee for what I've come to crave more than anything – a good, hard spanking.

I was getting it too, my bottom already on fire as the slaps rained down on my cheeks, with my legs kicking and my thighs pumping in my knickers, my body wriggling in an entirely instinctive and entirely useless effort to escape the pain, and in doing so showing off both pussy and bumhole behind. Not that I could help it, because it hurt too much, but it really was not the view I'd have chosen to present to the huge, bearded motorbike courier who walked in at the door without bothering to announce himself.

'Don't you ever fucking knock?' AJ demanded, and released her grip.

My face felt as hot as my bottom as I jumped up, torn between the need to cover up and to clutch at my poor spanked cheeks. Modesty got the better of me and I tugged my knickers up and adjusted my skirt, all so fast that the biker was still standing in the doorway gaping like a fish by the time I'd made myself decent. He'd seen me spanked, he'd probably seen pussy and my bottom hole, but there was nowhere to run to, and I was forced to stand there with my face the colour of a ripe cherry as AJ spoke again.

'What is it?'

'I've done the Transglobe job,' he managed. 'Can I knock off now?'

'Fuck off,' AJ told him, 'and next time, knock. Couldn't you hear I was spanking my tart?'

His face went as red as mine felt, and he left without saying another word. AJ shook her spanking hand, which was quite red too, and blew her breath out before speaking again.

'That's better. Now why don't you lock the door and do what you're best at?'

I knew exactly what she meant, and managed a weak nod in reply. My fingers were shaking as I fastened the catch on the door, and I gave a nervous glance to the window before turning to her once more. She was ready for me, her chair pushed back from the desk even further than when she'd spanked me, her leathers and thong pushed down, her long, lean thighs spread wide. As usual, she was freshly shaved, showing off the tangled barbed wire design tattooed on her pussy mound and the twin silver rings in her lips. Her hands were folded casually across her belly.

'Make it quick,' she ordered. 'Some of the others will be back soon.'

My cheeks had coloured up again at the thought of licking her while her riders waited outside. If it was the girls, they'd know what I'd been doing, an almost painfully embarrassing thought, but it didn't stop me going down on my knees in front of AJ. I could smell her immediately, leather and pussy and a touch of petrol, helping to bring up my excitement as I crawled quickly forward and buried my face in her sex.

'That's my Moppet,' she said, taking me by the ponytail and pulling me firmly in.

I was trapped against her sex, licking eagerly enough but knowing I wouldn't be let go until I'd finished my task whether I was eager or not. It was what I did, part of my duties, to lick pussy when and where I was told, which made it a thousand times more arousing that if I'd only done it when we were in bed and playing anyway. She was wet too, even before I got busy with my tongue, turned on by spanking me, just as I was turned on by being spanked.

My knickers were coming back down, even if she was in a hurry, and as I began to explore her pussy I'd quickly levered them off over my bottom and tugged my skirt up, once more baring my hot rear meat to the air. She gave a low, throaty chuckle as she saw what I was doing and called me a tart as my finger found the mushy, sensitive groove between my sex lips.

I thought of what she'd done to me, whipping me across her knee for an impromptu spanking just because she was cross with Morris Rathwell. It had hurt so much, and felt so shameful, especially when the man had come in, come in to see my bare red bottom bouncing under AJ's hand, my wet, excited pussy, my dirty little bottom hole. Maybe he'd even been able to guess that I was a virgin.

For one awful moment I imagined him plunging his cock up me as I licked AJ, but the thought was too scary to hold. I focused on how I'd been spanked

23

instead, how I'd imagined getting it in front of my little sister and how I'd been seen by a man for real. That was going to get me there, but AJ had tightened her grip in my hair, pulling me into her as she spoke.

'That's my girl ... that's my pretty little tart ... That's right, Moppet, lick my cunt and rub your own, you dirty little bitch ...'

She finished with a hiss and her hand twisted my ponytail harder still, hurting me as she came in my face. I kept licking, and I kept rubbing, my own orgasm already rising in my head as I thought of the overwhelming, delicious shame of being spanked in front of somebody else ... the biker, his eyes full of shock as he stared at my blazing, bouncing bottom ... Jem, laughing to see her big sister kick and squirm over another woman's knee ... anybody, and everybody, a huge crowd enjoying my pain and my shame as I was spanked bare for something I hadn't even done, which was the thought I held as I came with my face buried firmly in the wet flesh of AJ's pussy.

Two

The question that occupied my mind for the rest of the week, and the weekend too, was whether the Morris mentioned by Mr Todmorden was Morris Rathwell and, if so, whether the event on Saturday had been the spanking party AJ had been asked to attend. There was nobody to ask, not that I'd have had the nerve anyway, so I found myself brooding over the implications.

Dad definitely wouldn't have been involved, I could be sure of that, but if it was true, and Mr Montague and Mr Todmorden had known that I liked to be spanked, then somewhere between Dad and them my secret had leaked out. Not that they knew all that much, because there's a big difference between allowing my girlfriend to punish me and being willing to accept money to let my knickers down for a load of dirty old men I'd never even met.

All I knew was that the contact had come through Thames Vista Estate, a project Dad was involved with. They were represented by Montague, Montague, Todmorden and Montague, which presumably meant Richard Montague rather than his uncle, but Morris Rathwell had to be involved. The next question was: did Morris Rathwell know I got spanked?

Just thinking about it was enough to bring the blood to my cheeks, but I had to face the fact that he probably did. AJ was completely casual about our relationship and made no secret of the fact that she disciplined me, so she might well have told Morris, or more likely his wife, or one of the other girls who attended the parties. There were other possibilities too, and if he did know, that left a much simpler question: was he involved with Thames Vista Estate in any way?

I could hardly ask Dad, as he was bound to want to know more and the possible consequences didn't bear thinking about. It was embarrassing enough that Jemima knew, never mind my parents. What I could do was have a look on his computer, as he often brought work home, but he was very fussy about it and none of us were even allowed to touch it, let alone search for things. To do what I needed I'd have to be alone for at least an hour, and be absolutely sure I wasn't going to get caught, and I didn't get an opportunity.

By the Monday morning I was feeling distinctly apprehensive, with all sorts of alarming images floating around in my head. What would I do if Mr Montague, or even worse, Mr Todmorden, decided he wanted to spank me and made up some excuse to get me over his knee? I'd refuse, obviously, but it would still be intensely embarrassing, and if they thought I wanted it from them, the whole thing was sure to come out. Possibly my job even relied on me being available for spanking sessions, or worse, in which case when I refused I'd presumably get the sack.

I knew I'd refuse anyway, but it was impossible not to picture myself with my bum in the air across Mr Montague's knee, knickers down and kicking as Mr

Todmorden gloated over my rear view. My scenario also provided a possible explanation of old Mr Montague's curious remark about there being only four of them, and the four had included the clerk, Miss Phelps, and his secretary. Helen was young and pretty and seemed very gentle, even meek, so she presumably got it rather than gave it, but Miss Phelps looked almost as much a natural spanker as AJ.

On the train into London I was formulating a situation in which I accepted that I would be spanked, but only if Miss Phelps was the one to dish it out, with the others watching. After what had happened in AJ's office it was really rather horny, so horny that by the time I got to the office I'd turned myself on so much that I was willing to negotiate for real.

It didn't happen. In fact the day was excruciatingly dull. Miss Phelps showed me up to my top-floor cubby hole and the only even faintly sexual thing I got was a sadistic smile from her as she put an enormous pile of old files down on my desk. They apparently had to be arranged alphabetically, tied into bundles and taken down to Mr Prufrock in the archives. There were plenty more where they'd come from and she expected the job to take me several days.

I got down to work, telling myself it was probably some sort of test, and as I ground my way down the pile, sheet by sheet and file by file. I allowed myself to construct a fantasy around it, in much the same way that I'd always been able to distract myself from even the dullest of times at school. Back then, I'd usually either imagined what it would have been like to be given old-fashioned discipline, a spanking or caning in front of the class, or that one of the teachers I'd had crushes on would take me to bed. Now I imagined the exercise as a way to trick me into taking a punishment, expanding on the fantasy I'd had in the train. Miss Phelps would have arranged it, deliberately giving me the wrong instructions so that there would be a complaint from Mr Prufrock, who I imagined as some sort of grotesque gnome lurking in the basement. I would then be hauled before old Mr Montague and Mr Todmorden, where I would be lectured, put across the clerk's knee, and spanked.

It had been shortly after nine when I started, and by eleven I'd worked my way through a dozen versions of the fantasy and simply couldn't hold myself any longer. Nobody had disturbed me all morning, and the stairs outside creaked badly, so I had no compunction about letting my thighs come apart and easing my skirt up to show off the front of my knickers to the empty room. There was an ancient, cream-painted radiator under the window, and I used it to brace my feet, my legs well spread as I closed my eyes and slipped a hand between my thighs.

I spent a long moment just touching myself through my knickers, running over the fantasy as I felt the soft swell of my pussy lips and the gradually expanding wet patch between them. The original version of my fantasy was best – a plain, old-fashioned bare-bottom spanking from Miss Phelps while the two older men bore witness to my punishment. I focused on it, teasing pussy through my knickers as I played through the details in my mind; the awful moment when I'd be told I was going to get a spanking, the agonising shame as my panties were pulled down and my bottom exposed in front of the watching men, the pain as my meat was smacked up to a glowing pink, my tear-filled ecstasy as I ran to the loo and brought myself to a shivering, gasping climax, which was exactly what I'd now done, without even putting my hand down my knickers.

Tuesday started out much the same as Monday. I'd been trying to persuade Mum to let me stay with AJ, but she hadn't given in yet, so I was still taking the train. AJ had an early call in Bayswater, so gave me a lovely surprise by meeting me at Paddington and taking me to work as her pillion passenger. Montague, Montague, Todmorden and Montague used her courier company, so she knew exactly where to go, and I had the pleasure of dismounting from the bike and kissing her goodbye just as Mark James and two of the other men from the Blockhouse arrived for work. It was just a peck, but it made them stare, which kept me smiling as I went back to my tedious task.

The files were in a complete muddle, so I made a series of piles on the floor, each representing a different letter of the alphabet, which were growing gradually taller as I worked. There seemed to be an endless supply of the things too, and I knew I'd have to finish them before I could be sure I'd got all the letters complete, after which I could take the whole lot down to the archives. Miss Phelps seemed quite impressed by my system and even smiled at me as she left.

An hour and a half later I decided I deserved a break, and that it would be fun to explore the rest of the top floor, which seemed to be empty. I've always been fascinated by old, deserted rooms, ever since Jem and I used to explore Gran's attic when we were children, but Montague, Montague, Todmorden and Montague proved disappointing. The rooms were simply empty, save for a stack of old chairs in one and a box of Christmas decorations in another. I'd been hoping for some evidence of the partners' depravity; perhaps an elephant's foot umbrella-stand well stocked with canes, riding whips and other implements suitable for application to naughty girls' bottoms, or maybe a pillory, or a stool I could be bent over for a whipping.

What I did find was a ghost, or at least that's what my imagination told me would account for the faint voices I could hear in one of the rooms, until common sense got the better of me and I realised it was just people talking in the Blockhouse on the next floor down. That was still interesting, or at least more interesting than filing, and I soon found out how it worked.

There wasn't even a carpet on the floor, just bare planks, grey with age. A large, square hole had been cut out where the radiator had been fitted, and the bright sunlight coming in at the window allowed me to see down it into the space above the false ceiling of the Blockhouse. Kneeling down, I could even make out what they were saying, although it wasn't very interesting, just some of the men discussing a case which involved a dispute over how to calculate the floor area of an office block. It was still fun to listen, just for the sake of eavesdropping, but my knees had quickly begun to get sore when a new voice joined the conversation, also male, and highly excited.

'Would you fuck the new trainee?'

Even as my mouth came open in shock and outrage, one of the others answered him.

'Who wouldn't fuck the new trainee?'

A third agreed.

'I would. She's fucking gorgeous. I love the way her tiny tits stick up in the air, and when she walks it's like watching two cats in a sack.'

A different voice answered him, in a public school drawl I recognised as Clive Carew, the fat boy of the office.

'You're so poetic, Steve. Apple bottom, that's how you describe a girl like her.'

'Apple? More like a peach, and boy would I love to sink my teeth into it.'

'No, if you say a girl's got a peach it means her bum's big and round. Pippa has an apple bottom.'

'I still say it's a peach, maybe not big, but it's certainly round, and juicy, and oh so fuckable.'

'Do you normally go around fucking peaches then?'

'Call it what you like. I aim to fuck it.'

My outrage had been growing at every remark, also my embarrassment, until my fists were clenched in fury and my cheeks burning with blushes, but the final remark really took the prize. It was so arrogant, and insulting too, not merely to imagine that I'd give in to him, but to describe me as 'it', as if I was no more than the sum of my body parts, which was obviously how they thought of me.

I thought of stamping downstairs and confronting them, but I was sure they'd only laugh at me. If I tried to take it further they'd simply deny it all, and it would be the end of my job, so I was forced to clench my teeth and suffer, because I couldn't bring myself to stop listening. They were still talking about me, with the yobbish Den Coles scoffing at whoever had claimed he was going to have me.

'Fat chance, mate!'

'Why not?' the first man answered, aggrieved. 'I'm in with a chance.'

'Why not?' Den sneered. ''cause she's more likely to go with Claire or Gail than any of us, that's why not.'

31

'That I would like to see!' Clive put in.

'No way,' the first man exclaimed against a chorus of laughter as my cheeks burned hotter still.

Gail and Claire were the two female members of the Blockhouse, and obviously not present. I'd only glimpsed them when we were introduced, and neither had made any real impression on me, but the thought of the five men watching while I got off with them was painfully embarrassing. So was Den Coles's response.

'She's a fucking dyke, I tell you, a regular slit licker. Did you see the girl who dropped her off this morning. She looked like something out of Judge Dredd; six foot she was, easy, with piercings all over her face and tattoos right down her arms. That's what Miss Double-Barrel's into, cunt, and rough trade cunt at that.'

'That doesn't mean she won't fuck,' somebody else answered, the one who'd claimed he was going to have me, 'just that she hasn't found out how good it feels to have a cock inside her. She's just waiting for the right man, and that man is me.'

'Sure, Andy, in your dreams!' Den answered, and my mouth came wide once more in fresh outrage.

Andy Wellspring was about five foot four, shorter than me, and in his thirties, with a face like a rat and wispy red hair already going thin on top. If I'd been forced to choose between them, which would have taken a gun to my head, he would have been last on the list, even after Clive, who might have been fat but was nice, at least to my face, and also the tallest of them. Not that the other three were in the least bit appealing. Mark James reminded me more and more of a lizard every time I saw him. Den Coles was tall and quite good looking but an utter yob. Steve Frost would have been the best of them, except for his humiliating description of my breasts and bottom. It was he who spoke next.

'Face it lads, it won't be any of us. Richard'll have her knickers off before the end of the week, any money.'

'Why Richard? Why not me?' Andy demanded.

'Because,' Steve replied, 'Richard is a partner in the firm, looks like Pierce Brosnan, is single and is loaded, while you, my son, are a weedy little bugger with a wife, two kids and a mortgage.'

'Still . . . ,' Andy began, only to be cut off by Den.

'Yeah, I reckon you're right, Steve.'

'I am,' Steve insisted. 'A little thing like her, to him? She's so much cock fodder.'

'Maybe, maybe,' Andy replied, 'but he's going out with that fancy bit from Lloyds, isn't he, so I don't reckon he'll bother with Perky Tits upstairs. I will though, just you watch me go.'

'Not if I get there first, mate,' Den answered him, which led to a buzz of conversation.

It was too muddled for me to follow at all clearly, with all five of them claiming they'd be the first to have me, as if it was a foregone conclusion that I was available, with my lesbianism apparently forgotten or dismissed as unimportant. I was furious, with my head full of ways I could put them down, rejecting their advances in ways that would humiliate them as much as they had humiliated me. Still I was unable to pull myself away, and if I'd thought they'd plumbed the depths of arrogance and crudity, I soon realised I was wrong as Mark James spoke again.

'OK, OK, simmer down lads. I'm running a book on this, right? This is the deal. You can bet post or ante-post. Odds posted each morning. First one to fuck Miss Double-Barrel wins . . .'

'What if she's a virgin?' Clive broke in.

'Who gives a fuck?' Den demanded.

'I mean, if she won't go all the way but does something?'

'What do you care, Clive? It's not going to be you, is it, fat boy?'

'Why not? In fact I feel that she and I have rather more in common than . . .'

'Boys, boys,' Mark James interrupted. 'Let's keep on track here. OK, if she makes you come, it counts, hand-job, blow-job, one up the bum . . .'

'Oh yeah, to stick it right up that sweet little arse,' Steve cut it, 'then to make her give me bum to mouth.'

'You watch too much porno, Steve.'

'There's no such thing as too much porn.'

'What if I just fuck her?' Andy demanded.

'How do you mean?' Clive asked.

'You know,' Andy answered, 'catch her unawares, skirt up, knickers down and up goes the cock.'

'Will you lot shut up?' Mark insisted. 'No coercion, Andy, you bastard. Like I said, if she makes you come, on her own accord, you're the winner, and that doesn't mean wanking off over her, Clive. Only it's graded. If one of you bastards manages to squeeze a sympathy toss out of her I pay out half odds, three-quarters for a blow-job, full odds for a fuck, double if you put it up her bum.'

There was more laughter as I grimaced at the revolting thought of my bottom hole spreading to the head of one of their cocks. Mark was still talking.

'. . . and you've got to be able to prove it, no bullshit claims. These are the ante-post odds; Richard Montague, 3–1; Mark James, 5–1 . . .'

'In your dreams.'

'Shut up. Den Coles, 7–1. Steve Frost, 10–1. Andy Wellspring, 25–1 . . .'

'25–1? What, so you reckon I'm an outsider?'

'If you think the odds are good, put your money where your mouth is.'

'I will.'

'Hang on, I haven't finished. Clive Carew, 50–1. Right, let's see the colour of your money.'

I caught a grunting noise, probably Clive accepting his poor chances, then he spoke.

'How about the others?'

Andy answered him.

'What, old Montague and Lucius Tod?'

'No, I was thinking more of the girls, if she might be a lesbian.'

'Good point, Clive,' Den agreed. 'I'll have fifty on Helen.'

'I can do that,' Mark answered, 'if you want to waste your money. Miss Double-Barrel may be a dyke, but the others aren't.'

'No? Maybe not Helen then, but I reckon Maggie munches muff like Clive goes for the pies.'

'Could be. OK, Maggie is 10–1; and 100–1 the field.'

'How about old Prufrock?'

There was more laughter, fading only gradually as Mark spoke again.

'Fair enough, fair enough, always good to have one for the mug punters. Prufrock is 500–1.'

There was more laughter, and they all began to speak at once as they pressed their money onto Mark. I'd quickly lost the thread of who was doing what, and I no longer really cared. They were betting on me as if I was a horse or a dog, and worse, on which of them would be the first to have sex with me. Mark hadn't even had the decency to offer odds on my refusing all of them, a nasty detail that brought me to the edge of tears.

I walked back to my room thinking black thoughts of revenge, but I knew it was pointless. They would have their little game, and my only satisfaction would be in making sure nobody won the bet. I was sulking badly as I sat down, and spent a long while just staring out of the window at the trains coming and going on the bridge beneath, imagining all five of the men chained to the tracks while AJ and I took bets on who would get run over first.

Only gradually did my anger subside, and as it did a new thought came to me, so disgusting that I immediately forced it away, but so insidious I couldn't make it go away for more than a few seconds. They had no idea I knew about the bet, which gave me the opportunity to make a lot of money, maybe even enough to buy the bike I so badly wanted, just so long as I was prepared to do something dirty with one of them.

It really was truly disgusting, even the thought of taking one of their cocks in my hand and tugging him off. There were other problems too, especially how to place the bet without Mark growing suspicious. After all, I could hardly go up to him and put ten pounds on Steve Frost making me masturbate him, which was about the least repulsive of the options open to me.

Then there was his grading system. Even if I did manage to place my bet, and used as much money as I could get together, maybe £100, unless I did something really filthy I wouldn't get much in the way of return. Steve Frost was ten-to-one, so at half odds I'd earn £500 for masturbating him, nothing like enough for the sort of bike I wanted. At the other extreme, if I let Mr Prufrock stick his cock up my bottom I'd get £100,000.

I ran the figure over in my mind, a huge sum, almost worth it, assuming Mr Prufrock wanted to stick his cock up my bottom. He probably did, or at least, could be persuaded to try. Unfortunately Mark James would definitely be suspicious and refuse to pay out. I had to set my sights on something more realistic, perhaps sucking old Mr Montague's cock, which would earn me £7,500 and might be explained as giving in to my boss. That would work, and it would be very satisfying indeed to make Mark pay out so much money. How bad could it be? A stiffy in my mouth for a few minutes, a salty swallow and it would all be over, maybe after he'd given me a good spanking . . .

The thought of a spanking brought me up short. I was really considering doing it, surrendering my pride and my dignity for the sake of money, effectively whoring myself. It was an awful thought, unbearable, but as I went on with the filing it kept on creeping back, especially how I could manage to place a bet without arousing Mark's suspicions. Finally, I managed to tell myself that it was a purely intellectual exercise but I wouldn't really do it, and got down to working on the problem.

Only the men who shared the Blockhouse could bet, unless it was extended, but in any case nobody was going to tell me and it didn't seem likely they'd tell any other women. If they did, then I could try to make a deal with one of them, perhaps Helen, but it was far more likely I'd have to enlist a man. That meant one of four: Andy, Steve, Den or Clive. Nobody was going to do it for nothing. They either expected a share of the winnings or sexual favours, possibly both. That meant I'd end up handling not one cock but two, even sucking them, which was as far as I was prepared to go . . .

I'd done it again, considering the prospect as something real, and I had to tell myself firmly that it was only theoretical as I went on, considering the four men as animals, which made the thought of handling their cocks easier to cope with. Andy was a rat; small, aggressive, with filthy habits and a bad attitude. Steve was a wolf, or maybe a hyena; sly, cunning, impressive in a way but thoroughly untrustworthy. Den was a dog, an urban mongrel; handsome enough but potentially vicious and utterly ignoble. Clive was a panda; fat and soft and a bit silly, but still powerful physically.

There was really only one choice: Clive. The others simply couldn't be trusted, but he seemed honourable, and he'd been the least brash when they were discussing who was going to have me. His comments on my body hadn't been too bad either, because if AJ had told me I had an apple bottom I'd have been flattered. He also had the best odds, at 50–1, so perhaps I could even make a straight bargain with him and suck his cock. At three-quarter odds, and assuming I got him to put a hundred on and he let me keep the money, that would be £3,750, almost enough.

I was still trying to work out just how much of my pride I'd be prepared to sacrifice when I heard the stairs creak. A moment later Mark James poked his head around the door.

'Hello. How are you getting on?'

'OK, thanks,' I answered, ignoring my desire to throw something at his head.

'Fancy some lunch?'

'It's only just after eleven o'clock.'

'Oh don't worry about that. Only just now Maggie was saying what a fast little worker you are, and she won't notice at all if we nip out of the back.'

'I didn't even know there was a back way out.'

'There's a lot you don't know about this office,' he said, and winked.

That was as much as he knew, and I very nearly turned him down flat, only to reconsider. I didn't want to do anything to arouse his suspicions, after all, and if I suddenly became unfriendly for no obvious reason, it might well do that. Turning down sexual advances was another matter, as surely even an arrogant bastard like him would have to accept that I just wasn't interested. It might even be fun to string him along for a while, just for the satisfaction of turning him down.

'OK,' I told him, using my best schoolgirl voice, 'as long as you're sure I won't get into trouble.'

'That all depends what sort of trouble you mean,' he answered.

I gave him a blank look, pretending I didn't understand.

'We'll go to Champagne Charlie's,' he said. 'It gets crowded, but we should be able to get a table at this time of day.'

'OK,' I said, deciding to play the role of easily led little waif, which I was sure he'd accept.

The top flight of stairs was so narrow we had to go down in single file, me following, and I caught the smug glance he gave to the men who were still in the Blockhouse. Andy returned a look of annoyance and said something to Steve, but I was past the door and didn't catch it. The back door was at the end of a passage where the stairs started down towards Mr Prufrock's retreat. As we passed I caught an odd sound, somewhere between a cough and a grunt, which conjured up an image of him lurking in the dark as he peered up between the banisters in an attempt to see up my skirt.

With a friend I'd have shared the joke, but Mark didn't need any encouragement to talk. He was completely full of words, and full of himself, chatting casually about the skiing holiday he was planning in Val d'Isere and managing to subtly put down all four of his colleagues and Richard Montague as well before we'd even reached Champagne Charlie's.

It was a smart City bar, all chrome and pale, polished wood, with rank upon rank of bottles behind the counter, mostly champagne, but also other wines and spirits. There were several fridges as well, each with four tiers of bottles visible behind glass fronts, carefully arranged according to brand. I told myself it was just another bar, but it was hard not to be impressed, especially by the prices chalked up on a board. Even a bottle of the house champagne cost nearly half what Montague, Montague, Todmorden and Montague were paying me for a week's work. As Mark had predicted, it was still quite empty, but that didn't stop him making a show of clicking his fingers for the waiter.

'Good morning, Mariusz. A bottle of *La Belle Époque*, well chilled.'

The champagne he'd chosen cost some frightening amount, no doubt in an attempt to make me feel obliged to comply when he tried to get sex, but I wasn't going to be so easily led. He took me to a table by the window, looking out across the little square behind our building. Fancy as it was, Champagne Charlie's was built under the same railway that ran past Montague, Montague, Todmorden and Montague, so that everything shook a little every time a train passed overhead.

'The important thing with champagne,' Mark was saying as Mariusz eased the cork free, 'is always to buy a vintage. Otherwise you'll find it's too young and sharp.'

There was a faint pop as the cork came free, allowing a creamy white froth of bubbles to escape

40

the bottle neck and trickle down the sides. Mark winked and grinned, only for his expression to suddenly turn sour. He was facing the window and I turned to look. Andy, Den and Steve were coming towards us.

'Here are the boys,' Mark said with a strained attempt at jollity.

He poured the champagne before they arrived. I took a sip as they clustered around our table, Andy speaking first.

'What a surprise to find you here, Mark. Hi, Pippa, has this old goat been trying to get you in the sack then?'

'I thought . . .,' I began, immediately confused, but Mark stepped in.

'Ignore him, Pippa. You're with me, so you're fine.'

Andy gave a cynical chuckle. I took another sip of champagne, now confident that I was completely safe. Obviously they were going to try to seduce me, but altogether, in a wine bar, they could only hope to get so far. Steve went to the bar to get another bottle and the others sat down, Mark moving quickly to my side so that I had no choice but to sit with his leg pressed to mine or fall off the seat.

They began to drink, laughing and joking among themselves and with me, also trying to flirt. It would have been easy just to relax into it, as none of them were being pushy or particularly obnoxious, but I kept remembering the bet and what they'd said about me, and what they'd like to do to me. Steve in particular was being charming and friendly, enough to bring back my confusion over my sexuality, only this was the man who'd said he would like to make me suck his cock after it had been up my bottom.

I kept that firmly in mind as we finished the first two bottles of champagne and Den Coles ordered

41

another pair. They were trying ever harder to capture my attention, and I knew I was getting drunk, making me worry not so much about what might happen at the wine bar, but afterwards. Den in particular was an unprincipled bastard, and Andy wasn't much better. Maybe they were bad enough to come up to my room in the afternoon and try to make me toss them off, suck them, hold me down over the desk and stuff their erections rudely up me from behind . . .

The thought came with a little erotic shiver, and I pushed it down immediately, cursing myself for my own susceptibility. I do like men, sort of, sometimes, at least to watch, but it's not at all like the way I feel for girls, more a grotesque fascination. Grotesque maybe, but it's a fascination that makes pussy wet, and she was, fuelling my embarrassment as the four of them vied to get me out of my knickers.

I very nearly sent a text to AJ to beg for rescue. She would come, I knew that, but she'd be cross. I'd get punished, and not with a spanking, but with something both dirty and humiliating, one of her specials, which came in infinite variety and could be very hard to take. Instead, I told myself I was safe just so long as I was in the wine bar and there were lots of people around me, so when one o'clock came and I should have gone back I stayed, accepting yet more champagne, which was a mistake. Everybody had bought a bottle now, except me. I couldn't afford it, and they knew that.

'Whose round is it?' Andy queried, as if he didn't know.

'Pippa's,' Den answered, and I found myself digging in my bag to see if I could scrape together enough for a half bottle of the house champagne, only for Mark to come to the rescue, and to take his chance.

His arm had come around my shoulders as he spoke.

'Give the poor girl a break, you mean bastard. How's she supposed to buy a bottle in here on what old Montague's paying her?'

'A round's a round,' Andy pointed out.

'Yeah,' Den agreed, his voice slurred with drink, 'but I'm a fair guy. If she doesn't want to pay up, she can put out instead. How about it, doll?'

I couldn't speak, red-faced and open-mouthed in outrage, but both Mark and Steve quickly jumped to my defence, calling Den a prat and a jerk. Mark's arm pulled tighter around my shoulders.

'Look, it's OK,' I finally managed. 'I think I've got enough for a small bottle . . .'

'No, that's not necessary,' Steve insisted. 'The next one's on me. Come on guys, give the poor girl a chance.'

It was impossible not to feel relief, also protected by the strength of Mark's arm and the warmth of his body. He'd been right to give himself low odds as well, because while he might have been a lizard he knew far more about how to appeal to a woman than either Den or Andy, whose attitude was just plain creepy.

'Get a life, Steve, I was only joking,' Den insisted, but I knew he hadn't been.

Andy gave a nasty little snigger before he spoke in turn.

'Yeah, you can take a joke, can't you, Pippa?'

'Yes, of course,' I answered, but this time I allowed my voice to stay cold, a perfectly reasonable response.

My head was beginning to spin, but I swallowed what was left in the glass and accepted another when Steve brought back his bottle. I knew I had to stay,

43

but now the danger was different, and worse, that Steve or Mark would come up to my room and play on my sympathy and the state I was in to seduce me. Before long I'd be down on my knees with a penis in my mouth, saying thank you in the best way I could, a thought which again sent a thrill through me, sharper than before.

Again I pushed it down, but now with a weird sense of panic which I'd last known in the back of a car while watching my friend Sophie suck a man off through the open window. It had been frightening and exciting all at once, bearable only because the doors were firmly locked and my friends were there. I'd even gone as far as to pull up my top to show him my breasts, and there was no denying that I'd felt the urge to take his thick, dark erection in my own mouth. Fortunately my aunt had turned up before anything more could happen, which in a turn had led to my virgin spanking, an experience of such perfect ecstasy . . .

'Pippa? Earth to Pippa,' Steve's voice broke in, and I found myself mumbling embarrassed apologies as he went on.

'I was saying, once you've finished with that stuff you're doing for Maggie, why don't you join me on a visit to a client. It would be good experience for you.'

'Yes, thank you, I'd appreciate that,' I answered, truthfully. 'But what about Maggie?'

'You can ask her,' Den said, nodding towards the window.

I turned, to see Maggie Phelps halfway across the square. She had seen us, and she did not look pleased, filling me with exactly the sort of apprehension I thought I'd left behind at school. I made to rise, an apology already trembling on my lips, but Mark's arm was still around my shoulder and he eased me back into my seat.

'Relax, Pippa. You don't need to worry about Maggie.'

'Doesn't she?' Maggie herself responded as she turned in at the door. 'She's supposed to be gaining experience with us, Mark, and not in how to drink, or flirt. Come back to the office, Pippa.'

'Yes, of course,' I began, but Mark wasn't satisfied.

'How much experience do you think she'll gain sorting out the old files?' he asked. 'We could get a temp in to do that.'

'It's what I need her to do, at present,' Maggie answered.

'Fair enough,' Steve put in, 'but once she's finished I'd like her to come out with me for a few days.'

'That's not unreasonable,' Maggie agreed. 'Now come along, Pippa.'

I came, knowing it was what I should do and unable in my case to resist the authority in her voice. Mark let me up, and while Maggie didn't actually take my hand I felt very much that I was being led away as we left, led away like a naughty little girl caught playing with the wrong friends. I was sure the men were laughing at me as I crossed the square a couple of paces behind Maggie, leaving me red-faced, but my embarrassment flared higher still as she turned to me and spoke.

'I think we both know what you need, don't we?'

'A coffee?' I suggested, although I'd heard that tone of voice before and I had a horrible, thrilling suspicion I knew what she meant.

'A good spanking,' she answered, and my suspicion turned to certainty.

The shock and doubt in my face must have shown, because she went on immediately, her voice stern and commanding.

'Don't try to play the innocent with me, young lady. I know exactly what you are, and what you like.'

Sober, I'd have realised she really did know, and maybe told her I was in a faithful relationship with my girlfriend, maybe. Drunk and flushed with embarrassment, I tried to deny it.

'No, you've got it wrong, Miss Phelps, I don't . . .'

'I'll have none of that nonsense,' she interrupted me. 'You came with a reference from Morris Rathwell, didn't you? And we all know what that means.'

'Yes, but I . . .'

I'd been going to say that I had nothing to do with Morris Rathwell and that I only got spanked by my girlfriend, but both protests would have been lies and the second completely useless anyway. Instead I shut up, and Miss Phelps gave me a smug little grin, taking my hand as we turned and lost sight of Champagne Charlie's. She strode forward and I came meekly behind, full of confusion, scared and yet expectant, burning with resentment and yet full of arousal. There was a world of satisfaction in Miss Phelps's voice as she spoke again.

'I wanted to be the first to spank you, and it looks like I will be. Perhaps we'd better go in at the back? Otherwise I might have to deal with you in front of Lucius and Mr Montague, which would be a pity.'

She didn't say why, whether it was to spare my blushes or because she had further plans for me, but I suspected I knew the answer. I cast her a nervous look, already imagining the taste of her sex in my mouth, but she was walking straight ahead, towards the rear door of Montague, Montague, Todmorden and Montague. Inside, she hurried me up the stairs, applying a pat to the seat of my skirt to urge me up the final flight. It was no more than a touch, but it meant a great deal, her assumption of the right to smack my bottom, which I didn't rebuff.

My heart was beating fast as I entered my tiny room, and I was biting my lip for a moment before I managed to stop myself, trying to look composed as I awaited my punishment. She drew a key from her bag and quickly locked the door. For all my attempt at calm I felt very small indeed, and tried to be brave, speaking in an effort to show that I wasn't quite the pathetic little creature she assumed.

'How do you want me, over your knee I suppose?'

I'd put on my best sassy voice, but she answered quite casually.

'No, climb onto your desk and lie on your back, as if you were ready to have your nappy changed.'

All my efforts to appear cool and sophisticated collapsed in humiliation and the first words to enter my head spilt from my mouth.

'I don't wear a nappy!'

'No, but that should give you an extra little something to think about while your bottom is smacked.'

She was right. I was pouting furiously and quite unable to stop myself as I climbed onto the desk. It wasn't a position I'd been punished in before, but I could quite imagine how shameful it would be, with everything showing, while the thought of being made to wear a nappy and having it changed had inevitably got stuck in my head.

Determined at least to deprive her of the pleasure of exposing me, I began to tug my own skirt up, only to have a finger wagged in my face.

'Oh no you don't,' she warned. 'I'll get you ready. Now on your back you go.'

I went, turning over and lifting my knees as I knew I should. Even dressed, my bottom felt prominent and vulnerable, and Miss Phelps was smiling as she eyed the shape I made under my skirt.

'I'm going to enjoy this,' she said, taking hold of the hem of my skirt. 'It's been quite a while since I spanked a young one like you.'

She began to draw my skirt down my thighs, deliberately slowly. Her eyes were fixed on my legs as she exposed me, and when the tops of my stay-ups came on show she gave a nod of satisfaction and spoke again.

'I see you wear stockings. Sensible girl. Aren't tights horrid?'

I managed a nod, unable to speak for the lump in my throat. She could now see right up my skirt, to where the bulge of my sex was hidden by my knickers, my embarrassingly wet knickers. Her eyebrows lifted in amusement as she saw.

'Wet already? Quite the little slut, aren't you?' she said. 'Lift your bottom, darling.'

My obedience was automatic, and as I raised myself from the table she quickly pushed my skirt up over my hips, leaving my knickers on full show. Ever since my first spanking I'd been taught to associate a particular style of underwear with punishment, plain white, full-cut knickers, which was what I had on. Just knowing I was wearing them could be enough to turn me on, and Miss Phelps seemed to share my taste.

'Spanking panties?' she remarked. 'What a good girl you are.'

She stepped back a little, admiring the view of my thighs and bottom, no longer hidden by my skirt but bare save for where the taut white cotton of my knickers covered my most intimate secrets. It was a thoroughly ridiculous pose, and as she took hold of my ankles I thought of what she'd said about it being

48

the way I'd lie if I was having my nappy changed. Given the amount of modesty I was going to be allowed to keep, I might as well have been.

'Let's have those panties down then, shall we?' she said, her voice full of smug amusement as she took hold of me by the seat of my knickers.

One good jerk and they'd been pulled out from under my body. Another and my bum crease was showing. A third and they were around my thighs, exposing my spread bottom hole and the wet tart of my pussy. A hard sob escaped my lips as I was laid bare, and she gave a soft chuckle as she twisted her hand into my knickers, now at knee level, holding me firmly in place with my bottom stuck out and completely exposed. I was bare, and ready to be spanked, but she seemed to have other ideas.

Her eyes were lingering on what I was showing, and her hand had settled on the turn of my bottom cheek. I'd thought she might touch me up as well as spank me, and I closed my eyes, unable to resist the pleasure of having my bottom stroked and fondled for all the shame of my position. Only when her fingers began to move close to my anus did I open my eyes again, to find that she'd squatted down and was looking at my twin holes from just inches away. My surprise must have shown in my face.

'Aren't you used to having your bottom inspected?' she asked.

I shook my head.

'I always like to inspect a new girl before I spank her,' she said, and her hand had moved to my sex.

Another sob burst out as she inserted one long finger into pussy, just briefly, before extracting it and spreading my lips to open my hole for inspection.

'Not a virgin, then,' she remarked. 'Pity.'

'I am a virgin,' I managed. 'I just ride a lot.'

'Perhaps,' she replied, doubtfully, 'but I do like to see an intact hymen. Are you sure you haven't let your knickers down for some nasty little boy?'

'I promise,' I sobbed. 'I'm a virgin, I really am.'

She gave a little tut, then spoke again.

'Do you masturbate?'

'No,' I lied.

'I think you do, Pippa,' she responded, and she had begun to stroke between my sex lips.

My thighs tightened and my mouth came wide as she touched my clitoris. I began to wriggle, but she tightened her grip on my knickers and once more pushed a finger in up my hole.

'Do you masturbate?' she asked again, firmer now.

'Yes,' I admitted.

'How often?'

'Not often. OK, quite often ... nearly every day ... sometimes twice, or more ... I can't help it. My head always seems to be full of dirty thoughts.'

Her finger had been sliding in and out of me as she spoke, bringing my pleasure higher and breaking down what little resistance I had.

'Do you think about being spanked?' she asked.

'Yes,' I admitted, 'all the time.'

She pulled her finger free, but only to move it a little lower. I winced and gasped as she touched my bumhole, using a knuckle to rub in some of the cream which had begun to trickle down between my open cheeks. My ring began to twitch, and I was wondering if she was going to put a finger in when she spoke again.

'You play with your bottom hole, don't you?'

'No! Yes ... it's nice, and so is what you're doing.'

'Dirty little girl,' she replied, still rubbing my cream into my anus, 'but perhaps not all that dirty. Did you know that when a girl has been regularly sodomised her anus comes open a little at the slightest touch? I don't think you've been sodomised, have you?'

I shook my head, now shaking with humiliation and excitement. She continued to play with me, teasing my anal ring until I was open enough for the top joint of her finger to fit in.

'Then I'd watch out for old Lucius,' she said. 'He likes to collect girls' anal virginities. Unless of course you'd enjoy his cock up your darling little bottom?'

'No,' I managed, a weak sob as she continued to explore my anus.

'I didn't think so,' she went on, 'but I dare say you'll get it in the end, and I dare say you'll learn to like it. Now, as you like to play dirty, let's see if I can't find something to pop inside you while you're spanked.'

Her finger pulled from my anus and she reached to one side, where I'd left the stamp I'd been using to mark dates on the files for archiving. The handle was red painted wood, small and bulbous, just right for going in a girl's bottom hole, and staying in. She was smiling as she picked it up, and turned it over in her hand as she spoke again.

'These are perfect, I find. They look rather like dummies, too, don't you think?'

I nodded weakly as the image of me being put on my back to have my nappy changed rose up once more, only now as I sucked on a dummy. Not that the stamp handle was going in my mouth, it was going up my bum, the rounded tip already touching my ring. I was slimy with my own juice, and opened easily, my hole accepting the little plug and closing on the narrow part to hold it in with the date stamp protruding from my anus, both ridiculous and obscene.

'There,' she said, 'I expect you like that, don't you?'

'Yes,' I admitted.

'Time for your spanking then,' she said, and it began.

She was using her finger tips, applying little stinging slaps to the turn of my cheeks, hard enough to set me gasping and clutching at the table. I could feel my bumhole pulsing on the plug inside as I was smacked, and pussy felt open and vulnerable. The way she'd inspected me had turned me on so much I was quickly beyond the point of pain, wriggling my bottom to the smacks.

'You want to come, don't you?' she laughed, and I could only nod in urgent agreement.

'Not yet you don't, you little slut,' she answered me. 'First I want to punish you.'

As she spoke she changed the way she was spanking me, slapping hard across my cheeks so that every hit jammed the rubber stamp in up my bottom hole. It hurt, but it only made me wriggle all the more, and in turn she spanked harder still. Her expression grew stern and my legs had been hauled higher, to make a bigger target of my bottom. She began to slap my thighs and hips, bringing me real pain and making me yelp and kick in my tightly twisted panties.

'That's better,' she said, 'and you're getting nice and pink too.'

She was getting faster, and smacking just as hard, until I was writhing on the table top and biting my lip to stop myself screaming out and revealing to the entire office that I was having my bottom smacked. I knew I couldn't hold it in much longer, and perhaps she realised, slowing down, but tormenting me by lifting her hand over my bottom before applying single, hard slaps, so that each one had me twitching in anticipation before it was delivered.

At last she stopped, and began to rub my bottom instead, feeling my hot cheeks. I lay still, breathing heavily, my bottom glowing hot, my bumhole pulsing slowly on the intruding plug, my pussy dribbling juice down between my cheeks and around the slim wooden shaft in my anus. She continued to caress me, soothing my smacked bottom and occasionally brushing pussy to tease her, until I'd begun to arch my back in pleasure and need.

Seeing the state she'd put me in, she took hold of the rubber stamp and began to ease the handle in and out of my bumhole, pulling it free only to penetrate me once more, and again, and again, until I was whimpering with ecstasy and my fingers were locked tight on the sides of the desk. I was so well buggered my bottom hole had begun to stay open even when the plug was out, before she spoke again.

'I think you had better come now, don't you? While I bring you off I want you to think about what's been done to you, and in particular the position you're in, as if you still wear a nappy and I had to spank you while you were being changed. OK?'

I gave a nod, knowing full well that even if I tried I would be unable to get the awful fantasy out of my head.

'Good girl,' she said, 'and here's a little something to help you. Close your eyes.'

As I obeyed her command she drew the rubber stamp from my anus, but this time it was not replaced.

'Here's a dummy for poor spanked baby,' she said, and the handle which had just been used to plug my bottom touched my lips.

A violent shudder of disgust ran through my body, but I opened up and in it went, leaving me sucking on the taste of my own bumhole and whimpering with shame-filled ecstasy. She laughed at me, bringing my feelings higher still as my spanking began once more, only this time not on my bottom, but on pussy.

It wasn't hard, just pats, but perfectly delivered, each one sending a little jolt of ecstasy through me that could only end one way. I was going to come, and my head was already fixed on the image she'd provoked. She'd spanked my bottom, and to do it she'd put me in the same position I'd have needed to be in to have my nappy changed. Maybe she was going to put me in a nappy, and parade me around the office with the tell-tale bulge showing under my skirt so that everyone would know. Maybe she'd change me in front of the two dirty old men who shared our obsession, and spank me too, rolled up with my bumhole and pussy flaunted for them to gloat over, to toss their fat old cocks over. Maybe I'd have my bumhole plugged while they did it, with a real dummy, which I'd be made to suck on afterwards, with my mouth full of the taste of my own bottom as Maggie Phelps held me down and fat old Lucius Todmorden pressed his erection to my anus, penetrating me, buggering me, making me just one more girl on his long list of anally deflowered virgins.

I was coming, and I couldn't stop myself thinking about it, my thoughts fixed firmly on how it would feel to have my anal ring spread to his erection and my rectum fill with fat, hot penis. The humiliation was unbearable, but that was part of what was making me come as Maggie patted my juicy, open pussy to a steady rhythm and I sucked urgently on the tiny plug she had just that moment had up my bottom hole. It was a good orgasm, long and hard, and so emotional that the tears were running from my eyes as I came slowly down.

There was no question about what came next. Not a word was spoken as I spat out my impromptu dummy and climbed from the desk. Maggie went to my seat, her smart black office skirt already tugged up to reveal her stockings with slices of creamy white thigh bulging a little over the top of each and her knickers, black and lacy, pulled tight over the enticing swell of her sex. I went straight to my knees, crawling to her as she eased her knickers down and off. Her thighs came wide, presenting me with her neatly trimmed pussy, the centre pink and moist with excitement, the tiny bud of her clitoris showing ready for my tongue.

Three

AJ was going to kill me. I had broken her trust, which meant a severe punishment, and while in a way I was eager to take it, that didn't mean I wasn't scared. The only question was whether I should confess to her, and there was only one acceptable answer. If I kept it from her and she did eventually find out she would be genuinely hurt, which I didn't want at all.

I didn't see her that evening, and when we spoke on the phone I managed to convince myself that it was the sort of admission that should be made face to face. Not that it would be put off for long, because Mum finally decided to see sense and let me stay in London during the week. Jemima was green with envy, and once Mum and Dad were out of the way she wouldn't stop teasing me about what I'd be getting up to with AJ. Fortunately she only had the sketchiest idea of what that might be, although it was still deeply embarrassing having my little sister gloating over the thought of me getting a spanking.

The next day I packed a weekend bag to take with me, including several changes of clothes. At Montague, Montague, Todmorden and Montague I was greeted with a faint but knowing grin from Maggie and went straight upstairs. I now had the filing down to an efficient routine, and was eager to finish so that

I could go out with Steve Frost, although it was very hard indeed not to think about what had happened the day before, particularly while using the stamp Maggie had stuck up my bottom and made me suck.

I was also sure the men in the Blockhouse would be talking about me, and I couldn't resist listening in. There was even an excuse for being in the right room, because I now had so many files for the popular letters that I'd had to double up my alphabet and was rapidly running out of floor space. The room above the Blockhouse was the largest on the top floor, so it made sense to lay out my piles of folders there, and I could listen in safety.

There wasn't much to hear at first, because both Gail and Claire were in and, unsurprisingly, they didn't seem to have been included in the bet. Only when they went down to a meeting in the Boardroom did the conversation change, with Mark, Steve and Andy left in the room. After a moment of careful listening to make sure nobody was coming up the stairs I put my ear as close as I could get it to the hole in the floor. Steve was talking.

'You're a sneaky bastard, Mark, taking little Pippy off to Champagne Charlie's like that.'

First I'd been 'Miss Double Barrel' and now I was 'little Pippy'. I wasn't sure which was more insulting.

'All's fair, mate,' Mark answered, 'and besides, I have to protect my investment. Anyway, I'm making a few changes to the odds. She seems to like you, so you're down to 5–1, and I reckon I'd have made her yesterday if you lot hadn't pushed in, so I'm 3–1 and going down. After Den's performance, he goes up to 20–1, because frankly, I suspect after what he said she'd rather have sex with a syphilitic orang-utan. Andy's 15–1, and the others stay the same.'

They carried on talking, but about the bet and other similar bets they'd had before, which was all very interesting but only really served to confirm that they had no respect whatsoever for women. I'd soon gone back to work, which had become automatic, and I was again considering the best way to benefit from their dirty little game and to puncture their arrogance at the same time.

One obvious consideration was that I had to get my bet on before they found out I'd have sex with anyone, and with Maggie on a mere 10–1 I definitely didn't want them to find out about us. That meant acting fast, because she was sure to want to spank me again, and while I knew I ought to turn her down it wasn't going to be easy. After all, I'd accepted her once, so she might not accept any nonsense on my part, a thought that in itself gave me a delicious thrill. I also had to keep myself out of the clutches of old Mr Montague and Lucius Todmorden, so when I heard a slow tread on the stairs I was doubly apprehensive. It was indeed old Mr Montague, beaming paternally as he addressed me.

'Good morning, Pippa. I trust everything is going well?'

'Yes, thank you,' I answered, rising quickly in case the crawling position I'd been in gave him any ideas.

'And I trust Maggie is keeping you busy and out of mischief?'

There was a hint of amusement in his voice as he spoke and I found myself wondering if she had told him about the day before.

'Yes,' I told him, 'and she's very kindly allowing me to visit a client with Stephen Frost once I've finished this filing.'

He raised an eyebrow.

'Do you know who you will be visiting?'

'No.'

'Stephen is handling Stepney Customs, if I remember rightly,' he said. 'Would you like me to suggest he takes you there? I think you would appreciate Stepney Customs.'

'That would be very kind, thank you.'

'Always happy to oblige, my dear,' he replied, and glanced towards the stairs before continuing in a quieter voice. 'I was sorry not to see you on Saturday night. Another time, I trust?'

I hesitated, wanting to explain the situation and how I felt about men, still not entirely certain that he was talking about Morris Rathwell's spanking party and very eager indeed not to give myself away if he wasn't. A question seemed the best answer.

'Did it go well?'

Again he glanced towards the stairs, then shut the door before he answered.

'Yes, although your presence would have been a great asset, both for your own sweet sake and because he was down to three girls. However, when at the office, we make a rule of only referring to our mutual penchant in oblique terms; while however delightful the prospect might be, it is of course out of the question to actually indulge ourselves. Discretion must be our watchword.'

He had to be talking about spanking, in which case Maggie would seem to have broken the rules with a vengeance. I wondered if that meant she would get her own bottom smacked if I told on her, a thought I couldn't help but relish. That also implied that neither he nor Mr Todmorden was likely to be trying to get me across the knee at the office, which came as a relief.

'Although,' he went on, 'we have occasionally given in to temptation with Helen, but only when it was quite safe.'

I nodded, picturing the pretty secretary punished by the three of them as he continued.

'I trust you would be amenable to something similar?'

Now was my chance to back out politely, but as I struggled for the right words I realised that I could hardly claim to be faithful to AJ when he might find out I'd been spanked by Maggie. A claim of pure lesbianism seemed a better bet, but even more embarrassing, and I was quickly going pink. He smiled.

'You are blushing, how lovely. Well then, I shall not press the issue.'

He would have said more, and I still wanted to explain myself, but his phone went and he returned downstairs. I went back to work, my fingers now trembling slightly at what was expected of me, and the fact that I wasn't entirely against accepting my fate. Possibly I could let Maggie deal with me in front of them, a thought at once hideously embarrassing and deeply compelling, although it paled in comparison with the prospect of actually being put across a man's knee.

An hour later Steve came up to invite me out to lunch but I refused flat out, confident that it would be in character. I was approaching the end of the filing as well, and keen to get it done before the end of the day, so I pushed on, applying the final stamp to the final file just before four o'clock. It only remained to take them downstairs, so I worked out how many I could carry at a time and divided them into twelve neat piles.

As I took the first down, I was telling myself it was ridiculous to feel apprehensive at having to go into the basement, and that Mr Prufrock would be a perfectly ordinary old man. I still hesitated at the top of the staircase, which seemed unnecessarily gloomy, while the door at the bottom was firmly shut. Again I told myself not to be silly and went down, putting one foot firmly in front of the other and balancing the files against the door to free my hand as I knocked.

There was a creak from within, an odd shuffling noise and a rustle which I couldn't help but interpret as Mr Prufrock hastily doing up his fly. At last the door opened, but I found myself looking over the top of my bundle at nothing more alarming than some old shelves, each stacked with files. Only as a veined and liver-spotted hand pushed the door wider still did I realise that I was looking clean over the top of Mr Prufrock's head.

'You must be the new girl,' he said as I quickly turned sideways so that I could see him.

Mr Prufrock didn't look quite as grotesque as I'd been imagining him, but not by much. He was not only short, but broad and badly stooped with age, also completely bald, with the dome of his head shining yellow in the glow of the basement lights. His skin was rough and discoloured, his face a collection of small features squashed around a large, crooked nose, while his eyes bulged disconcertingly as they travelled slowly down my body.

'And aren't you a pretty one,' he remarked.

He gave a dirty chuckle, leaving me acutely aware that with the files in my arms there was nothing I could do to protect myself from a wandering hand. I tried to get past him as quickly as I could, but not fast enough as a gentle pat was applied to the seat of my skirt to urge me into the basement.

'If you could just slip those into the bottom shelf, over here,' he instructed, shuffling deeper in among the stacks.

I followed, between two high sets of shelves, to the corner of the basement, where the bottom three rows were empty. As far as I could see, my files should have gone on the highest of the three, and I was sure he'd chosen the lowest in order to make me bend down or kneel on the floor. Sure enough, he took up a position behind me, and I could feel his eyes caressing the shape of my bottom beneath my skirt as I put the files into place. My skin was crawling for fear he would touch me again, or even try to pull my skirt up, but he left me alone, contenting himself with watching my legs as I climbed back up the stairs.

He made me feel dirty, and I was very glad indeed that I wouldn't be associating with him very much, while it was intensely embarrassing to remember how I'd considered giving him some sexual favour in order to win the betting on my surrender. There was not any doubt in my mind, though, that he'd have accepted my offer, probably having me sit on his knee so that he could fondle my bottom while I pulled on his dirty little cock.

Not that it seemed all that little. When I came back down with the second set of files it was to find him seated on a chair which he'd used to prop the door open. His legs were set well apart with his nasty little pot belly hanging down between, but not far enough to hide a substantial bulge in the crotch of the threadbare suit of brown tweed he was wearing. I could even see the outline of his cock.

'Hurry along,' he said as I reached the bottom of the stairs, and I quickly turned to protect my bottom.

He gave another dirty chuckle, perhaps equally amused at my embarrassed evasion as at the little start I'd given previously. Once more he followed me, his eyes feasting on my rear view as I stacked the files, leaving me blushing pink and more conscious of my bottom than ever. I was only glad I was in a smart skirt instead of jeans, let alone a short skirt, which would have allowed him to look up it every time I climbed the stairs, maybe high enough to see my knickers.

As I climbed back up for my third load of files I was wondering if I should tell him what I thought of his behaviour, but decided not to. After all, what could I do except complain to the partners, and he was an old and respected member of the firm, while I was a mere trainee. It would be his word against mine. He only needed to make up some story about how I'd been rude to him and he'd told me off for my complaint to look like a piece of spite.

So I put up with it, doing my best to avoid his wandering hands and enduring his attention to my rear view. It was a lot of work too, and left me glad for all the long hours of gym and sports at school. I was still hot by the time I'd finished and straightened up from putting away the final set of files with considerable relief. Mr Prufrock was in his usual position, directly behind me, and I waited for him to start back between the shelves. Eleven times he'd gone first, but not the twelfth.

'Come along then,' he said. 'It's time I locked up, and what would people think, with you down here alone in the basement with me?'

'I'm sure they wouldn't think anything,' I answered, outraged that he dare imply that there was a possibility anyone might even think we would have done anything together.

He was still waiting for me to go past him. I made a vague gesture, intended to suggest he should go first, but he held his ground. He was smirking, quite obviously enjoying my predicament, as we both knew that if I passed him he would take the opportunity to pat my bottom. Standing there waiting, he looked like some kind of malignant little troll, and I was sure that even if I told him exactly what I thought of him he would only laugh, and enjoy my discomfort all the more. The longer I waited the worse it would be, and I finally gave in.

'Excuse me, then,' I said, and made to move past.

Immediately he moved to the side, pretending to be considerate so that he could get a better angle to my bottom, and sure enough, as I passed his hand found the seat of my skirt, only not with a pat, but with a definite little rub.

'Hey!' I protested, unable to hold back. 'Do you mind?'

He just chuckled, and I moved quickly on, burning with humiliation and resentment. I was still sure that any complaint would be futile, and that given what old Mr Montague knew about me he wouldn't even realise why I was making a fuss. Men never seem to understand that it's not what a girl will do that matters, but who she'll do it with. Now I was glaring, but he merely returned a nasty little smirk, and when he spoke it was far from an apology.

'Not at all, my dear, and nor should you, at your age.'

I couldn't help but answer him; what he'd said was just too outrageous.

'I suppose you think it's acceptable to go around patting girls' bottoms, do you? Well it isn't!'

He gave a peevish little grunt, then spoke again.

'Certain young ladies would do better to permit their elders and betters the occasional little courtesy, you know. It doesn't pay to be prissy.'

My mouth came open to answer him, but I just couldn't think of anything to say. His attitude was a complete reversal of everything that made sense, as if I should somehow be grateful for him pawing me and leching over my body. I could have slapped the revolting little gnome, but again I held back, telling myself it would only make matters worse.

Instead I simply walked away. Mr Prufrock was coming behind me, quite fast, so that I was forced to scamper the last few feet to the door. I made it, quickly said goodbye, and fled, his bulging eyes following the movement of my bottom under my skirt all the way to the top of the stairs, so that as I glanced back he was still staring up at me, grinning, and apparently completely unashamed of his unspeakable behaviour.

I was boiling with fury, and only very slowly came down as I made myself a coffee with trembling fingers. When Maggie came into the room I couldn't hold it, immediately blurting out my feelings.

'I've just met that horrible little . . . little creature in the basement! He kept staring at my legs and trying to touch my bum. He succeeded too.'

She responded with a sympathetic smile, then spoke.

'Oh you mustn't mind Mr Prufrock, he's just a bit old-fashioned.'

'Old-fashioned? He molested me!'

'Oh come, come, Pippa, do try not to be prissy. Just yesterday you were telling me you like to fantasise about being punished in front of an audience of older men.'

'Yes, but that's hardly the same thing as letting some old git touch up my bum!'

'But you like the fantasy, don't you?' she responded.

I made a face, unable to deny it when I'd already admitted to enjoying my own humiliation. What Mr Prufrock had done still felt wrong. In fact it was wrong. Maggie had come close, and kissed me gently before putting the two coffee cups she'd brought into the room down in the sink.

'You need to come to terms with who you are, Pippa,' she explained.

'I'm not a plaything for a load of dirty old men!' I protested.

'No?' she answered. 'I bet that's what you think about next time you masturbate.'

I promised myself firmly that it wouldn't be, but I was sure that if I said anything she'd only laugh at me. Instead I thanked her and took my coffee upstairs, where I drank it slowly, staring at the trains outside my window and brooding over my sexual feelings, which seemed to grow more complicated all the time. It had been bad enough coming to terms with my lesbianism, never mind my desire to be spanked. It seemed that I always wanted whatever other people deemed inappropriate, and just as I'd managed to accept one thing, another came along.

At precisely half-past five I put my things together and left the office. I was meeting AJ in Whispers, the lesbian bar in Soho where she was undisputed queen. As her girlfriend I was always treated with respect, at least unless she decided I needed to be punished, when my knickers would come down in front of maybe as many as fifty laughing, clapping girls. Now I had to admit to what I'd done with Maggie, which made a public spanking extremely likely, so that I was buzzing with a delicious mixture of excitement and fear as I pushed in at the door, a state of emotion that had absolutely nothing whatsoever to do with the way Mr Prufrock had treated me, or so I kept on telling myself.

Plenty of my friends were there, and Gina had an ice-cold vodka mixer on the bar for me before I even got there. AJ wasn't there yet, but to my surprise and delight Penny was, looking as neat and prim and intellectual as ever. She was at a table with her friend Jade, who waved for me to come over as I put down my drink after the first welcome swallow.

'Hi Pippa,' she greeted me, moving her chair up to make space.

'Hi Jade, hi Auntie,' I answered, sitting down.

'I wish you wouldn't call me that,' Penny told me. 'Not in here anyway.'

I kissed her and took another swallow of my drink. Jade had been telling a juicy story about some goings-on in Wales, which included several girls being made to wear nappies. That reminded me of my spanking from Maggie, and in turn how my secret had managed to leak out to Montague, Montague, Todmorden and Montague. I waited until Jade had finished before posing the vital question.

'Did either of you two tell Morris Rathwell I was into spanking?'

'No,' Penny answered immediately, her voice serious and even a little shocked. 'You know I wouldn't do that to you, Pippa.'

'Somebody has, because . . .'

I stopped. Jade had begun to giggle, making her enormous breasts quiver underneath her top. Both of us turned to her.

'Jade, you didn't?' Penny asked.

'I didn't mean to!' Jade laughed. 'It was just that he was going on about how he always gets to spank the new girls, and I couldn't resist teasing him. I said that because you were with AJ she'd never let him spank you, but . . .'

'But you didn't bother to tell him that I don't take it from men at all,' I finished for her.

'Yes,' she admitted, 'or it wouldn't have been any fun, not if he thought no man had a chance.'

'So what did you say?'

'Just that AJ sometimes passes you around to men ... to humiliate you, but that she'd told me she wouldn't let him have a go.'

'Thanks a lot, Jade,' I told her. 'Now he's told my boss, and ...'

'Your boss?' Penny demanded.

'It's complicated,' I told her, and began to explain the situation.

As I spoke, Penny's face remained both serious and sympathetic, but Jade was trying not to giggle, and when I told them how Maggie had treated me she burst out laughing.

'It's not funny, Jade!' I protested. 'Now I'm in trouble with AJ and there are a load of dirty old men who think they're going to spank me.'

'Oh it is funny,' she answered. 'Especially about you being in trouble with AJ. Looks like it's going to be show time tonight, Penny.'

'Don't be mean, Jade,' Penny answered. 'You know what AJ's like. Don't worry, Pippa. I'll have a word with her.'

'As if she takes any notice of you,' Jade laughed. 'Come on you two, lighten up. You know you'll love it, Pippa, and I'm right in the mood for a really dirty floor show. Hey, girls, AJ's going to take the Moppet into the back room for a punishment.'

She'd called out to the entire bar. Just about everybody there turned around, all looking at me as my cheeks flared through pink to red. Not one of them showed any sympathy, and most were grinning openly, or passing excited remarks about what was likely to happen to me.

'You've had it, Dumplings!' I told Jade, using the nickname AJ calls her.

'What are you going to do, Moppet, spank me?' she answered.

I hesitated. Most likely she would give in, but I knew I could strip her naked and apply every ounce of strength I had into smacking her fat white bottom without making her do more than purr in satisfaction. She was also a lot heavier than me, and if she chose not to give in I would be the one who ended up with a bare red bum, which would be unbearably humiliating when I'd set out to punish her. Fortunately there was an alternative.

'No,' I told her. 'I'm going to tickle you.'

The change that came over her face was wonderful to see, all her cheek dissolving in an instant, to be replaced by serious worry. I stood up and began to walk around the table.

'No, Pippa, not that,' she babbled, getting off her stool and retreating. 'That's not fair, Pippa. You know what will happen.'

'Yes, I do,' I answered her, snatching out for her arm.

I missed her by an inch and she darted around the table again, only for Penny to suddenly push her chair back.

'Penny!' Jade squealed.

'You deserve everything you're going to get,' Penny told her, and I'd caught hold of Jade's arm.

'No, Pippa,' Jade pleaded as I dug my fingers in under her armpits. 'No! I'll get you for this . . . both of you. Stop it! No . . . Pippa, please!'

Her voice broke to helpless giggles, her body shivering in my grip as I tickled her. She went limp, unable to control her muscles, still begging me to stop as she slumped to the floor, but her words barely intelligible through her laughter. I'd got her face down, and I sat on her bottom.

'You make a great stool, Jade,' I told her, 'very well upholstered.'

'You bitch!' she gasped, and tried to wriggle away, but I had her helpless.

She couldn't control herself at all, her body jerking beneath me, her hands beating on the floor in helpless frustration. I dug my fingers in deeper, thoroughly enjoying myself and determined not to stop until she'd disgraced herself, which was bound to happen. Sure enough, she began to babble again, her words broken and desperate.

'No, Pippa, please ... I'm sorry ... I'm really sorry, but stop, please stop! No, Pippa, I'm going to wet myself, you little bitch! No, sorry, I didn't mean that. I didn't ... I didn't ... you're not a bitch, and I'm sorry, no, no ... Pippa, stop. Stop! Oh shit!'

Her pleadings broke off in a wail of despair and I knew she'd done it, filling me with sadistic glee. I moved my bum onto her back and twisted around, still tickling. She was in army-green combat trousers, the seat tight over her big bottom, across which a dark stain was spreading as she peed in her knickers. I couldn't help but laugh, delighting in her helpless plight as the wet patch grew larger. As her legs came wide in her agony I saw that a little fountain of piss had begun to emerge from where the material of her trousers covered the fat bulge of her sex.

She was making a puddle on the floor, and the stain on her bum had grown to a big heart-shaped patch that made it quite obvious she'd wet herself. I was laughing at the sight, as was just about everybody else in Whispers. I heard Gina telling me I would have to clean up the mess and might get a spanking too, but there was laughter in her voice as well, encouraging me to continue tickling as Jade wriggled helplessly in her growing pee puddle. Somebody called out, suggesting I pull Jade's trousers

70

down and finish her off with a wet bottom spanking, only for her voice to die away.

I looked up as everybody else went quiet too, even Jade. AJ was standing over me, her hands on her hips, looking down with an amused smirk. Penny gave a nervous giggle and I managed a smile.

'Are you having fun?' AJ asked.

'I was just playing with Jade,' I answered, more than a little nervous.

Had I been the one on the floor with a wet trouser seat Jade would have been in serious trouble, but while I wasn't really supposed to play with other girls at all without specific permission, giving a punishment was a bit different. I hastily amended my excuse.

'Um . . . punishing Jade,' I said, 'for . . . for telling Morris Rathwell I like to be spanked by men.'

Now Jade really was in trouble, but it was the truth, and for all that I was really only being playful with Jade I was genuinely cross with her. Unfortunately she didn't want to accept her just deserts.

'Yeah, right!' she protested, wriggling around underneath me. 'I may have told Morris, but I didn't know he was going to pass it on to her boss, and even if I had it's not my fault Moppet let some hard old bitch from the office at her bum.'

'What?' AJ demanded.

'I was going to tell you,' I said hastily, the blood rushing to my cheeks. 'I . . . I got a bit drunk, and there's this woman at the office who likes to spank, and . . . and I let her . . .'

My voice had trailed off on the last few words and I hung my head, genuinely ashamed of myself and also frightened.

'Who was it?' AJ asked, her voice now cold.

'Nobody in particular . . .'

'Who was it? Tell me, Moppet.'

She'd reached down, taking a handful of my hair and twisting it in her hand so that I was forced to look up into her face.

'The clerk at my work,' I admitted. 'Maggie Phelps.'

'The old bitch!' AJ spat and dropped my head. 'I'll have her and, as for you, Moppet, what do you think I should do with you?'

'Punish me?' I said softly.

She squatted down to lift my head again, but this time just gently, with one finger underneath my chin. I found myself looking right into her eyes, making both my stomach and pussy tighten in reaction. After a while she spoke.

'You're a little tart, Pippa. What are you?'

'A little tart,' I admitted.

'A dirty little tart,' she responded.

'A dirty little tart,' I echoed. 'I'm a dirty little tart.'

'Yes,' she said, 'you are, aren't you, and you deserve to be punished, don't you?'

'Yes.'

'Punished hard.'

A quiet voice sounded from beneath me, Jade.

'Er . . . excuse me. Do you think I could get up now?'

'Shut up, Dumplings,' AJ answered.

Penny's voice broke in.

'Don't be too hard on her, AJ.'

'You can shut up too, Miss Muffet. So, Pippa, what's to be done with you? A good spanking, maybe? A bit of boot licking? Or shall I take you in the loos?'

'Not that, AJ,' Penny protested.

'I told you to shut up,' AJ snapped. 'She's my girl now, and I'll do as I like with her.'

Penny's face was set in determination, and she would have said more, but I shook my head.

'It's only fair, Auntie. I let myself go and I shouldn't have done.'

'Not down the loo, that's all,' Penny replied.

'Fair enough,' AJ answered, and got up.

I saw Penny swallow, and her eyes were wide with fear as AJ took her by the collar. Nobody spoke as Penny was hauled across the room towards the lavatory, even Jade staying as she was. The door slammed, but still everybody remained absolutely silent until we heard a new sound, the gurgle of a lavatory being flushed.

I got spanked. It wasn't even very hard, and really only done for the sake of the thing, knickers down across AJ's knee with all the girls looking on and Jade and Penny standing together in one corner with their faces to the wall and their hands on their heads, one with a wet bum and the other with dripping hair. Afterwards I was taken back to AJ's and she contented herself with making me lick her to ecstasy with my hands tied so I couldn't do myself.

That wasn't my punishment, and nor was the spanking, as she pointed out to me in the morning. For what I'd done it would have to be something special, while she was also determined to get her revenge on Maggie, indifferent to my protests that it had been entirely my responsibility. As far as she was concerned she had to punish Maggie, or risk losing face with the community, despite the fact that they seldom, if ever, moved in the same circles.

AJ was always direct, and decided to drive me in to work and speak to Maggie. She didn't tell me what she was planning to say, and although I was certain that not even AJ would dish out a spanking in the front office of a City law firm, my tummy was fluttering all the while. I was also determined to resolve matters one way or another, and hopefully not end up with a bad atmosphere at work for the rest of the year.

We got to the Minories nearly twenty minutes early, but Maggie was already there, visible through the window as she adjusted her spectacles to examine some document or other. AJ parked the bike and secured our helmets to it, then followed me up the steps.

'Wouldn't it be better to do this more privately?' I suggested.

'I don't know where the bitch lives, do I?' she pointed out.

'I could find out . . .'

I stopped, as the door had swung open. Maggie herself had opened it and, seeing AJ, naturally assumed we had a delivery.

'Good morning, Pippa,' she said brightly, then turned a haughty, superior look on AJ. 'Do you need me to sign?'

'No,' AJ answered. 'I need you to shut up and listen. I'm the Moppet's girlfriend, see, and nobody touches her without . . .'

'Not here, for goodness sake!' Maggie hissed, catching on instantly. 'Go away . . . or come into my office if you really have to.'

'I do,' AJ assured her.

Andy Wellspring passed across the corridor to the stairs, throwing us a curious look as we went into Maggie's office. She immediately turned on me, and AJ on her, so that they were speaking over each other with rising anger before Maggie finally went quiet.

'. . . fucking well listen!' AJ was saying, and went on. 'That's better. Now look, bitch. You punished my girl, and I'm not going to take that.'

I'd have been terrified, with AJ towering nearly a head height over me in her black leathers, but Maggie was a lot tougher and answered firmly.

'I'm very sorry, I'm sure, although I must point out that Pippa did not say she was expected to remain faithful. Indeed, I had understood very much the opposite.'

'What do you mean?' AJ demanded.

'What I mean,' Maggie went on, 'is that I had it under good authority that Pippa was regularly spanked by a variety of people.'

'Who the fuck told you that?'

'I am not at liberty to say.'

'It was Morris Rathwell,' I supplied. 'Stupid Jade told him you sometimes pass me around to humiliate me, for men as well.'

'You could have told me that last night!'

'I'm sorry, AJ, I . . .'

'Never mind,' she snapped, and turned to Maggie. 'Right you, I get that it wasn't all your fault, but if you touch her again you're going to be the one who gets passed around for spanking, among me and a few friends. Got that? I'll catch up with you later, Pippa.'

She stalked out, leaving Maggie open-mouthed with indignation and me with my tummy fluttering. If I'd been in trouble before, now it was going to be twice as bad, and there was also Maggie to worry about.

'I'm sorry,' I said, hanging my head.

'You might have told me,' she responded. 'That woman's a gorgon.'

'She can be a bit rough,' I admitted.

'I suppose I had better leave you alone then,' she said.

'I'm sorry,' I repeated. 'I did like what you did with me, very much.'

'I know,' she said, and kissed me.

I kissed her back, and our lips stayed pressed together for perhaps half a second, no more, but as I pulled away it was to find AJ standing by her bike outside the window, looking directly at me with her face frozen in astonishment. Immediately I began to make frantically apologetic signals, but she simply pulled her helmet on and kicked the bike into life, disappearing along the Minories without a backward glance. I was left feeling sick to the stomach, and would have phoned her immediately had not Steve Frost appeared outside at that moment. He let himself in and I met him in the corridor, knowing he'd expect to speak to me.

'You're good and early,' he said. 'Ready to go then?'

'Yes,' I managed, although what I really wanted to do was to burst into tears.

'I'll need a few minutes to get my papers together,' he said. 'If you could get a cab for us, perhaps?'

I nodded and went outside to flag down a cab. A few minutes later we were driving down the Commercial Road as I tried to pay attention to what he was saying about the case, which involved copyright law.

'. . . so the question becomes; to what extent does copyright apply to a customised car, and specifically the paintwork.'

He continued to talk, and I continued to listen, or at least try to, until we reached a low row of railway arches, most of which had been blocked off, with corrugated iron, masonry, or in the case of Stepney Customs, old doors topped with barbed wire. When I'd first heard the name I had assumed they were something to do with Customs and Excise, and even while Steve had been explaining the case to me I'd been imagining a serious and up-market business, not the seedy garage outside which we had been dropped off.

Inside wasn't much better, with three dodgy-looking mechanics in greasy overalls and a lot of dirty equipment. I now knew they specialised in customising cars, and there were three vehicles in. One was an ancient Ford of some sort, with a long bonnet, which had been stripped right down so that it was little more than a shell. Another was largely hidden behind a system of screens, with just a small area of gleaming chrome and brilliant scarlet paint visible. The third was a Triumph Bonneville halfway through being restored to its original glory, with the chrome work immaculate but the wheels and petrol tank off.

Steve was sharing a few male-to-male witticisms with a man who looked like a gorilla, and I took my chance to examine the bike, moving towards it in reverent awe. Another of the mechanics immediately stepped close, a tall, skinny man with a long face and acne, speaking as he came.

'Don't touch, love, it's on blocks.'

'I know,' I answered him. 'I just want to look. She's beautiful.'

'It's a 1969 T120 Bonneville 650,' he said with evident pride.

'I don't suppose it's for sale?'

'Nah, love. Custom job, ain't it. Cost you five grand, that would.'

The implication was that I wouldn't be able to afford it, and he was right. I found myself making a sad face as I admired the beautiful machine, and once more wondering if owning such a marvel would be worth accepting some dirty old man's cock in my hand or mouth. Even at half odds, if I took old Mr Montague in my hand with a £100 bet on, I'd have had enough. He wasn't all that bad, rather a nice old man really, and very clean and neat. How awful could it be, just to take hold of his penis and pull on it until he came off in my hand, maybe after a gentle spanking on the seat of my knickers . . .

'Would you like to come into the office, Pippa?' Steve asked, interrupting my fantasy.

'Yes, of course, sorry.'

I did my best to concentrate as Steve and the gorilla look-alike, Mr Mulligan, went through the case, but it was hard, with my thoughts constantly slipping to AJ and the motorbike. For all I knew by that evening I'd no longer have a girlfriend, but on the other hand, while the bike outside might not be for sale I was sure I'd be able to buy something similar and have them do it up. Perhaps they'd even give me a discount.

The way they'd been looking at me they were more likely to demand sex as an extra, but that was just one of those things. I could always refuse. The skinny man in particular seemed to be fascinated with me, and kept glancing towards the glass window of the little wooden cabin we were in, even though he could only see my head. He also made several comments to his colleague, a younger gorilla whom I took to be Mr Mulligan's son.

He was indeed, as I learnt when we finally left, while the tall skinny man was called Fitch. All three of them seemed keen on me, and assured me we'd meet again soon as we said goodbye. Steve was oblivious, or possibly assumed that I always got that level of attention. He was trying to flirt in the cab back to the office, but I was in no mood to respond one way or the other, and declined his offer of dinner.

The rest of the day passed painfully slowly, but at long last five-thirty rolled around and I left the library where I'd been trying to concentrate on reading about copyright law. As I made my way towards the door I wasn't sure which I was dreading more, AJ being there, or AJ not being there. She was there, already straddled across her bike, and my heart gave a little jump. I hadn't been dumped, but I was undoubtedly in trouble.

She didn't speak to me, and kept her visor down, so I quickly put on my helmet and threw my leg across the back of the seat. As I adjusted my skirt to get comfortable I was showing a lot of thigh, which drew a wolf whistle from the open window of the Blockhouse above us. I didn't see who it was, and AJ responded with a casual V sign before pulling out into the traffic.

I was accustomed to her driving, but she was faster even than usual, weaving in and out of the traffic and using both accelerator and brakes with a will. All I could do was cling on tight, with both my adrenaline and my apprehension soaring as we headed north. I'd half expected her not to make for Kingsbury, and sure enough, she stayed on the A1, picking up speed as the traffic began to clear beyond the North Circular. I knew where we were going, to The Pumps, an ex-filling station turned bike garage just south of Hatfield, and what that was likely to mean.

AJ never so much as acknowledged my presence until we arrived, and I hung my head meekly as soon as I'd taken my helmet off. She took no notice, instead walking towards the back of the main building, and I followed. Several girls were already there, most of whom I knew, including her friends Sam and Naomi, also the huge Chinese girl, Xiang, but none of the femmes, only butch girls. They looked up in surprise to see me trailing behind AJ instead of walking by her side.

'Has the Moppet been misbehaving?' Sam asked.

'She's been unfaithful,' AJ answered, and turned to me. 'Strip, unless you want your clothes cut off.'

I didn't, and hastened to obey, my hands shaking badly as I began to scramble out of my clothes.

Nobody else could see me, unless they came around the end of the building, but I was still going nude in public. Once I'd kicked my knickers off, the temptation to cover my breasts and pussy with my hands was overwhelming but, when I did, it only made me feel small and stupid. I put my hands on top of my head instead, to stand trembling and exposed on the warm, oil-stained concrete, examining my feet in embarrassment and fear as the girls gathered around. AJ came close, tilting my chin up with one finger to force me to look her in the face.

'So,' she said, 'you like a bit of variety, do you?'

'It . . . it wasn't like that!' I managed.

'No?' she queried. 'That's how it looked to me. So what did she do with you?'

I hesitated, but only for a moment. Jade knew pretty well everything and it was more than likely she'd had it squeezed out of her.

'She spanked me,' I said, 'for taking too long over lunch. She spanked me and made me lick her out.'

'And? Did she get you bare?'

'Yes.'

'Completely?'

'No. She . . . she pulled my knickers down.'

'What position did she spank you in.'

I was already pink faced, and going rapidly pinker as I confessed.

'Um . . . she did me . . . on my back . . . on my desk, in nappy-changing position.'

Somebody behind me giggled. AJ gave a knowing nod and I realised Jade had definitely been made to tell.

'Any other dirty little details you'd like to tell us about?' AJ asked. 'How she made you come, perhaps?'

'She . . . she spanked my pussy.'

'And?'

'Um . . . she fingered me, and . . . and tickled my bumhole.'

'And?'

'She . . . she put a little plug up my bottom, one of those rubber date stamps, while she spanked me.'

'And what did she do with it after your spanking? Did she leave it up your bottom?'

'No. Oh, AJ, please, no . . . oh, OK, she made me suck it.'

'She made you suck it? After it had been up your bottom?'

'Yes!'

There were giggles and sounds of both delight and disgust from around me. AJ smiled, her face full of cruelty and lust as she leant closer still to speak again.

'And did you enjoy that, Pippa? Did you enjoy sucking on a plug you'd just had up your dirty bottom?'

'I wasn't dirty!'

There was a chorus of laughter, leaving my face burning so hot my cheeks must have been beetroot coloured.

'Did you enjoy it?' AJ demanded.

'Yes,' I admitted, close to tears, my head filled with panic and confusion as I was made to admit my filthy behaviour, but not my filthiest, because I hadn't told Jade how I'd imagined myself being buggered by Lucius Todmorden at the very peak of my orgasm.

'At least you're honest,' AJ said, 'or is it just that you know that little slut Dumplings would have told me everything already? Yes, it is, isn't it?'

My eyes had given me away, and she gave a satisfied nod before she continued.

'OK, Moppet, so you like a bit of variety. Fair enough, so do I, and just to be kind I've arranged for you to get some. Take her indoors, girls.'

'What are you going to do?' I asked as Sam and Xiang took me by the arms.

'It's more what you're going to do,' AJ told me. 'You're going to satisfy all of us.'

I swallowed hard. There were fourteen of them, all bigger and older than me, most of them into spanking or bondage or worse. Yet I couldn't refuse, and I couldn't even resist, only stumble after AJ as I was dragged across the rough concrete and inside the old garage. The air was thick with the smells of petrol and grease, the light dull and greenish where it shone through algae-encrusted windows. Several half-dismantled bikes and cars stood around a clear space where a grubby mattress had been laid out on the floor, with a chair beside it. I was pushed towards the mattress, where I stood, biting my lip as the girls made themselves comfortable.

'Go on then, AJ,' Naomi urged. 'Teach the little slut a lesson.'

'I don't want to be greedy,' AJ answered. 'I'll go last. The rest of you can draw lots for her.'

She'd gone across to the far wall, and pulled a page out of an old calendar that showed a blonde girl lifting her top. I waited, ever more conscious of my nudity as she carefully cut the page into pieces, separating out the first thirteen number squares, on which she closed her hands, shaking them as she turned back to us.

'Sam's number one,' she said, 'Naomi's two, then three and four and so on round to Xiang, who's number thirteen. Got it?'

They obviously had, and she quickly drew out a number from the now scrumpled bundle of paper in her hands.

'Seven,' she announced.

A girl stepped forward, someone I only knew by sight. That didn't matter. I was hers to do with as she pleased. She was dressed as a man, but in a style out of date by fifty years, with a formal suit and a hat. I was just glad I hadn't been given to one of the hardcore diesel dykes first, and as she stepped onto the mattress I managed a nervous smile.

'Go for it, Trilby,' one of the others urged, 'but leave something for us, yeah?'

The girl nodded, not bothering to turn around, but fixing me with a disconcerting stare. Her eyes were steel-grey, and although she was just an inch or so taller than me and slim too, I knew I'd be putty in her hands. After a moment she spoke.

'Ever been fucked?'

I shook my head, then halted in confusion as I realised what she meant and made a vague gesture towards AJ. Trilby smiled and spoke.

'Well you're going to be now. Get on your knees, arse high.'

As she spoke she pointed to her feet and I got quickly down, lifting my bottom into the required position, kneeling low on the mattress with my cheeks up and open to show off the little hole between and pussy too. Trilby began to walk around me, stopping when she was directly behind.

'Are we going to need any lube?' she said. 'Are we fuck!'

A sob broke from my lips. She was right. I was quite wet enough already, my pussy creaming so well the juice was running down my thighs as I held my position. They could all see, laughing and joking amongst themselves for the state I was in, and clapping as Trilby pulled down her trousers to flop out a thick rubber cock. It was bright red, and fashioned in grotesque detail, with a bulbous head and great thick veins crawling up either side of the shaft.

I was staring in horror at the thing she was about to put inside me, or attempt to. As she got down I tried to crawl away, but she caught me easily, holding onto my hips as she pressed the thick dildo against my sex. I felt pussy spread to the fat rubber tip, and up it went, tight in my hole, but not so very tight. It didn't hurt at all, and as she begun to fuck me I was soon gasping and clutching at the old mattress in helpless excitement. Trilby laughed and called out to AJ.

'I see you've already got her nice and open.'

'I fuck her regularly,' AJ answered.

'If you want it tight, Trilby, stick it up her bum,' somebody called, causing fresh laughter.

'She's just tight enough to hold my strap-on in, thanks,' Trilby answered, and she'd pushed herself deep in up me. 'Hold still, slut.'

She'd begun to rub herself on the base of the dildo, making it squash in and out of my open hole, while her open trousers were rubbing on pussy. I put my face in the mattress in a vain effort to hide my pleasure, but I knew that if she kept the motion up for long I was going to come. She was taking her time, exploring my bum and slapping my cheeks, occasionally pulling out to penetrate me again or fucking in my hole for a few short strokes. Soon I was panting and wriggling myself onto the dildo inside me, much to the delight of the crowd, and long before she'd come my own orgasm rose up in my head and burst, to leave me sobbing and whimpering into the mattress. It took another long minute before Trilby finished off and pulled free, leaving pussy to close with a soft burping noise as AJ called out.

'Well done Trilby. Next we have, number four. That's you, Phil.'

I knew Phil, or Philippa really, like me, a massive, busty blonde who rode a 1,000cc bike and liked to tie her girlfriend into awkward positions for punishment. She was already drawing a handful of cord from one pocket as she approached me.

'Not too long, Phil,' Sam joked. 'There are fourteen of us.'

'Don't worry,' Phil answered, 'just a quick hogtie.'

She'd squatted down as she spoke, and quickly rolled me onto my back. My legs were pulled up and lashed together around my ankles, my wrists fastened the same way, but under my knees so that not only was I completely helpless, but my bottom and pussy were spread to the audience. It had taken her no more than a few seconds.

'Just do as you're told,' she instructed, and her hands had gone to the button of her jeans.

I watched as she undid them and pushed them down, her knickers too, to lay bare her full, soft bottom, heavy hips and bulging belly, her sex too. She didn't waste any time, swinging one leg across my body to squat over my face, her fat, hairy pussy and the deep, dun-brown dimple of her anus just inches in front of my face, which she was about to sit on. I closed my eyes, just in time before I was smothered in warm, moist flesh, her pussy directly over my mouth.

'Lick,' she ordered.

My tongue came out and I was doing it, lapping at the wet folds of her sex as she wriggled her fleshy bottom into my face and explored my body, teasing my breasts and pussy, slapping my thighs and tickling my anus until I was squirming in helpless, frustrated ecstasy. Only when she was near her climax did she stop tormenting me, instead sitting herself firmly onto my mouth, so that I could barely breathe and the tip of my nose was in up her bumhole.

I could hear the others laughing and joking to see me hogtied with her bum in my face, setting me sobbing with humiliation even as I struggled to lick. Phil was coming anyway, squirming her bottom in my face and sighing with pleasure, until at last I felt her muscles contract against my skin and I knew she was there.

As soon as she'd climbed off I was alternately gasping for air and begging to be untied, but they ignored me, AJ pulling another piece of paper from the bundle in her hand. She called out the number one and Sam stepped forward, her hands on the thick leather belt that secured her trousers. It was quite obvious what she was going to do with it, and as she stepped onto the mattress my bottom cheeks and anus had begun to squeeze and open in fear.

She doubled the belt over, grinning down at me, and took hold of my bound ankles to make a better target of my bottom. I closed my eyes, shaking badly as I heard the whistle of the belt and the smack of leather on meat, my meat. The pain hit me at the same instant and I cried out, wriggling in her grip as she brought the belt up once more, and down. Again I heard the meaty smack of leather on bum flesh and felt the sting of the impact, and again.

I lost control as she began to thrash me, writhing in my bonds as my bottom was beaten to an even, steady rhythm. Only when my anus opened in a long, rasping fart did she stop, joining in the chorus of laughter for my degradation. She let go of my legs too, and I collapsed onto my side, gasping and sweaty, desperate to touch my beaten bottom and clutching for pussy with my tied hands.

The meat of my bottom felt hot and tender, my whole body ultra-sensitive, with the ties on my ankles and wrists seeming to trap me not just physically, but mentally too. When Sam rolled me over and put my face to her pussy I licked as best I could in my awkward position, revelling in my own pain, exposure and restriction. She soon came, leaving my face even stickier than before, while my body was slick with sweat.

I heard AJ call out the next number and I was being used once more, now with a thick, knobbly vibrator slid in up my pussy while I was made to lick. The next girl untied me and put me across her knees for an old-fashioned spanking before I went down on her, the one after made me beg like a dog and put my tongue to her pussy as she stood over me. Naomi made me masturbate in front of them before she took her own orgasm, and after that it seemed to blur into one.

They spanked me, slapped me, tickled me. They tied me into awkward positions and stuck things up me. They made me suck on fingers which had just been in their pussies. They smothered my face between their breasts and between their bottom cheeks. Above all, they made me lick, again and again, until my tongue was aching and sore while every movement of my jaw hurt like fire.

My bottom was a throbbing ball, my breasts red with pinches, both nipples painfully erect. My skin was filthy, wet with sweat and smeared with oil and grease, spittle and pussy juice. My bumhole was open and smarting, dribbling fluid from being lubed up with some sort of heavy grease. My pussy was open and slippery, both with juice and oil.

At last I realised it was AJ coming up onto the mattress. One of them had tied my hands behind my back to stop me touching myself, but I managed to wriggle around into a kneeling position, looking up at her through the bedraggled strands of my filthy hair. She smiled down at me.

'Are you sorry?'

I nodded my head.

'Time for a little change in the rules then,' she went on, 'seeing you can take it, and you're such a tart. From now on you can let other women have you, but only after you've got my permission, and you're to stay away from Maggie Phelps. Got that?'

Again I nodded.

'Good,' she said, and began to undo her trousers.

I let my jaw come open and poked out my tongue, determined to do her justice for all my aches and pains. Never had I felt so used, or so submissive, a beautiful high I'd only come close to achieving a very few times. I watched as she opened her leathers and pushed them down, exposing the bare, tattooed mound of her sex. I caught the scent of leather and pussy and perfume, strong in my nose as she came close. I pressed my face to her sex and began to lick, lost in ecstasy as I served my girlfriend and owner.

As I licked I could picture myself, naked and filthy on my knees, my face smeared with pussy juice from the thirteen girls who'd already come in it. My wrists were bound, secured firmly behind my back to stop me playing with myself. I had my bottom thrust out, my reddened, bruised cheeks spread to show off my anus and pussy from the rear. My breasts were swinging forward, jiggling to the motion of my head as I lapped at AJ's sex.

She came, pressing her belly to my face as her muscles went into contraction, never giving out so much as a whimper to show her pleasure, but placing a hand on the back of my head to make sure I kept busy until she was finished with me. When she let go I rocked back on my heels, looking up once more. She was still just inches in front of me, and as I saw her tummy tighten I realised what she was going to do an instant before she let go, pissing in my face.

I took it, my mouth wide, drinking her urine in filthy, abandoned ecstasy, letting it fill my mouth and deliberately swallowing so that they could all see I was drinking her piss, moving my body to make sure it went all over my tits and ran down my belly to wet my pussy, and again to be sure my hair got soaked and some went down my back to soil my bottom. AJ was laughing as she watched me degrade myself, which made her pee come in little spurts, splashing in my face and hair, on my breasts and legs. I opened my mouth once more and came close, drinking direct from her pussy and swallowing over and over again, until at last her stream died to a trickle.

Some of the girls were clapping as I rocked back on my heels, with AJ's piddle still dribbling from either side of my mouth. My belly felt round and heavy, filled up with her piss, and I was dizzy with reaction and need, my thighs cocked wide to spread pussy open in the hope of a touch. AJ saw, and nodded, put out one booted foot and pushed me over.

I sprawled on the mattress, now sodden with pee, and lifted my legs, showing off my pussy to her and the audience. She stepped close, to press one rounded boot-tip to me, spreading my sex lips onto the hard leather. I began to wriggle, rubbing my slippery, dirty cunt on her boot-cap, to smear black polish on my skin, and to bring my clit into contact. That was how I came the last time, tied up in the nude, spanked and tortured, my legs cocked wide to show off my bumhole to thirteen other girls, squirming in my lover's piss as I rubbed my cunt off on the toe of her boot.

Four

I was in a fine state the next day, but I still managed to get into work. In fact it was rather nice having a bruised bottom, as the tenderness kept me constantly in mind of what had happened. I had been punished, properly, not in play, and although I assumed I could have called a halt if I'd needed to I knew that would have marked a downturn in my relationship with AJ. She had little time for anyone who wouldn't play by her rules.

Just that knowledge was enough to give me an exquisite little thrill every time I thought about it, and every time I sat down I thought about it. I also kept nipping down to the loo to inspect my bottom, admiring the colourful blotches where bruises had come up and the red marks where they'd scuffed my skin. In addition to the belting from Sam I'd been spanked over the knee three times, had a bath brush and a custom-made leather paddle taken to me, and been pinched and slapped repeatedly.

It felt both ridiculous and shameful to be proud of having my bottom beaten, but those feelings made it all the nicer, keeping me on a pleasant high all day. I was even polite to Andy, and spent lunchtime with the boys in Champagne Charlie's. When old Todmorden commented on my sunny disposition I just smiled, ignoring the temptation to tell him that I was happy because I'd been so well spanked.

After all, it would only have given him ideas, and if AJ had given me permission to play with other women subject to her approval, that definitely did not apply to men. With that in mind, I began to reconsider my prospects for winning money on myself. A search of the net revealed plenty of old Triumphs, which I'd now set my heart on. Most were pretty beaten up, but with the assistance of Stepney Customs I could not only get myself a truly superb machine, but do it without help from AJ or the girls, which I knew would impress them.

My choice was Helen, who might not have been a lesbian, but I knew she shared my secret, and if she enjoyed a spanking, possibly she wouldn't mind a lick afterwards. There was still some tricky manoeuvring to be done, and the question of how to get my bet on safely, but she was being offered at 100–1, so it had to be worth a try. I made a point of being friendly to her, and by careful timing managed to bring her a cup of tea while both old Mr Montague and his nephew were out. Lucius Todmorden was around, but engrossed in paperwork, so it seemed unlikely that we'd be disturbed.

'Here we are,' I said, putting the tea down on her desk.

'Thank you, Pippa,' she said. 'You're in a very bright mood today.'

It was too good an opening to miss, although I could feel the blood rising to my cheeks as I spoke.

'That's because I got spanked last night.'

She went abruptly pink, but her eyes were wide with interest for all her blushes, and her voice was low and breathy as she replied.

'Did you? You know we're not supposed to talk about it in the office, but . . .'

She trailed off, glancing at the door, which I'd closed on purpose, then speaking again.

'Who by? Lucius?'

'No, by my girlfriend, and some of her friends.'

A little purring noise escaped her throat.

'Mr Montague had me OTK on Monday night,' she said. 'We worked late. He wants me to come to Mr Rathwell's next party too. Will you be there?'

'No. I'm not really into older men . . . or men at all for that matter.'

'I heard that from Maggie. I prefer older men. They know what to do.'

'So does my girlfriend, believe me.'

She gave a nervous smile, still blushing with embarrassment for all her obvious enthusiasm. I was too as I put my next question.

'Do you? With other women? Maggie maybe?'

'Maggie? Yes,' she answered as her blushes grew darker.

I wanted to ask if she'd let me, or better still, do me, but she spoke again before I could get the words out.

'In front of Mr Montague and Mr Todmorden, of course. I'm not really keen on woman to woman spankings, but I don't mind in front of men.'

I nodded, trying to look understanding instead of disappointed. Still, we at least had one thing in common, even if for me getting it with a male audience was only a fantasy and likely to remain that way. Unfortunately that made my wicked plan next to impossible, but I continued to talk, not wishing to give the impression that I'd just been trying to chat her up.

'I don't mind the idea of getting it in front of men,' I admitted, 'but I never have. I'd not sure I'd dare, and there's always what they'd expect afterwards.'

'You should let Maggie do it in front of Mr Montague, that would be perfect for you. He's never pushy at all. Lucius . . . Lucius expects things.'

I knew exactly what Lucius expected, and found myself blushing again.

'But really you should come to a party,' she went on. 'Morris and Melody look after the girls really well.'

That wasn't what I'd heard, at least, not in the sense of making sure nobody got more than she'd bargained for, but I just shrugged.

'My girlfriend wouldn't let me,' I told her.

'That's a pity.'

'But she did say Maggie could do me, if I asked. Well, not Maggie in particular, but women other than herself, so maybe . . .'

I caught myself, realising that if I admitted to her that I'd be willing to be spanked in front of old Mr Montague it was likely to lead to an offer of exactly that. AJ would not be happy about it, and I didn't even have the excuse of trying to win my bet, only my own dirty fantasies.

'You should,' she urged, and her voice sank lower, to an excited, conspiratorial whisper. 'Maggie's very good at it, actually. She likes to slip something up my bottom while I'm being punished, but you know that, don't you?'

I nodded, now with a catch in my throat for the memory and blushing red because Helen had obviously been told all about my little session on my desk.

'It's even better in front of old Mr Montague,' Helen went on, 'so embarrassing . . . you understand that, don't you?'

'Of course.'

'Sometimes he takes pictures and shows me afterwards, or even a piece of video, so I know exactly what he saw, and he always makes sure to sit right behind me, so everything shows.'

She gave a little shiver as she finished, then an embarrassed smile. I responded in kind, imagining how she'd look across Maggie's knee, her knickers well down, her bottom rosy with smacks, as the handle of a stamp was eased in up her bumhole. She was right, it was embarrassing, hideously embarrassing, especially to be filmed like that and then made to watch her own punishment.

I had to get out of there, or I was going to proposition her. Fortunately somebody passed the door, which broke the mood and I was able to make an excuse and slip away without seeming hurtful. I was burning with frustration as I climbed the stairs to my room, with rude images flickering across my mind in endless succession, and I knew I would have to masturbate.

My room was safe enough, as always, because I could easily cover up before anyone caught me. As soon as I'd shut the door I pulled my skirt up, leaning back as I slipped a hand down the front of my knickers. I was wet and ready, still a little sore, too, but I didn't care. Not even bothering to sit down, I slumped to the carpet with my back against the door and my eyes closed in bliss. I had to come, and I had to come over Helen.

I wanted her badly, but that hurt, because I knew I couldn't have her, yet at least I could share her. Even if I was the one doing the spanking it would be good, better still if I was across her knee. We could take turns, maybe, or best of all, we could be done side by side, bent over a desk, close together as our skirts were raised ... as our knickers were pulled down ... as our cheeks were pulled wide to show off our bumholes ... as we were penetrated with the little stamps, and spanked, and spanked, and spanked ...

Just as I was about to come my mind slipped, imagining not only Maggie, but old Mr Montague, watching us as we were given our humiliating punishment, with a camera in his hand to record the very rudest details. I remembered that Maggie had said the next time I masturbated it would be over dirty old men, and tried to push the thought aside, gently circling my clit with one finger as I struggled to focus. Whatever I thought about when I came, it would not have anything to do with dirty old men.

Yet Maggie had planted the seeds in my head, and Helen too. Besides, if I was to be spanked side by side with Helen I wanted an audience, and I wanted my shame to be captured on camera. Maybe it would be OK if Maggie filmed us to show Old Montague and Lucius Todmorden later? No, they had to be there. They had to watch my bottom cheeks spread and my anus penetrated, and once Helen and I were spanked and juicy and too far gone to stop it, they'd bugger us . . .

Again I tried to pull back, but I couldn't, sobbing with frustration for my own helpless, dirty imagination even as I began to rub myself again. My orgasm was already rising up in my head, and I had to come over the fantasy I'd evolved, nothing else would do. I bit my lip to stop myself screaming when it happened, and let go.

In my mind's eye I was bent over Mr Montague's big desk, after hours, with Helen beside me. Our skirts were up, our knickers down around our knees, our pussies on show, our bottoms bare with the ends of date stamps sticking out between our cheeks where our bumholes had been filled. Maggie would be spanking us and the two men watching, old Mr Montague with his camera, on which he'd already have recorded a close-up of my bottom hole being plugged to show me later, and Lucius Todmorden with a fat, straining erection sticking out of his trousers, ready for that same rude, dirty hole once I was vacant.

They'd do Helen first, making me watch as the stamp was extracted from her bumhole and replaced with old Montague's cock. I'd see the pained ecstasy on her face as her hole came wide, and the shame as she began to grunt and pant to her buggering. I'd hear her beg for more as her rectum filled with cock and her satisfied gasp as his balls pressed to her empty cunt. I'd smell the heat of her sex and beg to be allowed to lick her out while she was buggered, even offering to attend to old Montague's balls as well.

I'd be ignored, and I'd be buggered. Maggie would pull the plug out of my anus and guide old Todmorden's cock in. I'd feel it touch my ring. I'd be begging him not to even as my hole spread to the pressure, but I wouldn't mean it. I'd stay just as I was, bent over with my bum stuck out, whimpering, sobbing, maybe in tears, but all too eager for his fat penis to be jammed right up my bottom, jammed as deep as it would go, with his fat ball sack pressed to my empty cunt.

He'd bugger me. He'd bugger me in front of Maggie and Helen and old Montague, and I'd be filmed, close up, so that afterwards I could be made to watch in detail as I moaned and gasped my way through the buggering and even watch the taut ring of my bumhole pulling in and out on his cock shaft. He'd bugger me until he'd spunked in my rectum and pull out to leave me masturbating in his mess as it dribbled out of my gaping bumhole and over my cunt, all of which would be caught on film.

My orgasm was so strong I nearly fainted, but I had filled up with self-recrimination long before it was over, and was left sobbing on the floor in exhaustion and shame.

Travelling home on the Friday evening, I felt as if I'd been away for months rather than a few days. Everything was exactly as I remembered it; the delphiniums in the garden on the corner, taller than me, the plum tree overhanging the road outside No. 61, from which Jemima and I had always loved to steal the fruit, even Mr Pott's broken down lawnmower, which stood exactly as it had at the beginning of the week. It felt different, no longer somewhere I yearned to escape from, but a sanctuary to which I knew I could always return.

Mum and Dad were out, but Jemima was there, in her room, face down on her bed and still in her school uniform, the long white socks halfway down her skinny legs. She turned her head as I said hello, and padded after me as I went into my own room, folding her arms across her chest and cocking her head a little to one side as she spoke.

'Well?'

'Well what?'

'Well, did you get spanked this week?'

She smacked her lips on the word 'spanked', as if her sister being punished was both highly amusing and desirable. I opened my mouth to deny it, only to close it again. She was a sight too happy about my spankings, so happy in fact that I could not help but wonder if she wasn't developing an interest in having her own bottom attended to. If there was one thing guaranteed to put a stop to that, it was what had been done to me.

'Yes, I did, as a matter of fact,' I told her. 'Hard. It hurt. A lot.'

'Let's see then,' she demanded.

'No!'

'Go on, Pippa, show.'

'Jemima!'

'Come on, I want to see. Please?'

There was altogether too much excitement in her voice, but if she saw the state I was in it was sure to change her mind. I nodded and began to undo the button of my jeans as I spoke.

'OK, Jemima, I'll show you. I'll show you what it looks like when you get a proper spanking.'

I turned my back and quickly pushed down my jeans and knickers, sticking my bottom out a little to let her see the full extent of my bruising. Her mouth came slowly open as she took the sight in, and her lower lip began to tremble before she suddenly rushed from the room. I allowed myself a quiet smile. There would be no more talk about spanking from my baby sister.

The mirror showed what she'd seen, and although the bruises had begun to fade both my cheeks were still pretty colourful and it was obvious I'd been given a severe spanking. Again a little thrill ran through me at the memory, and I was humming happily to myself as I went downstairs, despite feeling a little guilty about Jemima. I made myself an instant coffee and went into the garden, sipping it on the patio and watching Mr Porter prune his hedge.

I'd known him all my life, as a large, taciturn man who seldom spoke save to say good morning if we passed in the street. Never once had I given the slightest thought to his sexuality, but now, as he worked the clippers and the beads of sweat formed on his bald patch I found myself thinking of him as the sort of man who'd attend Morris Rathwell's parties, paying for the privilege of dirty little shows like schoolgirl striptease and spanking some unfortunate girl's bottom before she was sent upstairs to suck him off.

From what Penny and others had said, that was generally the sort of thing that happened, and a shiver of excitement and disgust ran down my spine at the thought. Determined not to start fantasising about Mr Porter, of all people, I swallowed the last of my coffee and went indoors. As I put my mug in the dishwasher it occurred to me that Jemima ought to have got over herself and come downstairs, but she hadn't. I called out, feeling guilty again, but there was no response. With a long sigh I started up the stairs, wondering what I could possibly say to her to make things right.

I stopped on the landing, trying to put my thoughts together, when I heard a soft, somehow liquid noise from her bedroom. She was crying. I hesitated, wondering if I should wait a bit before speaking to her, but her door was slightly open and I decided to look through the crack and see just how bad a state she'd got herself into. I stepped close, as quietly as I could, and pressed my nose to the wood, peering in.

Jemima was lying on her bed, as I'd expected, but she wasn't crying. She was on her back, her shoes off, her socks around her ankles, her jacket gone and her blouse undone to show her breasts, her school skirt pulled up around her waist and her knickers taut between her calves, her thighs cocked wide to show off her little pink cunt, which she was busily masturbating. I could only stare, transfixed, my mouth open as I watched her fingers move, patting and snatching at her sex.

She was about to come, her back arched tight, her eyes closed in bliss, her spare hand teasing one stiff little nipple. I could even smell her arousal, and had to remind myself exactly who I was watching before my own hand went between my legs. That didn't stop

99

me, even when she suddenly flipped herself over onto her tummy and stuck up her bottom, into exactly the same rude pose I like best when I do it lying down. Now I knew just how rude I looked.

Her knees were still cocked wide, her lower legs slightly lifted, so that her bright pink panties hung between her ankles. She had lifted her bottom, just as I did, allowing her cheeks to part and show off the tiny pink dimple of her anus, also her pussy, moist and puffy with excitement as she worked her clitoris. Now she was coming, shivering in her ecstasy, her thighs and bottom cheeks in powerful contraction, her anus winking lewdly between, white juice oozing from her open pussy hole.

The instant she'd finished I pulled myself away from the door crack and retreated as fast and as silently as I could, back downstairs. My head was spinning, full of shame and confusion at my own desperate need to masturbate, and worse, for the fact that I could be very sure indeed that I knew what she'd come over, my own well-spanked bum.

All weekend I was telling myself I ought to have a serious talk with Jemima, but I could never find the right words to say. After all, she was old enough to think for herself, and for sex, while her behaviour wasn't really so very different from my own when I'd first begun to explore my feelings. How could I criticise Jem for doing the same?

Besides, she probably hadn't been thinking about me as such, not even me being spanked by AJ. More likely the sight of my smacked bum had merely triggered a fantasy of getting the same from one of the men she was seeing. She tended to go for muscular, sporty types, who no doubt could dish out a good spanking if it was called for. In fact the way they drooled over her they'd no doubt be prepared to do anything whatsoever if it involved playing with her bare bum.

So I left it, but I was still feeling guilty and cross on the Monday morning as I made my way into London. I was supposed to be going out with Steve Frost again, this time to attend a court hearing, but it had been postponed, leaving me at a loose end. I'd heard that Mr Prufrock had asked if I could help out with the archives, a job I was very keen indeed to avoid, so I went up to the Blockhouse before Maggie could catch me, intending to see if any of the others were prepared to put up with me for the day. Only two people were there, Gail, who was busy at her desk with an expression of such deep concentration I immediately decided not to disturb her, and Clive Carew, who was sucking on the end of a long yellow pencil and staring out of the window.

'Hi,' I ventured. 'Clive?'

He hadn't realised I was there, and started visibly, dropping the pencil and going abruptly pink.

'Pippy . . . Pippa, hello,' he managed, extending one plump paw and promptly thinking better of the gesture. 'How can I help?'

'I was supposed to be going out with Steve,' I explained, 'but the hearing has been postponed. I was wondering if any of you were doing anything? I'll be as good as gold, I promise.'

'Um . . . er, I'm taking a client to lunch, as it happens, because Mr Montague's not well, um . . . Mr Montague Senior, that is. I'm sure you could come along. It's always nice to have a pretty girl about . . . not, that is, that I mean to suggest you . . . I mean . . . I'm sorry.'

'That's alright,' I assured him, trying not to smile. 'Is Mr Montague OK?'

'Just a head cold, I believe. Would you like to come?'

'Please, yes.'

It didn't sound a very interesting outing, but it had to be better than being cooped up with Mr Prufrock all day. Clive at least didn't seem likely to molest me, even if he did think I had an apple bottom and therefore was presumably quite keen to get his hands on it. Unfortunately he wasn't leaving the office until midday, and I spent the morning trying to evade Maggie and look busy. I succeeded, and met Clive in the Blockhouse shortly before noon to make sure I wasn't forgotten.

'I have a table at Casa Azul,' he told me. 'I think their tapas is some of the best in London, and the *jamon serrano* is beyond the reproach. They do a rather good Rioja too, from one of the smaller bodegas you don't often see in the UK . . .'

He stopped talking as we reached the top of the stairs, because Maggie was coming up and obviously wanted to speak to me. I had a nasty suspicion that she wanted to send me to Mr Prufrock, out of pure cruelty, and it was quickly confirmed.

'There you are, Pippa. I've been looking for you all morning. Mr Prufrock needs your help down in the archives.'

'Clive was just taking me to see a client,' I said, defensively, and wondering if her sadism extended to enjoying having me molested.

She thought for a moment before replying.

'Very well then, but you're to go straight down to the basement as soon as you're back.'

'OK,' I promised, telling myself that I'd be back at exactly twenty-nine and a half minutes past five even if it meant flirting with Clive Carew all afternoon.

We left the building and caught a cab, which dropped us only a couple of blocks away, where the restaurant stood in the shade of the enormous glass tower everyone called the erotic gherkin. It was certainly phallic, and Clive tried to make a joke, only to break off in blushing confusion before the end. He obviously found my company deeply embarrassing, and yet had been desperately eager to please, holding the door for me to get in and out of the cab, and at the restaurant too.

Casa Azul was rather nice, a cool, airy space smelling of unusual spices and grilled meat. The client wasn't yet there, and I allowed Clive to steer me to a table, where he ordered glasses of ice-cold sherry and a plate of olives and nuts. He seemed determined to talk, but his embarrassed, halting conversation was almost impossible to follow and I contented myself with nodding and smiling at appropriate intervals. Every now and then he would glance at his watch or out of the big window beside us. Finally his increasingly concerned looks gave way to a smile.

'Here he is,' he said.

I followed his gaze across the board plaza, to find a man approaching from the direction of the gherkin, a man I recognised. My stomach went tight and I bit my lip. I'd only seen him a couple of times before, but there could be no mistaking the curly, grey-white hair, the prominent nose or the expression of absolute self-confidence. It was Morris Rathwell, and he had to be the client.

At least, I was praying he was, because from what I'd heard he was quite capable of striking up a conversation about spanking or even more embarrassing things, and Clive knew nothing of my little secret. Even if he was the client I had to hope he knew the situation at Montague, Montague, Todmorden and Montague, or the lunch might prove one of the most embarrassing incidents of my life.

There was no escape. He came in, glanced around, and as his eyes settled on me his mouth turned up into a smile at once so knowing and so lecherous that he might as well have offered to turn me across his knee then and there. I found myself grinning nervously in response, and rising by instinct as he approached the table.

'Pippa!' he exclaimed. 'What a nice surprise! And Clive, how are you, you lucky young goat. Landed little Pippa as your trainee, have you?'

Clive was obviously deeply embarrassed, and mumbled something about me only being with him for the day, which Morris ignored completely.

'Let's see about lunch then,' he declared happily. 'These nuts won't go very far, will they? If you could tell them to get a bottle of the Gran Reserva breathing, Clive, and I'll have a Manzanilla while you're about it.'

Morris turned his attention to the menu as Clive attempted to signal a waiter, failed, and went to the bar instead. I sipped my sherry, turning to glance from the window once more, only to look back and find Morris staring directly at me.

'You are beautiful. You look like butter wouldn't melt in your mouth, and all the time so dirty underneath. What is it Alice calls you, "the Moppet"? It suits you.'

'Don't call her Alice, Morris. She hates it. Anyway, I . . .'

'I'll call her what I please,' he interrupted. 'Silly cow, for instance. What's her problem, that she won't come to a party? It's not like she's never been spanked before.'

'She has not!'

'She's been over Mel's knee.'

'Your wife?'

'Sure.'

He had to be lying. AJ never went down for anyone.

'Not that she got much say in the matter,' Morris continued, 'but she came, and that says it all really, doesn't it?'

'She came?' I asked quietly, still not sure I believed him, even though I could imagine Melody Rathwell doing it. She was as tall as AJ and solid muscle.

'Sure,' he said casually. 'OK, so Mel frigged her off, but she came, so you know she likes it deep down, whatever she says.'

'No . . . I'm sure that's wrong,' I answered, although I couldn't immediately convince myself that it didn't make sense, 'and anyway, even if Melody did spank her, that doesn't mean she wants to have it done by some dirty old man at one of your parties, does it? Never mind what else goes on.'

I expected him to argue the point, but he just grinned.

'You'd love that, wouldn't you? A nice slow bum-roasting followed by a portion of cock right up that darling little tushie.'

I didn't know if he meant me or AJ, but I'd gone bright red on the instant, completely taken aback by his sudden change of tack, and how he seemed to have plumbed into my most secret fantasies.

'Are you still a virgin?' he asked. 'Nah, that would be asking too much. Some greedy little git will have had you.'

My cheeks were ablaze, but I had to answer him.

'Yes I am, actually, and could you not talk so loudly, please? People will hear!'

'You are?' he said, no less loudly than before. 'Don't fancy earning a few grand do you? There's almost no limit to what I could charge people to see a sweet little thing like you get it for the first time, and as for what I could get from the guy who popped your cherry, we're talking as much as old Montague will be paying you all year.'

I couldn't believe he'd said the words that I'd heard. My mouth was opening and closing in outrage, while I struggled for something to say that would even make the beginning of a suitable response. He appeared not to notice, not even bothering to lift his eyes from the menu, and I finally subsided, defeated by his sheer nerve. Besides, Clive was coming towards us.

'Mr Carew is coming back,' I pointed out, before Morris could make some awful suggestion in Clive's hearing, maybe that I be auctioned for a public buggering or put on a sex show with a troop of chimpanzees.

Morris merely gave a dry chuckle and accepted the glass of sherry as it was passed to him. His appalling suggestion was buzzing in my head and I knew my face was red, but Clive either didn't notice or was too polite to say anything. They began to talk business, but instead of listening I sat brooding over male arrogance.

The meal eventually arrived, and was every bit as delicious as Clive had said it would be. So was the wine, and by the time it arrived they were deep in conversation about whether it would be possible to challenge a government directive on what constituted contaminated land. Morris, it seemed, wanted to build on some. I half listened and sipped my wine, mindful of what had happened to me last time I'd got drunk over lunch but still feeling ever so slightly tipsy by the time we'd finished.

I'd been bracing myself to tell Morris what I thought of him, and the wine had certainly helped.

Clive finally waddled off towards the Gents, but Morris spoke up before I could.

'The next party is the Saturday after the one coming. I hope I can rely on you?'

'No!' I answered him, seizing my chance. 'I think you've got the wrong idea about me, Morris, whatever Jade may have said. In fact . . .'

'Have I?' he broke in. 'I hear you entertained fourteen of London's toughest dykes last week.'

'How did you know that?' I demanded, colouring up one more time.

He simply tapped the side of his nose. I sat back, furious and embarrassed, not knowing what to say. Morris chuckled.

'You look even prettier when you blush, Pippa, and you'll look prettier still when you're blushing at both ends.'

'That's not something you're ever likely to see,' I told him.

He merely gave another dry chuckle, but continued watching me. I stayed silent, my arms folded across my chest, my face set in stony distaste, or what I thought was stony distaste. He was grinning.

'You look prettier still when you're sulking,' he said. 'Do you pout like that during spanking?'

'Will you shut up?' I snapped. 'You're not going to see me spanked, you dirty old goat, so you needn't bother to think you'll ever find out.'

'No?' he queried. 'I beg to differ. I know a spankee girl when I meet one, and the young ones usually take a while to accept their true nature, but you'll get there, and believe me, it makes a lot more sense to enjoy it while you're fresh and young. Then you'll be the centre of attention, you see, which of course is what all women crave, but if you put if off until you're older, there's bound to be some other cute little poppet around, and the boys will be chasing after her instead. You'd hate that, wouldn't you?'

'You don't know anything about me,' I answered.

This time he laughed out loud and I found myself blushing again, just in time for Clive to see as he came back to the table. Morris did know about me, an uncomfortable amount. Not only did he seem able to read my darkest, most private thoughts, but he'd found out about what had happened at the Pumps, which was supposed to be strictly between those who'd been there. Somebody had told him, obviously, but I couldn't image who, and if AJ caught her she was going to get the same treatment herself, butch or not.

Clive had ordered brandies, which turned up in huge, balloon-shaped glasses. I sipped mine cautiously while Morris went into a lengthy tirade about not being allowed to smoke a cigar in the restaurant. It was already gone one o'clock, and they didn't seem to be in any hurry, so I let them talk, far preferring to sit back in comfort with a drink than be chased around the archive stacks by old Mr Prufrock.

Half-an-hour later I was beginning to feel drowsy. It was hot outside, and in, while I'd definitely drunk more than I should have done. Returning to Montague, Montague, Todmorden and Montague was best avoided, although a long, rude punishment session from Maggie would have been rather nice. I began to imagine how she'd deal with me, spanking me in nappy-changing position as she had before, only this time putting me in one afterwards to add to my humiliation as I went down on my knees for her. It was a good fantasy, and just developing nicely when I was brought out of it with a jerk by Morris slapping both hands down on the table.

'Work to do, people to see,' he said, suddenly brisk. 'Thank you very much for lunch, Clive, and I'll expect your report on the Creekmouth coal-gas site sometime next week. A pleasure to see you, Pippa, my dear, and don't forget about Saturday.'

As I was next to the window I was unable to avoid him as he bent close to kiss me goodbye, and with Clive present could only accept it with as much good grace as I could manage. He winked at me as he left, and I just had time to stick my tongue out at him, but was left feeling silly and juvenile for making the gesture. It only made him laugh anyway, and I was seething with anger and embarrassment as he walked away across the plaza.

'Just let me deal with the bill, and it's back to work, I suppose,' Clive said.

I really didn't want to go.

'Could I have a coffee, please?' I asked. 'I'm not used to drinking so much, especially at lunch time.'

'Um ... yes, certainly. In fact I'll join you,' he offered, and reached up to signal the waiter's attention.

This time he got it, if only because our table was one of only three still occupied. It was well gone two, so I had three hours to kill. When our coffees arrived I asked Clive to explain the laws on building on brown field sites, which he did, in detail. As he talked his shyness vanished, and I realised that underneath his awkward manner and faintly comic appearance he was not only intelligent and resourceful but not all that scrupulous. Moral issues, such as building a housing estate on land contaminated with coal-tar by-products, didn't trouble him, so long as he could operate within the letter of the law. Long before he'd finished his explanation I'd realised than if I did want to go ahead with my little money-making scheme, he was the ideal partner. I was drunk enough to put the proposition to him as well.

'Clive,' I said, when he'd finally wound down. 'I have an offer to put to you, a proposition, a rather private one.'

'Um . . . a private proposition?' he asked, his shyness flooding back in an instant.

'Yes,' I told him. 'I know about the book Mark James is making, you see, the one about who'll be the first to get me into bed. I overheard you talking in the Blockhouse.'

He obviously thought I was trying to blackmail him, and his features had begun to twitch between cunning and concern, so I continued hastily.

'I don't mind, Clive . . . well, I do, but that's not the point. The point is, that I know, but nobody else knows I know, so I thought, maybe, we could strike a bargain?'

Now he understood, although not perfectly, as his face had gone bright red and he was stammering unintelligibly as he struggled to reply.

'I don't mean with you,' I told him, and his face fell so badly I found myself reassuring him, 'not because I don't like you, Clive, but because you're only on 50–1 and there are better odds available.'

It sounded horribly mercenary, but I was beginning to realise that if I wanted to succeed as a lawyer I needed to put some of my finer moral values to the side. He understood anyway, and nodded.

'Unfortunately I can't spare all that much money,' I told him, 'but if you were prepared to put a bet on for me, I'll be willing to guarantee the result and we can divide our winnings.'

Again he nodded, and his voice had become firmer as he replied.

'Um . . . all right. I see what you're driving at, but we can do better. I can fund the bet, except that Mark's no fool and is bound to be suspicious if, say,

110

I were to put a thousand pounds on Mr Montague Senior.'

'I'd thought of that, also that there must come a point at which he'd simply refuse to pay out.'

'Yes and no. Mark quite often runs books, on all sorts of things, and he can't afford to lose his reputation for paying out on winners. So he'd be good for quite a bit, but yes, I suppose there must be a limit, only he wouldn't just refuse, he'd claim there was a fix.'

'Which is exactly what I want to avoid.'

'Naturally. We need to maximise our profit. I would say we're safe up to £10,000, maybe even £20,000, although he would not be a happy man.'

'That's part of the plan, and I hope to have at least £5,000 for myself.'

To my surprise he wagged a fat finger at me.

'Don't let your emotions get involved, Pippa. After all, from what I hear you're not particularly keen on men anyway.'

'I'm a lesbian,' I told him.

'But you would be prepared to consider performing a sex act with a man in order to let me win this bet?'

I winced.

'Yes, if I have to, but nothing ... nothing too extreme.'

'A pity,' he said thoughtfully, now very much the lawyer, 'because as I see it our ideal strategy would be for me to lay a series of relatively low-value bets on all the outsiders, ten pounds, let us say, and as I suppose you know, the odds vary according to what you actually do.'

It was my turn to blush.

'I do know, but ... but I'm still a virgin, and I'm not prepared to go that far.'

'I assume the same applies to sodomy?'

Now I was really blushing as I shook my head in a definite no.

'A pity,' he repeated, this time not quite so lawyerly. 'I take it you'll accept fellatio?'

I nodded, ignoring the sudden sick feeling in my throat as I thought of how I would feel with a penis down it.

'Which is three-quarter odds,' he mused. 'If we aim to win £10,000, we would therefore need to place a bet of, let me see . . . at least £134 at odds of 100–1. Hmm . . . I suspect Mark would be suspicious if I was to place a £150 bet on a 100–1 outsider, especially just after taking you for lunch. He's not stupid. On the other hand, we'd only need £30 at 500–1 . . .'

'Oh God, not Mr Prufrock.'

'Emotions, Pippa. Do you want your £5,000 or not? I could just about get away with £30 each on the three male outsiders, especially if I put a larger bet on Steve, who's the favourite now, and claimed I was hedging.'

'Yes, but, Mr Prufrock . . .'

'Just close your eyes and think of England.'

'But he's awful, like some sort of creepy gnome. Anyway, would Mark believe I'd do that?'

'He wouldn't have much choice, so long as there's proof, but that's a problem. Mark's assuming one of the younger lawyers will succeed and it will be obvious from your attitude to him that he's done the deed. Even there's the problem of proving how far you went, and we're supposed to get a picture of you performing on our mobiles.'

'Bastards!'

'They do it all the time, Den and Andy in particular.'

'The dirty . . .'

'Never mind that, Pippa, let's concentrate on how to do this. You're right, Mark might well be suspicious, unless he thinks you're into older men . . .'

112

He went quiet, frowning in thought. I sipped my coffee, also thinking, and curiously detached, as if it wasn't me who was going to have to take a big, dirty penis in my mouth and suck it until the spunk came out, but some other girl. That made it easier to accept that Clive's reasoning made sense, and when he spoke again he had slotted the final pieces into place.

'It can be done,' he said. 'Mark just needs to think that you had some good reason to fellate old Prufrock. It can't be blackmail, because the rules exclude coercion of any form, but it could be money. Mark would believe that.'

'That I'd take money for sex from Mr Prufrock!?'

'I'm afraid that a lot of men believe all women are prostitutes at heart, although I do not, I hasten to add.'

I made a face. If Morris Rathwell was anything to go by, it was true. I even wondered if what we were planning counted, but I wasn't actually being paid for sex, not as such.

'In fact,' Clive went on, 'if Mark learns that you've fellated Mr Prufrock, he will automatically assume that money has changed hands, but that doesn't affect the bet. It's only because you look so innocent that he hasn't set the odds to allow for something like that happening anyway. Then there's the question of proof. The best way would be to ensure you get caught at it.'

'Caught at it? Who by?'

'It might raise Mark's suspicions if it was myself, but it would be easy for me to text you when one of the others is likely to have to visit the archives. You'd have to leave the door unlocked, of course, and hope Prufrock doesn't hear whoever it is coming. Hmm . . . tricky, but by no means impossible. We might not succeed immediately, but it would actually be more convincing if you were to be doing it regularly.'

'Regularly?' I echoed in horror.

Not only was I going to have to suck Mr Prufrock's cock, but several times, and I'd be seen doing it too.

'I'm not sure I can do this,' I said.

Clive spread his hands and shrugged.

'Whether to act or not is your choice,' he said, 'but that's my best advice. I don't suppose you'd care for another brandy?'

'Yes I would, if that's OK, thanks.'

He ordered the brandy, which was warm and strong. My fingers were shaking just at the thought of what I was taking on, and while part of me was screaming that it was an outrageous impossibility, I still had that odd sense of detachment. If I was going to do it, I needed that, because Clive was right that I had to get over my emotions. Ever since I first decided to study law I'd realised that in order to succeed I'd need to learn to be completely objective, and this surely was the perfect test of that ability? To judge by the way I felt, I seemed to be on course for an F.

'I always get As,' I said, not meaning to speak out loud.

'I beg your pardon?' Clive asked.

'Sorry, I was talking to myself,' I replied, 'and trying to decide if I want to do this.'

'You must weigh the benefits against the costs,' he replied. 'On the one hand, you have £5,000, on the other, one or more perhaps unpleasant but hopefully brief experiences. You must decide which way the scales tip, and act accordingly.'

'I have to think about it.'

'My advice, for what's it's worth, would be that the benefits vastly outweigh the costs.'

'You're a man, you would think that. Would you do it?'

'Fellate Mr Prufrock for £5,000? No.'

'Well then.'

'But if I was a woman, and on trainee wages, I would.'

'Do you think I'd be prostituting myself?'

'No, not by the legal definition of prostitution.'

'But Mark and the others will think I am, won't they?'

'There is that, but I feel I should point out that to them much of your appeal lies in your innocence. If they think you have already been corrupted they are less likely to pester you, and of course the bet would be closed. In fact, may I make a suggestion?'

'Go ahead.'

'Once you have moved on to university I could tell Mark the truth, or at least a close approximation of the truth. You would then no longer be the girl who fellated old Prufrock for money, but the girl who took Mark James for £10,000. The way in which you did it would merely add lustre to your reputation.'

'The story would run for years, wouldn't it? I want to go into law after uni.'

'Then I suggest we follow the full plan. You might find some of the more stuffy chambers looking down their noses at you, but most firms would snap you up. Mark has quite a reputation, you know, and to have outwitted him so thoroughly ...'

He left the sentence unfinished, and me feeling more confused than ever. Did it really work that way? Maybe it did. Presumably it did. If so I'd have a huge advantage, or would I just be dismissed as a dirty little tart? As Clive said, it all depended on people's attitude, so I'd be a dirty tart to some and the Iron Lady to others. I only needed one.

'I'll do it,' I said, and felt my stomach go tight at my own words.

'Good for you,' Clive answered, and raised his brandy glass.

I chinked mine against his and swallowed the contents, which made my vision go fuzzy.

'Another?' Clive offered.

'I think I need it,' I told him.

He smiled, no longer shy, but confident and friendly. We spent a while over the next brandy, talking law and more personal things. I discovered that he'd been to a public school just a few miles from my own, and knew the River Pang and the Thames at Henley and above Reading. He even remembered the village where my grandmother lives, and the cantankerous old colonel who lived across the road in what is now my aunt's house.

It was after four when we finally left Casa Azul, with the midday heat just beginning to fade and the giant gherkin reflecting rich yellow glitters from the sun. I didn't feel at all steady, and when Clive laughed and offered his arm I took it. He slowed down, but we were walking towards the Minories and Montague, Montague, Todmorden and Montague. In the basement would be old Mr Prufrock, the dirty-minded, wrinkly old gnome whose penis I had to offer to take in my mouth.

I remembered how big it had looked, bulging beneath the crotch of his brown tweed trousers. His balls had looked pretty large too, and I wondered if he'd make me suck on them as well, a thought that made me gag a little. Maybe men always expected that? I didn't know. Nor did I know much else, save what I'd picked up from friends, least of all how to make a man come quickly, which I could see might be very valuable knowledge in the days to come. It would be my first time.

Firsts are important to me, especially sexual firsts. My first spanking had been a wonderful experience I

116

would remember with pleasure for the rest of my life, over Penny's knee in an old pill-box beside the Thames with my school skirt lifted and my knickers well down. The first time I'd had pussy licked was equally intense, and when I'd first returned the favour. I could even remember the first time I'd put something inside myself, the mouthpiece of my recorder, and how I'd been so excited I'd done the same with my bumhole just hours later, holding my cheeks apart in the bathroom mirror as I squeezed a blob of toothpaste onto the tiny pink hole to help a finger go in, only to discover that toothpaste stings. Now there was another first on the horizon, the first time I sucked a man's cock, my first blow-job, a disgusting, crude expression that always made me shiver, and it looked like it would be for Mr Prufrock.

I couldn't bear it, not the first time. Yet I was headed for Montague, Montague, Todmorden and Montague, where Mr Prufrock lurked in the cellar. I was drunk, and feeling vulnerable, horny too, although I didn't want to admit it to myself. Once I got there, down I'd go, in more ways than one, quite possibly, down the steep old stairs and down on Mr Prufrock, taking his fat, wrinkly cock in my mouth, sucking until it began to swell, doing whatever dirty things he told me to until he was ready, and then taking his load. For the rest of my life I'd know that had been my first.

'I don't really want to go back to the office,' I said.

'It might be an idea to sober up a little, certainly,' he agreed. 'We could stop for another coffee? Or I only live down by St Katharine Dock, if you'd prefer to sleep it off?'

I nodded and took him by the hand, signalling a cab with the other. The journey took just minutes, which seemed to pass in a dream. His flat was in a squat, brick block, overlooking the water and a cluster of yachts and motor launches. One of them was his, and he wanted to point it out to me, but I wasn't interested. I knew that if I hesitated I'd lose my nerve.

'I don't want to see your yacht,' I told him. 'I want to suck your cock.'

He looked at me in astonishment, but I cuddled him, hugging him with one arm as I burrowed for his fly.

'Er ... um ... Pippa, I think you're drunk,' he spluttered.

'I know I'm drunk,' I told him, 'so you'd better get your cock out and pop it in my mouth while you have the chance.'

'But, Pippa, I think you might regret what you're doing, so ... oh God!'

I'd pulled his fly down and my hand was inside his trousers, squeezing at the fat, soft bulge in his underpants. He made an odd little whimpering sound in his throat as I kneaded him, the same way I'd have kneaded a girl's pussy with my hand down her knickers, because it was all I knew. Not that he was going to stop me, his eyes closed in guilty bliss, one podgy hand now on my back, and moving lower.

He gave a sob as his fingers closed on my bottom, and I let him fondle me for a moment before pushing him gently back to the huge, cream-coloured sofa. I always licked AJ on my knees, and I got down into the same position for Clive, with him sprawled on the sofa, his legs wide apart. He was mine, completely, staring in delight and in awe as I finished unfastening his trousers to expose white underpants beneath, lumpy with the mass of his genitals.

'You're going to have to teach me how to do this,' I told him. 'It's my first time, with a man.'

'Oh God,' he repeated. 'I think I've died and gone to Heaven.'

'I'm not sure they do this in Heaven,' I said, and slipped my hand into the opening of his Y-fronts.

He felt warm and soft, silky too, really rather a nice feeling. I began to explore him, stroking his balls and taking hold of his cock, which had begun to swell, making a long bulge beneath the white cotton. He was watching, enraptured, but silent.

'You're supposed to be teaching me how to do this,' I reminded him.

'You . . . you're doing very well,' he assured me. 'Don't feel you need to rush. Just pull up and down . . . yes, like that, and feel my balls, if you like.'

The bulge in his pants was growing rapidly now, his cock extending to one side as I began to stroke his balls once more. They felt strange, shifting under my fingers as if they had a life of their own, and it was amazing how big his cock was getting.

'You'd better take me out,' he sighed.

I nodded and tugged the hole in his Y-fronts open, to pull out his cock, a plump, pink tower of meat, almost as heavily veined as Trilby's dildo. A thick collar of wrinkled skin surrounded the top, with the tip of a moist, bright pink helmet just beginning to poke out. I could smell him too, a scent very different from pussy, which made my nose wrinkle but which seemed to be helping send little shivers down my belly to my sex.

'Take my balls out too, please,' he instructed, his confidence rising to my obvious enthusiasm.

I complied, scooping his balls sack out of his underpants to leave it lying fat and heavy on a bed of plain white cotton with his cock rearing above, now maybe halfway to being hard. It looked rather nice, and very rude, hideously ugly, but still desirable. I

119

took him in my hand and began to pull up and down as I had before, stroking and tickling his balls at the same time.

'A little harder,' he sighed, 'and roll my foreskin back, please. Yes, like that, only with your finger and thumb in a ring. Yes, perfect . . . oh God . . .'

'Do men like that?' I asked.

All he seemed to be able to manage was a nod, and his mouth was slack with pleasure, so presumably they did. It looked rather comical to me, with the big pink hat of his cock head popping in and out of his foreskin as I rolled it up and down, but he was soon too big to keep it in. He was hard too, his cock shaft now curving up from his belly with the big veins standing out blue on his pale skin.

'Are you fully erect?' I asked him, and he gave a weak nod.

'Then I suppose I'd better suck you off,' I said doubtfully.

'Yes, please,' he answered. 'If you want to.'

'I do,' I assured him. 'I really do, just not yet.'

I continued to masturbate him, wondering if I'd ever seen anything at once so repellent and so attractive as his erect cock and heavy balls. Girls are pretty all over, not men, and I was supposed to put the hideous thing in my mouth, and suck. I was going to do it, too, just as soon as I'd plucked up enough courage. My mouth came open and I was telling myself I'd put him in on the count of ten, then twenty, then thirty, all the while tugging at his now straining shaft.

'You'd better do it, Pippa,' he gasped, 'or I'm going to come in your hand.'

'Hang on,' I told him, 'not yet.'

'Stop it then.'

He took over from me as I let go, opening his eyes to stare down. I smiled back, nervous and embarrassed, but excited too, and rather enjoying myself. He spoke.

'Would you . . . would you mind taking your top off? A lot of men like a girl to do it topless, or at least with her breasts bare.'

I wasn't doing that for old Prufrock, but now I didn't mind. Nodding my agreement, I quickly shrugged off my jacket and undid my tie, with Clive staring all the while, as if he couldn't bear to miss a single instant of my little show. I did my blouse buttons slowly, teasing him just the way I'd teased the girls when AJ had me perform a striptease at Whispers. His eyes stayed glued to me, and he was nursing his erection as he watched.

'Is this good?' I asked.

He nodded dumbly. I eased my blouse off down my arms, wondering how best to show my breasts. AJ likes to make me strip quickly, or to pull my clothes off herself. Penny likes to flip my bra up before she spanks me, and I tried the same, taking hold of the undersides of my cups and tugging them up. Clive gave a soft moan and began to wank faster.

'Good?' I asked, although the answer was pretty obvious.

'Perfect,' he sighed. 'I love to see a girl play peek-a-boo with her tits, and yours are no nice, small and perfect . . . and your little rosy nipples, so stiff . . . and . . . oh God, suck my cock, Pippa . . . suck it, I'm going to come.'

'Hold on!' I urged.

I moved quickly forward, determined to do it, and this time my urgency got the better of me. His hand came away and mine had replaced it, holding his big, silky shaft as I opened my mouth, to take him in, sucking a man's penis for the first time in my life. He groaned, and I thought he'd come, but there was nothing extra in my mouth. If anything, he seemed to have got himself under better control, and I drew back, once more tugging gently at his shaft.

'Come on, Clive, teach me,' I urged.

'Like you were,' he sighed. 'Come on, Pippa, finish me . . . be my little cock sucker.'

A sharp pang ran through me, shame and excitement. That was what I was now, a cock sucker, maybe what I would be once he'd come, but it was what I wanted. Again I rocked forward to use my mouth on him. I still didn't know what to do, so I began to lick, the same way I would a girl if she had a really huge clit, kissing the bulbous helmet and lapping under the shaft. Again Clive groaned, and this time he came, a fountain of thick white spunk erupting from his cock to catch me completely by surprise, full in my mouth.

It tasted horrible, salty and slimy and male, but before I could spit it out a second spurt caught me in the face and hair, forcing me to close my eyes and leaving me spluttering spittle and come over my bra and my bare tits, which was where he finished off, wanking himself to spray gobbets of sticky whiteness into my cleavage and both little mounds, before wiping the last drop off on one nipple.

Finally he collapsed back onto the sofa, leaving me with spunk dribbling down my face and chest, my eyes closed to avoid the sticky streamer laid over one lid and my mouth open in disgust. I heard him speak.

'Oops! Sorry, Pippa, I got a little carried away. Let me get you some loo roll.'

I shook my head, and climbed unsteadily to my feet. Opening my single clear eye, I made my way over to the bathroom, a big, white-tiled affair. I locked the door very carefully and went to the loo, not to wipe my face, but to tug my skirt up and slip my knickers down to my ankles, then to sit down. He'd spunked in my face, maybe the most disgusting thing I'd ever had done to me, worse than being peed on, worse than being made to suck things I'd had up my bum. I simply had to come, and I had to come still filthy with his mess.

After all, it was what I deserved. I was a cock sucker, his little cock sucker, so it was perfectly right for me to have my face spunked in, and my mouth. I could feel it, and taste the salt and slime, filling my mouth and wet on my skin. As I began to masturbate I was touching my breasts, rubbing the spunk into my nipples and scooping up the bigger blobs so that I could suck them from my fingers.

As I soiled myself the same phrase was running through my head again and again, what I now was, Clive's little cock sucker, and as I came in a welter of shame and ecstasy it had changed, to what I was going to become, Mr Prufrock's little cock sucker.

Five

It didn't seem nearly so easy the next day, not least because I'd spent a night of glorious mucky lesbian sex with AJ and was wracked with guilt. She'd been amazed by how horny I was, but I could hardly explain that it was because I'd just sucked my first cock, while I knew it was pointless to ask permission to go down on Mr Prufrock. What I did tell her about was my meeting with Morris, and how he knew what had happened at the Pumps, which put her in a foul mood until I managed to drag her out of it by crawling around her kitchen floor in the nude and pretending to be a puppy.

She was still talking about it in the morning, going through the thirteen girls over a bowl of cereal and trying to decide who was the traitor, which was how she saw it. I had to point out that any one of them might have told their girlfriends, who in turn might have told somebody else, or even Morris directly, so that in the end she had to admit defeat. She drove me in as usual, but dropped me in Fenchurch Street, where she had an early collection to make. I walked to work through the back streets, past Champagne Charlie's and to the rear door of Montague, Montague, Todmorden and Montague.

I had to knock twice to get any attention, but was eventually admitted by Andy Wellspring. He made some remark about my figure, but I barely heard. My attention had been drawn to the gloomy well of Mr Prufrock's stairs. The door at the bottom was shut, and he probably wasn't even in, but it was impossible not to imagine him crouched down there, thinking his dirty little thoughts, or even masturbating to pictures of girls being rude on some smutty website. I was sure it was the sort of thing he'd do.

Andy obviously knew he was out of the running, because he didn't linger, leaving me to walk through into the hallway. I knew I should go and see Maggie to find out what she wanted me to do, but I was dreading the answer. In the end I told myself I ought to wait until Clive had a chance to get his bet on, otherwise the whole thing might go wrong, which was enough of an excuse to delay my fate. I went upstairs, to meet Steve Frost just coming out of the Block-house. Clive was there too, at his desk, but I ignored him. We'd agreed it was the best course of action the day before. I'd also explained to him that his blow-job was strictly a one-off. Mark was there, talking to Gail, so a little flirtation was obviously a good thing.

'Hi, Steve,' I said brightly. 'Are we going anywhere today, like out for lunch maybe?'

A distinctly stern voice answered me – Maggie, who was coming upstairs behind me and must have been in one of the partners' offices.

'You've had quite enough long lunches for one week, young lady. At the very least you might have checked in with me before going home.'

'I just missed you,' I explained. 'I was with Clive.'

'I know,' she said, 'and I know what you were doing.'

She didn't, but I wasn't about to correct her.

'So it need not go any further,' she continued, 'not officially.'

The last two words had been spoken softly, and Steve had already gone into the Blockhouse, out of earshot. It wasn't safe to say anything specific, so I merely gave her a nervous smile.

'What should I do?' I asked.

'I need you to collect something for me, from Stepney Customs.'

'Oh, I thought . . . Mr Prufrock?'

'Never mind Mr Prufrock, this is important. Come upstairs for a moment.'

She took my arm and led me quickly up to my own room, where she shut the door. I was already beginning to feel nervous, and it got worse as she fixed me with her sternest look.

'This is one of those tasks,' she said. 'Mr Mulligan's account is badly overdue, and he is being deliberately difficult, but only so that he can take advantage of our special relationship . . .'

'Sorry,' I broke in, 'I don't understand.'

'For goodness sake, Pippa,' she sighed. 'Mr Mulligan comes to Morris's parties, as do many of our clients, which has allowed us to build up a useful network of contacts and business. Think of it like the Rotarians, or the Masons, only with spanking instead of funny handshakes.'

'Spanking girls? And in this case me?'

'Yes, of course. You're not going to be prissy about this, are you, Pippa?'

'Prissy! Maggie, I . . .'

'Yes, yes, I know, you're a lesbian, etc. I've heard it all before, Pippa, and I'm not impressed. We both know you like it . . .'

'No I don't! And why me? Couldn't you send Helen?'

'Mr Mulligan has asked for you personally. He's one of those men who likes to try something fresh, I'm afraid, and that something fresh is you.'

'But I don't want to be spanked by Mr Mulligan!'

'Pippa, you're beginning to sound like a brat. It probably won't even be bare bottom, not in front of his son and the other mechanic. He may not ask to spank you at all, but you're to be prepared for it, and you're to tell him you'll be at Morris's next party, and to promise him he'll get to do you there.'

'But I'm not going to Morris's party!'

'That hardly matters, once his cheque is safely in the bank. We can say you caught Mr Montague's cold or something.'

'Yes, but . . .'

'I'm not asking you to have sex with the man, Pippa, just to flirt a little. The most you'll get is a few pats to the seat of your skirt, and that won't hurt, will it? Or if you really have to be a little madam about it, tell him you're on your monthly and promise you'll be willing at Morris's party. Is that too much to ask?'

I didn't answer, and I knew I was pouting badly.

'And you needn't put on that face to me, young lady,' she said. 'Now come along, bend over your desk and I'll warm you up a little. That will make it easier.'

'But if he's not going to . . . ,' I began, only to break off with a squeak as she pulled me firmly across my own desk.

She had me by the wrist, and twisted my arm up behind my back, forcing me to stay in position as she groped for my skirt and I began to babble.

'Maggie, no! This isn't fair . . . and anyway, you're not allowed to . . . you're not . . . AJ said so, and . . . and . . . ow! Not so rough!'

My skirt was already up, and she'd yanked my knickers down, pulling them out from where they'd ridden up between my pussy lips on the bike. It hurt, and so did the smacks she began to apply to my bottom, one cheek at a time, hard and accurate, to set me kicking my feet and struggling in her grip.

'I'll tell AJ!' I warned, realising how pathetic the threat sounded even as I said it.

She didn't even bother to reply, but twisted my wrist a little harder, keeping me firmly pinned down across the desk as she spanked me, now full across my cheeks before beginning to pepper the meat of my bottom with little hard slaps of her fingertips. I knew I'd be going pink, and was praying I wouldn't have to take my knickers down in front of Mr Mulligan, but I was getting warm too, with inevitable consequences. By the time she finished I could smell my own pussy.

'That should do,' Maggie said, releasing me, 'and there's a certain natural scent about you too, which should appeal to him, if only subconsciously. Now come downstairs and I'll get the paperwork ready for you.'

I quickly adjusted myself, pouting furiously as I followed her, my bum warm in my knickers. My gusset was soaking wet by the time she was ready, but I did my best to compose myself before stepping outside to find a cab. She'd really got to me, making me angry and excited at the same time, with my resentment for the spanking hot in my mind even as I yearned for more. One thing I was sure about was that Mr Mulligan wasn't going to be giving me what I needed, and I promised myself I would get the job done, but with the absolute minimum of personal humiliation.

When I got to Stepney Customs they had the big double doors wide open and Fitch was driving out the Ford I'd seen to a waiting customer. I'd had the cabbie drop me some way down the line of arches on purpose, and was glad I had done so. The owner of the Ford was there, and his girlfriend, and while it didn't seem likely that Mulligan would simply up-end me then and there, I didn't want to take any chances. I pretended to study some graffiti in one of the empty arches until they'd gone, then walked cautiously forward. Mr Mulligan himself emerged from the doors just as I reached them. He smiled and rubbed his greasy hands on an equally greasy cloth as he spoke.

'Ah ha, what have we here!'

'Good morning,' I said brightly, fighting to keep the tremor out of my voice.

'So they've sent you to collect, have they?' he asked, leering at me.

'Yes,' I admitted, 'if you could just sign a couple of things, and . . .'

'Come in the office,' he said, cutting me off.

I followed him into the garage and across to the little shack he used. His son looked up from where he was putting the finishing touches to the Bonneville, watching my progress with what seemed to me an unhealthy interest. My cheeks began to colour up as I wondered how much they knew, if anything, and I was glad to find the shelter of Mr Mulligan's office. He sat down and motioned to the chair opposite the desk, which I took. I wasn't at all sure what to say, but he had no such reserves, leaning back and putting his hands behind his head as he spoke.

'So you want your money? That's fair enough, but seeing as I'm being so generous, I think it's only fair if I get a little something in return, don't you?'

'What might that be?' I asked, trying to sound coy and flirtatious despite the hammering in my chest and huge lump in my throat.

'Ooh, I don't know,' he replied. 'It all depends on what you want to give, don't it? Morris tells me you like a good spanky, in public?'

'No!' I squeaked before I could stop myself. 'I mean, yes . . . maybe, for the right person, in the right place . . .'

'Am I right?' he asked, grinning.

I began to stammer an answer, my efforts to remain calm collapsing in ruins at the prospect of him spanking me in front of his son and Fitch, but he cut me off again.

'I'm not one of these bastards who likes to hurt a girl,' he explained. 'With me it's nice and slow, knickers down easy, a bit of cuddling, and I know how to warm a girl properly too. So how about it?'

'I, um . . . yes, that sounds nice,' I managed, 'but not right now, please? It's a bit embarrassing, but I'm on my period. Perhaps at Morris's party though, if you're going?'

'I'm going,' he assured me. 'Wouldn't miss it for the world, not now I know you'll be there. So you'll give me first go, yeah?'

I nodded, my hope rising. He seemed perfectly content with my suggestion, and had reached out to take my documents. I handed them over and watched as he signed, then reached for his cheque book. It had been easy, far easier than I expected, or so I thought, until he stopped short of signing the cheque and laid his pen down.

'Give us a little preview then,' he said, 'just a little twirl, bare bum. Then I sign.'

My heart was back in my mouth, my hope shattered. He had sat back again, in the same position as before, waiting.

'Now?' I asked, and immediately realised what a stupid question it was.

'Yeah, sure,' he said. 'Nobody can see.'

That wasn't strictly true, because if I stood up both his son and Fitch would be able to see me, or at least

130

my top half. Neither of them were visible though, and I quickly stood up, knowing I had to do it and keen to keep my exposure to a minimum. Mr Mulligan was smiling broadly, no doubt enjoying my red face and shaking fingers as I stepped clear of my chair. I turned my back, quickly tugging my skirt up and pushing down my knickers to show him my bare bum, only to realise that both mechanics were now in the garage, both could see me, and both were close enough to the window to get a full moon of my bum.

'Heh, heh, give us a chance,' Mr Mulligan said as I snatched my panties up. 'Go on, pretend you're getting ready for a spanking. Stick your bum out and push 'em down, nice and slow, then just a little twirl and you're done. Nice panties, by the way, and did anyone ever tell you how gorgeous your arse is?'

I didn't answer him. I couldn't, because I was biting my lip to hold in the sobs of humiliation as I stuck my bottom out a little and took my knickers down once more.

'Slowly, doll, slowly,' he urged. 'What's the rush?'

'Your son's watching,' I sobbed, 'and the other man.'

'Let 'em,' he said, 'they deserve a treat now and again. One more time, nice and slow, and stick it out properly. I like to see pink.'

I was choking on the lump in my throat as I pulled up my knickers again, close to panic, but determined to bring the cheque back to Maggie. Yet he wanted to see pussy, which meant he might realise I didn't have a tampon in, and he'd tell me to get over his knee, and he'd spank my bottom in front of his son, and they'd take turns to fuck me . . .

'That's my girl,' he said, 'out with your bum, and down they come.'

My bottom was thrust out, and I hadn't even realised it. I hadn't even pulled up my panties properly either, half my crease already on show, and more as I began to push them down, sure he'd only complain if I didn't do it slowly enough. His eyes were glued to my bottom, drinking in every inch of bare white flesh as it came on show, and I was praying I wasn't still pink enough for him to realise I'd just been spanked. I was wishing I had a fatter bum too, because even stuck out a little way my anus shows, and at the thought that he'd be the first man ever to see the tiny pink bud between my cheeks I lost my nerve.

'Oh you little sweetheart,' he sighed, as I hurriedly pulled my panties up. 'Oh you little tease. I am going to enjoy spanking you, Pippa, I am going to love it. One last show then, and this time, pull your knicks right up first, so they're nice and tight over your cheeks. I love the sight of a nicely shaped bum in white panties, I do.'

'You said just once!' I protested, turning, and my mouth came open in shock.

Both mechanics were at the window of the office, grinning at the display I was making, still with the seat of my panties on show.

'Mr Mulligan . . . ,' I began.

'Come on, doll, don't be shy,' he interrupted. 'Not like it's the first time, is it?'

'I . . . I'll pull them up tight for you,' I said, ignoring what he'd said, 'and you can . . . you tell me what to wear for Morris's party, but that's all for now. I'm on my period, Mr Mulligan!'

'Oh that's the problem, is it?' he responded, not unkindly.

'Yes! I told you!'

'OK, pull 'em up, pull 'em down, quick twirl and you're done. I promise.'

I didn't hesitate, pushing my bottom out and pulling my knickers up tight to lift my cheeks in the cotton pouch, holding the pose for just a moment and then easing them down, but turning before my bumhole came on show, to provide him with the briefest possible flash of pussy before hastily covering myself up. I was now facing the grinning mechanics, who were laughing at me, making my blushes more furious still.

'Beautiful, and so shy,' Mr Mulligan commented. 'Who'd have thought you were one of Morris's girls?'

I very nearly told him I wasn't, but managed to hold back, grabbing the cheque and the documents I needed the instant he had signed. The mechanics were still outside, and I fled in confusion, scampering across the oily floor in my heels and thrusting one leaf of the big doors wide. It hit something, bounced back and nearly knocked me over. I just managed to keep my balance, and ran, only to turn at the sound of a bang followed by a metallic clatter from directly behind me.

The door was swinging slowly back, to reveal the 1969 Bonneville, almost on its side, the gorgeously painted petrol tank against the low iron bollard which marked the boundary between the properties. I slowed to a stop as what I'd done sank slowly in, my mouth falling wide in horror. The bike was obviously dented and scratched, the brand-new paint job ruined, and possibly the tank as well. Mr Mulligan wasn't going to want to spank me any more, he was going to want to murder me, crucify me, stick a spit up my bum and roast me for dinner.

He'd come out, and the others, staring aghast at the damage I'd done. I made to run, only to stop. They knew who I was, where I worked, everything. It was all their fault anyway, and I tried to hold that thought as I walked slowly back towards them, but I didn't manage to express it.

'I'm sorry,' I said. 'I'm really sorry. I didn't know it was there!'

'You stupid little cow,' Mr Mulligan mouthed.

'That's hardly fair,' I answered him, but I could hear the whining note in my own voice. 'You freaked me out!'

'We were only having a laugh with you,' he answered. 'Oh for fuck's sake!'

Fitch and the younger Mulligan had lifted the bike. As I'd feared, the petrol tank was badly dented, along with a long, deep scratch where bright metal showed beneath the paint. I made a face, feeling sick to the stomach for what I'd done and the trouble I was in, despite the little insistent voice telling me over and over that it wasn't my fault at all.

'You're going to have to pay for this,' Mr Mulligan said.

'That's not fair!' I protested, now close to tears.

'I suppose you think we should?' he demanded.

'Well, no . . . yes . . . no . . . I don't know, but . . . I haven't very much money, and . . .'

'What, a posh piece like you? Get Daddy to fork out.'

'I'd rather he didn't know,' I answered, 'but if . . .'

I stopped, realising that if I told Dad what had really happened I would end up in far more trouble than I was already. He'd call the police, immediately, and Mr Mulligan would inevitably defend himself by saying I'd agreed to show him my bum and was into spanking anyway. After that it would become a nightmare.

'How much will it be?' I asked weakly.

Mr Mulligan sucked his breath in between his teeth.

'All depends. Looks like we might need a new tank, and they're not so easy to get nowadays. And then there's the labour. Skilled job, that. Big Mel's not going to be too happy about it either, and I'm sure you know what Morris is like about getting a discount.'

'Morris? Mel? Is it Melody Rathwell's bike?'

'Yeah. Maybe she'll take it out on your hide, if you ask her nice?'

He wasn't joking. He was completely serious, sympathetic even. Unfortunately it was out of the question. AJ would never allow it, not with Melody. It was worth calling AJ though, if only to get an expert opinion on the cost of repairs, because I was sure Mr Mulligan would try to take advantage of me.

'Give me a second,' I told him, and stepped away to make the call.

AJ grumbled a bit but said she'd come over, and I spent an embarrassing half-hour waiting. When she saw the bike she was nearly as horrified as Mr Mulligan, but she wasn't standing for any nonsense about the estimate, and he realised she knew what she was talking about. The final figure they agreed was still far more than I could comfortably afford, and I had to promise to pay it by instalments.

'What happened?' she asked as we walked back to where she'd left her own bike.

I could see a world of trouble opening up if I told the truth, but I didn't want to lie.

'I was collecting a cheque,' I explained, 'and when I came out I pushed the door open a bit hard.'

'Hard enough to knock a motorbike over?'

'Maybe it wasn't on its stand properly?'

She gave a doubtful cluck and went silent for a few seconds. 'Mulligan's a spanker, isn't he? Did he try it on?'

'No!'

There must have been something in the tone of my voice, because she gave me a distinctly puzzled glance, then spoke again.

'What's been going on, Pippa?'

'Nothing!'

'Show me your bum.'

'AJ, we're in the middle of the street!'

'Get in there then.'

She was pointing to the arch with the graffiti. Too shallow to be of any commercial use, it had filled up with dirt and leaves blowing in from the tiny park opposite. She pushed me forward, towards the back of the arch, which was covered with graffiti in black, silver and a brilliant spectrum of reds and oranges. Nobody could see us unless they came directly past the opening, but we were still in the street, and I was shaking as I levered my knickers down underneath my skirt. They immediately fell down to my ankles, increasing my resentment and feelings of exposure as I tugged up my skirt to show her my bare bum. She bent close, examining me, then stood up again, to lift my chin beneath one crooked finger, her eyes boring into mine. I wasn't sure if I was pink behind or not, especially as the bright sunlight pouring into the arch was sure to show up even a faint flush, and could only return her stare as best I could.

'Have you been behaving yourself?' she asked.

'Yes!' I insisted. 'AJ, you know I would never . . .'

'Do I?' she interrupted. 'You let that Maggie Phelps spank you.'

'She is a woman, AJ.'

Her finger stayed where it was for a moment more, before she released my chin, only to lift her hand and plant a single, firm smack on my bare bottom. I stayed as I was, spanked in the street, shaking badly. She spent a moment more looking at my bum, then spent a moment playing with a strand of my hair before finally stepping back. I quickly tugged my skirt down and pulled my knickers up underneath, following AJ out of the arch to find her staring thoughtfully at nothing in particular.

'OK?' I asked.

'No,' she answered me, 'but I'm sorry I doubted you. I just can't stop wondering who told Morris about your punishment.'

'Don't worry,' I said, and went up on tiptoe to kiss her on the cheek.

'What do you mean, don't worry?' she demanded. 'Now it looks like I can't have any fun with the girls without Morris fucking Rathwell finding out. Come on, I'll drop you back at work.'

I had at least got my cheque, and what had happened with the Bonneville was none of Maggie's business. She was nowhere to be seen anyway, so I put the documents and the cheque on her desk and went up to my room, where I sat looking out of the window at the trains and sulking over the events of the morning. It really wasn't fair that I should have to pay for the damage to the Bonneville, and it wasn't very nice of AJ to be so suspicious either. She'd been right, or course, but that wasn't the point. I'd also been spanked, made to show my bum and pussy to Mr Mulligan and put on display in the street, all within the space of under two hours. That gave me every right to be sulky, but I wished it hadn't also made my knickers quite so damp, something AJ must have realised.

She probably assumed, though, I had wet knickers pretty much all the time, which was true when I was with her, because she turned me on more than anybody else. It was a shame she'd had to go back to work, because it wouldn't have taken long for her to turn my bad feeling around, and she could have had me in some quiet nook, or even at her office. As it was I had ended up all alone, and I didn't even want to masturbate, because I knew full well I'd end up coming over one or another of my humiliating experiences, which would have felt like a surrender to those who'd inflicted them on me.

Normally I'd have ended up doing it anyway, but with the repair bill looming over me I just wasn't in the mood. I began to think about my arrangement with Clive Carew instead, and whether he'd managed to get his bet on. I went into the other room to listen, but all I could hear was a faint clicking, suggesting that there was just one person in the Blockhouse, and he or she was working at their computer.

Presumably he had put the bet on, and I knew I should really go downstairs and volunteer to help Mr Prufrock, but I couldn't bear the thought of being with him, let alone going down on his wrinkly old cock. If I did it at all I would have to be feeling very strong, and probably get drunk first as well. Mr Prufrock would just have to wait, and yet now I needed the money more urgently than ever.

I felt as if I'd been staring out of the window for hours when I heard a tread on the stairs, but the clock showed that barely ten minutes had passed. It was Steve Frost, looking smart in a new and obviously expensive suit.

'Lunch?' he offered.

'Thank you, yes,' I answered immediately, with real gratitude, because it was exactly what I needed to bring me out of my black mood, and all I could have afforded would have been a sandwich from the shop under the bridge.

'Come on then, we'll beat the rush,' he suggested.

'OK, but I have to get back by one,' I insisted, 'or I'll be in trouble with Maggie.'

He just laughed, and began to explain the case they had helped win that morning, some complicated job involving supposed financial irregularities which had involved most of the Blockhouse. It seemed to have earned him a good-sized bonus too, because at Champagne Charlie's he ordered a magnum bottle of some frighteningly expensive champagne. I'd supposed he wanted me alone, but Mark James, Clive and Gail were already there.

'I brought Pippa over, to brighten the place up a bit,' he explained, earning both himself and me a dirty look from Gail. 'She's more than just a pretty face too. This morning, she managed to get old man Mulligan to pay, in full.'

The others looked genuinely surprised, and I found myself blushing and looking at my toes in gratified embarrassment.

'I better watch my back,' Mark said, 'or they'll be making her a partner before me.'

'It didn't go all that well,' I admitted, eager to let out my feelings to what I knew would be a supportive audience. 'I accidentally knocked over a motorbike, the restored Triumph Bonneville you saw, Steve, and I have to pay for the damage.'

'Ouch!' Steve sympathised. 'But look, maybe we can have a whip round? What do you think, lads?'

Clive nodded. Mark began to reach for his wallet. Gail spoke up.

'I don't mean to be nasty, Pippa, but I really think you should take responsibility for your own mistakes.'

'I agree, absolutely,' I said, praying they'd ignore me, 'I did the damage, so I should pay.'

'That's a very sensible attitude,' Gail agreed.

'Maybe,' Mark said, 'but you're to let us know if you get into difficulty, Pippa, OK?'

'OK, thanks,' I promised.

'At least let me take you out to dinner this evening,' Clive put in. 'That should cheer you up.'

'No, thank you,' I answered, my voice deliberately cold. 'I'm busy.'

Clive's face fell and Mark gave a brief, dry snigger. Steve had filled a glass for me and I drank from it, the cold champagne flowing down my throat to bring a wonderful sensation of relief, for all that it made no difference whatsoever to my troubles. Another couple of glasses and I was beginning to get my confidence back, and to play a little. Andy, Den and Claire had come in, allowing me to adjust my attitude and body language to each of them; friendly and a little deferential to the two women, indifferent to Clive, cold to Den and Andy, but flirtatious with Mark and Steve. I even allowed Steve to put his arm around me as we stood at the bar, and laid my head on his shoulder for a little while, in full view of Mark.

By the time we left I was back to my old self, laughing and joking with them as I walked between Steve and Mark, each vying for my attention. It was only just after one, but there was still no sign of Maggie and I didn't quite have the courage to go down to volunteer my services to Mr Prufrock of my own accord, so I went up to the Blockhouse with them. Richard Montague emerged from his office as we passed, to congratulate them on their morning performance, and joined us. I could see why they thought I'd have been an easy target for him, with his looks and air of absolute confidence, but he didn't show any particular interest, and I ended up sitting on Steve's lap as we talked together.

He was actually being really nice, and brought out my ambivalent feelings, so that I had to remind myself that the charming, handsome man who could make me laugh so easily had said he'd like to put his cock up my bottom and make me suck it afterwards. A little voice came back, reminding me how I'd sucked on the handle of Maggie Phelps's rubber stamp happily enough, after it had been up the same dirty hole, but at least it was only a couple of inches long. Steve's cock, no doubt, was three or four times the length, and he would be sure to stick it in as deep as it would go before transferring it to my mouth.

At length Richard Montague persuaded everybody to go back to work, myself included. I knew I had a perfect opportunity to go down to the basement, but I went upstairs instead, and down again, one flight, and up again, and down again, two flights, which was where Maggie caught me as she came out of Mr Todmorden's office.

'There you are, Pippa,' she said. 'I understand it went well this morning?'

'Yes,' I admitted, trying not to sound sulky.

'And did you?' she asked quietly.

'A little bit,' I admitted. 'He . . . he made me show him my bum.'

Her expression flickered to a truly sadistic joy, but only for a moment, and then she had composed herself again.

'Good girl,' she said. 'And I don't suppose it was so very terrible, really, was it?'

I made a face, unable to express my true emotions on the landing where anyone might have come past, but not wanting to claim I'd liked the way Mr Mulligan had treated me either. Maggie gave a knowing smile.

'I understand,' she said. 'I was the same once, but believe me, it's best to get over your bad feelings and not to be too prissy.'

'I'm not prissy,' I answered, but I could hear the sulky tone in my voice, and she just laughed.

'You are a little bit prissy, Pippa, but I dare say you'll grow out of it, with experience. Speaking of which, I want you to go down to the basement and help Mr Prufrock this afternoon, and this time, do be nice to him.'

'Nice?' I queried.

'You know very well what I mean, Pippa,' she said impatiently. 'Just don't make a fuss if his hand should happen to stray to your bottom, or anything of that sort, and be prepared to show him little courtesies, the sort a gentleman might like.'

I began to protest, only to shut my mouth again, my outrage tempered by what I knew full well I was supposed to be doing.

'OK,' I answered.

'Don't sulk, Pippa,' she told me. 'It's very unbecoming. Just think of it as a charitable act towards a lonely old man, and do stop making those faces. Try and act like a lady.'

'A lady wouldn't let Mr Prufrock touch her up.'

'A true lady never makes a fuss over such things, but unfortunately true ladies are very rare indeed, these days. Now run along.'

She was talking rubbish, not only about ladylike behaviour, but about being charitable too. There was more to it, I was sure. For one thing she kept calling me 'prissy', a word Mr Prufrock also used, and they'd both used the phrase 'little courtesies' in just the same way. He wasn't a spanker, or at least not according to Mr Montague, but perhaps he and Maggie had some sort of arrangement. In any event, I was going down to the basement.

As I descended the stairs I was trying to tell myself it was what I'd decided to do anyway, but that did nothing for the weak feeling in my stomach or the trembling of my hand as I knocked on the door. It opened, and Mr Prufrock's face appeared, his little dark eyes twinkling in the light as he took me in, his toad mouth twitching with pleasure.

'I was told to help you this afternoon,' I announced.

'Come in then,' he said, moving aside as he opened the door to place himself in the perfect position for applying a pat to my bottom.

I knew he'd do it, and couldn't help but wince as I came close. Sure enough, out came his hand and I winced a second time as I was given a gentle pat to steer me through the door. This time I kept my feelings to myself, swallowing my shame and resentment. Mr Prufrock closed the door with what seemed a horrible finality and I was alone with him.

'What should I do?' I asked.

'Now there is a question,' he answered. 'I can think of some very interesting things a little popsy like you might do, were she rather less prissy than she is, and in return she might find a gentleman really quite generous.'

I wondered if he was offering to pay me for sex, which made me feel sick.

'You . . . you don't need to be generous,' I told him. 'I've spoken to Maggie.'

'Ah ha, have you indeed,' he replied, 'and what did she have to say?'

'She said . . . she said I wasn't to make a fuss if you asked for any little courtesies,' I answered him.

He sat down in his chair before answering, looking up at me with a little doubt and a great deal of lust.

'You made a fuss last time you visited me,' he said, 'a most unladylike little fuss.'

'I won't this time,' I said, and hung my head.

'I'm very glad to hear it,' he replied, 'but after your behaviour, I'm sure you'll understand if I'm a little doubtful. Come a little closer, and turn around.'

I did so, forcing myself to take a step towards him and turn my back, just as I had for Mr Mulligan.

Obviously Mr Prufrock had something similar in mind, only more intimate still. My trembling had grown hard to control as I waited for his touch, and when it came my stomach lurched.

He'd begun to explore my bottom, his short, podgy fingers stroking my cheeks through the material of my skirt, to feel out their shape, tracing a slow line down the gentle valley over my crease, following the contours where my cheeks tuck under, and again, a little more firmly, and this time pushing in to feel where my bum meets my thighs, directly over pussy. A sob escaped my lips as I felt a knuckle press in towards my pussy hole, making me think of penetration.

Mr Prufrock merely chuckled and continued to enjoy my bum. It was hardly the first time I'd been touched up, and I wasn't even bare, but he was a man, and not just any man, but a dirty, lewd, old pervert, who was clearly enjoying my embarrassment and shame as much as the feel of my flesh. There was something awful about his touch too, something horribly intrusive, which made my stomach churn and my knees feel weak, but still I kept my hands on my head and my thoughts to myself.

I thought he was going to strip me, to lift my skirt and pull down my knickers and have a good grope of my bare flesh, probably pull my cheeks apart to inspect my anus and check pussy to see if I was a virgin, which I knew would be more than I could stand. Fortunately he contented himself with fondling me through my clothes, and finally stopped.

'So it is true,' he said. 'Well I never.'

'What do you mean?' I asked.

'Never you mind what I mean,' he said, 'just you get those little knickers off, and your skirt. I think I'll have you work bare bottom today. In fact, I think I'll have you work bare bottom every day. Just let me lock the door.'

I hesitated, wondering if I could negotiate, perhaps agreeing to go bare if he promised not to touch me too intimately, or whether I'd only succeed in revealing my darkest fears and encourage him to take advantage. He locked the door, twisting a huge iron key in a lock that looked as if it had been in place since the building was first put up.

'Come along, let's have you bare,' he said as he turned again, his tone of voice suggesting he was talking to a not very intelligent child, or a dog.

Again I wondered if I should try to bargain, but decided against it. Struggling not to make faces, I reached up beneath my office skirt, took hold of my knickers and levered them down. He watched, his little piggy eyes bright with pleasure, as I removed my panties and hung them on a peg by the door, alongside his musty old overcoat. Now I was bare under my skirt, and as my fingers went to the zip they were trembling so badly I fumbled it twice before catching hold. I pushed it down and felt my skirt grow loose around my waist, bringing me a sharp sense of exposure, and worse as a little bit of my hip came on show; so bad I realised my courage was about to fail me and hurriedly pulled it down and off before it did.

'Very pretty,' Mr Prufrock remarked.

I hung my skirt up with my panties, trying not to show too much as I moved, and failing. The tails of my jacket and blouse almost covered my bum, leaving just the turn of my cheeks showing beneath, but I was quite bare at the front, pussy peeping out naked between my thighs, and I couldn't resist shielding myself with my hands as I turned back to him.

'Oh no you don't,' he chided, wagging one fat finger at me, 'there's no need to be shy, not in front of me. Yours won't be the first bare fanny I've seen, you know.'

Very hesitantly, I took my hand away, to show him the tight pink V between my thighs. AJ likes me to shave, and I was bare, which made him raise his eyebrows and smack his lips, a gesture at once so dirty and so expectant I quickly covered myself again. This time he chuckled, and spoke with immense satisfaction.

'Oh I do like them shy,' he said, 'dirty but shy, the best possible combination. Are you a virgin, dear Philippa?'

'Yes,' I admitted.

'Not for long, I'll be bound,' he replied, chuckling again, and I just had to speak out.

'Mr Prufrock, I ... I don't mind ... don't mind providing what you call little courtesies, but I'm afraid I'm not going to allow you to go that far.'

'Oh you needn't worry about that, my dear,' he laughed. 'Not that I would turn down a chance to pop that delightful little cherry, but I fear I have been unable to manage an erection for some years, rather over a decade in fact, and I dare not resort to medical assistance for fear of the condition of my heart. My doctor advises against it, you see, and ...'

He went on for some time, describing his medical symptoms as I stood there with my hands shielding my pussy, feeling increasingly foolish. In the end I took my hand away, because it just seemed silly to be guarding my modesty when he'd already seen so much. As I exposed myself he stopped talking about his ailments, which was well worth giving him a flash anyway.

'That's my girl,' he said. 'It's silly to hide yourself from a gentleman of my age and condition, isn't it?

Now, I believe you were sent down here to do some work, so if you wouldn't mind going through this stack here and rearranging the files so that they're in order of archive date instead of alphabetical, that would be most kind. You'll stay bare, of course.'

I hadn't imagined for an instant that I'd be allowed to cover up, and it was just the sort of dirty trick I'd have expected him to play on me, but that didn't stop my resentment and sense of shame building as I went about my task. The work seemed pointless, at least as far as filing was concerned. From the point of view of making me show off, it was anything but pointless. I constantly had to stretch up and bend over, displaying my bum and pussy from all angles, while he sat in his chair and enjoyed the view.

At first I tried to show as little as possible, but it just made the work harder and more tedious than it already was. Gradually I gave in, at first keeping my body sideways on as much as possible, but soon abandoning that in favour of squatting down instead of bending so that I didn't show too much behind, only to give in because it made my knees hurt. The last of my resistance came at the thought of him being the first man to see my bumhole, but I was forced to get into so many awkward positions I soon couldn't be sure that he hadn't. At last I gave in, too humiliated to care any more as I bent to pick up a pile of files and let my cheeks spread behind, showing off the little pink knot to his dirty, leering gaze. After that, I didn't even bother to keep my legs closed. The damage was done, he'd seen it all, and if he wanted to examine my bumhole and the folds of my pussy lips in minute detail then that just made him a dirty old bastard.

I was hot and sweaty too, with stiff nipples and a creamy pussy despite myself. He'd made me humiliate myself in front of him and I was aroused, there was no point in denying it. I felt bewildered, even that I'd betrayed myself, but before too long I had to accept that I was ready for cock. Nor was it just for the bet. I wanted to be dirty, or better still, I wanted him to make me be dirty. That way I'd have fun and could win the bet too, while I could at least pretend to myself that I'd been cajoled into it, but he seemed content to watch.

He was sitting sprawled in his chair, his thighs open to show the bulge in his trousers, and if he wasn't stiff then he was certainly big. As I worked he'd been touching himself occasionally, but that was all, and not enough, although goodness knows what the Blockhouse boys would have thought if they'd caught me working with my bum and pussy on show and Mr Prufrock watching me. I had to do something, so I told myself I'd sit on his knee and take him in my hand, which surely counted even if he couldn't get an erection?

For maybe ten minutes more I continued to work, stretching and bending and squatting to expose myself to him, now deliberately in order to make my feelings stronger still. I even bent to retie a stack of files with my bottom full towards him, holding my pose and knowing full well he'd have a clear view of pussy pouting out between my thighs and the wrinkled pink knot of my bumhole above. Just knowing he could see that had me breathless, and finally allowed me to speak the words that would make me a complete and utter slut.

I stretched up to put the files on the shelf, making my tails lift to show my bare bum one last time, then turned to face him. There were plenty more shelves to do, but we both knew the work was pointless, and created only to provide plenty of opportunity for me to make a display of myself.

'Er ... Mr Prufrock,' I said, 'if you want a little favour, I don't mind. Perhaps you'd like me to sit on your lap, and ... hold you for a bit ... hold your penis?'

I heard the words, but it was hard to believe they were coming from my own mouth. Even Mr Prufrock looked doubtful, but that didn't stop him nodding and putting his hands to his fly. I watched, every second bringing me closer to making a tart of myself, as his zip peeled down, his trousers came wide, and he pulled open the hole in his underpants to flop out a fat, dark-skinned cock and a heavily wrinkled set of balls. Now ready for me, he spread his thighs a little further to leave the whole obscene mass dangling down between, and patted his leg.

'Come along then, my dear.'

I realised I'd been holding back, but forced myself to step forward, to settle my bare bottom on his knee, and as his hand found the curve of my meat, to take his cock in mine. Now I'd done it, really done it. There I was, quite the little tart, sat bare bottom on a dirty old man's lap, tugging his cock as he fondled me, and not minding in the least. Far from it. It felt lovely, to have my bottom bare and his hand kneading my flesh, to feel the heavy bulk of his penis in my grip, and to wonder if I could get him erect after all, to make him spunk up all over my hand.

'Maggie was right, you are a dirty one,' he said, 'and what a firm little bottom you have. You don't mind me feeling, do you?'

I shook my head, unable to express myself, or to admit out loud that I was enjoying the rude, intimate way he was fondling my bum. He had one hand cupping a cheek, so that his little finger was just an inch or so from my bumhole, which had begun to twitch and squeeze as I wondered if he'd get ruder still and touch it. I pushed my bottom out a little more, telling myself I was just getting comfortable on his lap, but in reality to make pussy available for his fingers. He gave his dirty little chuckle, and suddenly I could feel that his cock had begun to grow firmer and fatter in my hand.

'I think you're getting stiff, Mr Prufrock,' I told him, and began to wank faster.

He was, his cock definitely swelling, and a wet pink helmet had begun to peep up from his foreskin at every tug. His hand moved a little, wringing a gasp and a sob from my lips as his little finger found my bumhole. I wanted to say no, to tell him he'd gone too far, but my instinct was the opposite, to push out my bottom even more. He began to poke at my anus, making it open a little, and with my hole slippery with pussy juice the tip of his finger was soon in.

I was sobbing with shame even as I began to wriggle my bottom on his intruding finger, wanting more. He obliged, slipping his hand beneath me to cup my bottom, now with a longer, thicker finger touching my anus. I tugged harder, the way Clive had explained I should wank a cock after I'd brought him off in my face, and in return had the new finger slipped in up my bumhole. He began to wriggle it around in my ring, filling my head with filthy thoughts, of being sodomised on my knees, or sitting fully in his lap with his erection up my bum, even of taking his dirty penis in my mouth once I'd been well and truly buggered.

'That's my darling,' he rasped as I began to squirm my bottom on his finger. 'You like a little attention to your botty hole, don't you?'

Again I could only nod in agreement, the shame burning in my head as I admitted the awful truth. He pushed deeper and I gasped, my anus squeezing on his finger as he began to explore my rectum. His cock was nearly hard, flopping just a little with each tug of my hand, and long, and thick, far thicker than my bumhole could accommodate, I was sure, but I still wanted to try.

'Do whatever you like to me,' I sobbed, 'anything at all.'

'Then I'll show you a little trick,' he said, 'a little trick you'll thank me for the rest of your life.'

As he spoke he had begun to extract his finger from my anus. I lifted my bum, expecting to be shifted onto his erection as my bottom hole closed with a soft, bubbling fart, but he simply slipped his hand between my thighs, cupping pussy and starting to rub her with the finger he'd just had up my bum. He was going to masturbate me, and maybe he thought I'd never come.

I was going to now, my muscles squeezing even as he found my clit, and in a moment I was tugging furiously on his cock, still wishing he'd try to fuck my bottom, or fuck my cunt. He had me completely, his fingers working in the wet, mushy flesh of my sex as I squirmed my bare bottom on his hand and wanked him as hard as I could. I'd have done anything, let him spank me and grope me and take down my panties whenever he liked, as often as he liked, let him up my bum and suck his penis clean, let him take my virginity and fill my willing little hole with spunk . . .

He gave his filthy little chuckle as I came under his fingers, but that was it. His cock still wasn't fully hard, certainly not hard enough to get in up my tiny bumhole, while the moment my orgasm had died all my feelings of shame and resentment came flooding back. Not that I said anything, because it would have seemed ridiculous after the way I'd behaved, and I knew I'd be back the next day, and with my knickers off.

Six

I had a lot of trouble coming to terms with what I'd done, and especially my own reactions. So many times I'd allowed the thought of dirty, humiliating sex with men to creep into my fantasies, but I had never imagined the reality could break down my resistance so absolutely. Not that I was any more attracted to men than before, let alone the appalling Mr Prufrock. It wasn't the men who turned me on, it was the humiliation.

Two other things helped, that I was doing it to win my bet, and that I could try to see what I'd done as a act of charity. Take away the sex, and I had provided a lot of pleasure for a lonely old man, which was just the sort of thing I was always told I should be doing in Guides, although it very definitely did not include showing them my bum, let alone wanking them off. For the bet, everything was going to plan. Clive had the money on, and it was just a matter of me getting caught, although we had agreed to wait awhile to avoid arousing suspicions.

So for the rest of the week I followed the same hideously embarrassing routine; down to the basement, off with my panties and skirt, a little show for Mr Prufrock, an hour of work done bottomless. The work was the worst of it, because he invariably chose things that meant I had to stretch up or bend down, so that I was repeatedly showing off my bum, and quite often my anus and both front and rear views of pussy. He lapped it all up, his bright piggy eyes drinking in every rude detail of my body and every embarrassing little display I was forced to make, while I had to suffer the gradual build-up of my arousal and the inevitable consequences.

Unfortunately there was a problem. He was always careful to lock the door as soon as I came in, and once he had turned the big iron key in the lock he would put it in his jacket pocket until I was once more decent. Never once did he vary the routine, until I began to think that we would have to find some other way of getting me caught.

We also talked occasionally, generally once I'd been brought off under his fingers. Because I could never make him come, he was always at his horniest, and wanted to know all about my sex life, which he imagined as a series of bedtime romps with my school friends and clumsy fumblings by inexperienced boys. I pretended to be shy, which only made him all the more eager.

On the Friday morning I got him to confirm something I'd suspected all along. Maggie had substituted me for herself, ending an agreement to come down into the basement twice a week and pose for him while he played with his cock. I was not best pleased, especially as she was supposed to keep my secret between the four spanking enthusiasts, and Mr Prufrock was not included. She'd also broken the rules about spanking in the office, which tempted me to take my revenge by reporting her to Mr Montague.

The opportunity came almost immediately. I'd come up from the cellar for lunch, and Mr Prufrock had made me leave my knickers with him, so I was bare under my skirt, and perhaps Maggie had been made to do the same thing, as she smiled and raised her eyebrows when she met me on the stairs. All she got in return was a scowl as I wondered if I dare express my feelings then and there, but it merely seemed to amuse her.

'Mr Prufrock is very pleased with you,' she said.

'I bet he is,' I told her. 'I don't think it's very fair, Maggie . . .'

'Sh,' she urged, lifting a finger to her lips. 'After all, it's what you like.'

'No it is not!'

'I think we both know you rather better than that, Pippa, don't we?'

'No . . .'

'He tells me you like to sit on his knee and play with his cock, that you even suggested it, and that you like him to call you his "little tart".'

I felt my face go scarlet, instantly betraying myself. She gave me a knowing, sadistic smile and went on.

'Perhaps I should tell him you enjoy playing spanking games? I don't think he's into it, but I'm sure he would be happy to oblige you.'

'That's not fair, Maggie,' I blustered, but stopped as her smile grew broader and more evil still. 'Please don't?'

We reached the second-floor landing, and she stopped.

'Then perhaps I should take you back upstairs?' she suggested. 'I miss your pretty little behind, and I suspect you're overdue a spanking.'

'I don't want to be spanked by you,' I answered. 'AJ says I mustn't, and . . .'

'Then perhaps she'd be interested to hear how you let me warm your bottom before your little encounter with Mr Mulligan?' she said. 'Or perhaps she'd even like to know what you did for Mr Mulligan, flashing your little tail for him and the mechanics.'

'You bitch!'

'You will not call me that, Pippa. Get up to your room, now, and wait for me there. I'm going to spank you so hard . . .'

She stopped at the sound of a cough and I saw her face go pale. I spun round, to find Mr Todmorden standing behind me in the open door of his office.

'Come in here, both of you,' he demanded.

We went, and I was fidgeting badly as he closed the door behind us, sure he was just going to whip me across his knee and spank me pink whether I liked it or not, but when he spoke his words were addressed to Maggie.

'For goodness sake, do you have no sense at all?' he demanded. 'I heard every word.'

'There's nobody in on the third floor,' Maggie said hastily.

'And what if young Mr Montague had been in conference with me?' Mr Todmorden enquired. 'Or a client, God forbid. Which is all beside the point in any case, as unless I'm greatly mistaken you threatened to take Pippa up to her office for a spanking?'

Maggie didn't answer, but hung her head, and she too was fidgeting with her fingers.

'Don't you have any patience?' he went on. 'Damn it, woman, don't you think I'd like to do the same? Certainly I would, but I have the common sense to wait until Pippa is ready and the circumstances allow.'

'I'm sorry,' Maggie answered, sounding utterly pathetic.

'Sorry won't do,' he answered. 'What you need is a dose of what you were threatening to dish out, don't you think?'

The consternation on Maggie's face was wonderful to see, and she was going to refuse when I spoke up.

'I think that would be fair,' I said, 'and I don't mind, as long as it's done by a woman.'

'Hardly fair in my case . . .' Maggie began, but I cut her off.

'Why not? I think you deserve it, and hard.'

Her expression turned to outrage, but she must have caught the look in my eyes. I was taking a risk, because I had no idea what his reaction would have been to my revelations about Mr Prufrock, and it might well have ruined my plan with Clive, but Maggie fell for my bluff.

'Very well,' she said. 'If I have to.'

'Good,' Mr Todmorden said, and put his fat hands together in what I hoped was preparation for walloping her skinny bottom while I looked on. 'Not here, of course, but Morris has made an offer for the next party, free entry for anyone who brings a willing girl. Mr Montague will be taking Helen, of course, and I had planned to ask you, Pippa, but Morris tells me you're coming anyway, so you will do nicely, Maggie.'

I'd have liked to spend a moment drinking in the expression of utter horror on Maggie's face, but I was more worried on my own behalf.

'Sorry . . . Mr Todmorden. You said Morris told you I was coming?'

'So Morris said,' he replied. 'Aren't you?'

'No.'

'How peculiar. He seemed so sure.'

'You should come,' Maggie said nastily. 'I'm sure you'd love to see me get it.'

'I would, only I'd get it myself, wouldn't I?'

'Oh, you can count on that, my girl.'

'Ladies, please,' Mr Todmorden interrupted. 'I shall call Morris and find out what is going on.'

'Please tell him I'm not coming,' I put in.

'As you wish,' he answered. 'You may go, both of you.'

We left, and I made a point of going downstairs, just in case Maggie had any ideas about following me up to my room. I felt annoyed, for several reasons, and frustrated too. Had she taken me upstairs I knew I'd have ended up enjoying my punishment, which was pretty humiliating in itself, while I'd also lost the chance to see her get it, which would have been immensely satisfying.

I bought a sandwich at the shop under the bridge and went to eat it on a sort of observation platform outside Tower Hill Station, with a view over the Tower itself and the river beyond. It was only when I caught a look of astonishment from an elderly American tourist that I realised that the people passing below only had to glance upwards to see right up my skirt to my bare pussy. Pink-faced, I retreated to a nearby park where I could finish my lunch without providing a peep-show at the same time.

With Maggie told off and facing a spanking, I wasn't under any obligation to go back to Mr Prufrock that day, and she'd given me no other instructions. As I walked back to Montague, Montague, Todmorden and Montague I was wondering what would happen if I simply took the rest of the day off, but decided not to risk it. I went up to my room instead and had hardly sat down when the ancient black telephone attached to one wall rang, making me jump as I hadn't even realised it was connected. Somewhat gingerly, I answered it.

'Hello?'

A female voice answered, her accent an odd blend of the East End and New Yorker, her tone commanding to say the least.

'Pippa?'

'Yes.'

'This is Melody Rathwell. What's this I hear about you not coming to the party?'

'I never said I was!'

'Mr Mulligan seems to think you are.'

'Er . . . that's all a bit complicated, but I'm not coming.'

'Then how are you supposed to work off the money you owe for my bike?'

'I can do that . . . in time.'

'What do you mean, in time? I've already paid him, and you're going to work it off over his knee, and mine.'

'No I am not! You can't make me, Melody. Anyway, AJ says . . .'

'Sod AJ, any shit from her and she goes over too, and you both know I can do it. You've got a straight choice, Miss Pippa. You pay for the damage, or you come to the party.'

'I'll pay for the damage, thank you.'

'With what? Or are you going to run to Daddy to help you out?'

The contempt in her voice had me blushing, but I managed an answer.

'I am earning.'

'I don't want it in instalments, Pippa. I want it paid off, now.'

'I can't, not now, but I will as soon as I can.'

'You pay before the party, or you come to the party.'

'No. I . . .'

She had put the phone down, leaving me trembling. There was only one thing for it, to make sure I was caught with Mr Prufrock early next week, which would allow me to solve my problems with one

158

stroke, or at least, most of my problems. Somehow I would have to make sure the basement door remained unlocked, that or arrange some other indiscretion. Unfortunately it was not easy to see how it could be done, while I'd also have to suck Mr Prufrock's cock to get the most out of it. The thought of Andy, Den or even Mark catching me with my skirt and knickers off and Mr Prufrock's cock in my mouth made me feel weak and sick.

I spent most of Friday evening at Whispers, an ordinary night out with the girls, from which I felt strangely detached. My knickers were still in Mr Prufrock's lair, and inevitably AJ found out I was bare, so that I first had to suffer the embarrassment of having my skirt lifted so the entire bar could see, then was forced to make up a story about how I'd wet myself and had nothing to change into.

They lapped it up, especially Jade, and I ended up being taken into the loos and made to pee in front of them, then put on my knees to lick AJ while Jade brought me off from behind. That left AJ in the best mood she'd been in all week, because she was still brooding about Morris knowing what had happened at the Pumps, and she offered to take me home on her bike. I accepted happily, and we stayed in Whispers until closing time, so that it was gone one when we finally arrived in Sonning.

The house was dark, but then it had been dark the time Jemima had caught me too, so I found myself looking suspiciously at her window as I dismounted. AJ had taken off her helmet, and as I fastened my own to the bike she leant out to kiss me. I gave her a peck on the cheek.

'That's no way to say goodbye,' she protested. 'Come here.'

'Better not,' I advised. 'Last time my sister saw, and now she keeps asking questions about spanking and stuff.'

'That's cool. She's cute, is Jemima.'

'AJ! She's my little sister!'

'Not so little she can't make her own mind what she's into. Bring her down to Whispers one night, why don't you?'

'She prefers boys.'

'What a waste. Oh well, if I can't do her, I'll just have to do you in front of her.'

She'd grabbed my wrist, and a moment later I was across the petrol tank, my skirt had been bundled up and my bottom laid bare to the moon, then smacked, a dozen times, to leave me tingling behind and blushing as I once more glanced at Jemima's window. AJ laughed.

'There, and tell her she can have the same anytime she wants. Hey, how'd you like me to do her in front of you? That would wipe the smile off her face!'

'No, AJ, please . . .'

'Hey, I'm joking. Lighten up, will you.'

She ruffled my hair and reached down for her helmet.

'See you Monday night, yeah?'

'See you then.'

I went in, expecting to find a smirking Jemima in my room, but she'd been asleep all the time. She was still asleep when I got up, and stayed that way until Mum finally got fed up with her. It had been a long week, and I spent most of Saturday lazing in the garden and riding, while Jemima was off somewhere with some friends from school. Her exam results had arrived, and she'd done almost as well as me, failing to get her star in just one subject, so she was in the mood to celebrate.

We were going to Granny's for lunch on the Sunday, which hopefully meant I could nip across the road afterwards and swim in Penny's pool. Jade might even be there and, even if she wasn't, there might be interesting possibilities, just as long as I could get rid of Jemima. That didn't seem likely, and I resigned myself to not getting my bottom warmed again until the Monday night.

As usual, we went over quite early, and I joined in the usual family routine of helping prepare the dinner and drinking sherry in the garden. Penny was there, as I'd hoped, and managed to get me alone long enough for a kiss and a gentle squeeze of each other's bums, which left me hoping for more. Lunch was roast beef and Yorkshire pudding, with all the trimmings, followed by apple pie and cream, leaving me feeling replete and a little sleepy, which wasn't helped by the wine I'd drunk. With the washing-up done, Penny invited anyone who wanted to come across the road and swim, but just as I had expected, Jemima jumped at the chance.

Watching her change I was reminded of what AJ had said. People call me skinny, but she was like a broomstick, with barely enough flesh to fill out her tiny blue bikini, either at top or bottom. Yet she was undoubtedly a woman, with a rich growth of dark brown hair over her pussy and full, puffy nipples that seemed to be permanently erect. I really had no business to try to stop her from doing as she pleased, and yet it was impossible not to feel protective.

I spent a while sunbathing to let my lunch go down, telling myself there was a chance Jemima would get bored and go back to Granny's so Penny and I could strip off for mutual spankings and whatever else came to mind once we were warm behind and turned on for sex. Penny didn't seem to have read the script, messing about with Jemima in the pool until I finally gave up and jumped in myself. It was impossible not to have fun, and I was soon splashing about as enthusiastically as the others, when Penny's bell went.

'Jade?' I asked.

'She's not coming up this weekend,' Penny told me.

She got out, pulled on a gown and went to the door, so that I had my back turned to Jemima just too long. I got jumped on and my head pushed under water, so that I was still grappling with her in the hope of revenge when Penny came back with her visitors, Morris and Melody Rathwell. I tried to stop playing and immediately got ducked again, leaving Morris chuckling with amusement and Melody looking smug, but I finally managed to push Jemima off and make her stop it.

'Don't mind us,' Morris assured me, then turned to Jem. 'You must be Pippa's sister. I'm Morris, and this is my wife, Melody.'

'Hi,' Jemima answered enthusiastically and extended a wet hand up from the pool.

Melody looked like a tiger with its eye on a spring lamb as she grasped Jemima's hand, and Morris was worse. Penny had gone in to get drinks for them, and I realised what the girls had meant about her being servile to Melody.

'I had a bottle of Provençal Rosé in the fridge just in case you dropped in,' she said, 'as I know it's a favourite. So what brings you over?'

'We were in the area,' Morris said, obviously lying, 'so instead of phoning we thought we'd drop in and try to persuade you to come to next Saturday's party. You haven't been for ages, and everybody's been asking after you. It'll be a good one too.'

'I'm er . . . I'm not sure,' Penny responded, trying desperately to signal the presence of Jemima with her eyes, but if they saw, they ignored her.

'Oh come on, Penny,' Melody urged, 'we're even letting the girls choose, and you can go first. How's that for an offer?'

'We wanted Pippa to come too,' Morris added, 'but she's being a stick-in-the-mud. I'm sure you could persuade her.'

'What's the party?' Jemima asked innocently. 'Do I get invited?'

'Absolutely,' Morris responded on the instant. 'If you'd like to come?'

'Yes, please,' Jemima answered.

Penny and I exchanged a terrified look. One of us had to speak up, but it was hard to know what to say.

'You wouldn't like it, Jem,' I tried. 'It'll just be a load of boring old people talking about golf and mortgages. That's why I'm not going.'

'That,' Morris said, 'is hardly a fair description of one of my parties, but fair enough, if it's not your thing. I suppose your sister and your auntie have told you . . .'

'No, we have not!' Penny broke in.

'What?' Jemima demanded.

'Let's just say,' Melody replied, 'that the reason big sister won't come to the party is that she doesn't want her chubby little tushie smacked, which is what she deserves for denting my bike.'

'What?' Jemima demanded. 'Is it some sort of sex party? Do people get spanked?'

I'd hidden my face in my hands, but Penny answered.

'Yes, they do, Jemima, and it hurts, a lot. Did you have to say that, Mel?'

'Why do you go then, Auntie Penny?' Jemima asked, and Penny blushed crimson.

163

'Because she loves it!' Melody said when she'd got her laughter under control. 'And so does your butter-wouldn't-melt-in-her-mouth big sister. Don't you, girls? Nothing like a good spanky, eh?'

Penny looked as if she was about to burst into tears, but Morris was chuckling, and raised a calming hand.

'Relax,' he advised, 'what red-blooded girl doesn't enjoy her bottom warmed from time to time? It's nothing to be ashamed of, is it? Come along, if you like, Jemima . . .'

'I warn you, Jem, don't,' I broke in. 'It's nothing but a load of dirty old men, and they won't just smack you gently on your clothes. They expect to take your knickers down, and they expect to have a good feel too, and afterwards, the girls get taken upstairs.'

I was looking daggers at the Rathwells as I spoke, and Jemima had finally begun to look uneasy when Morris spoke up again.

'There's a stop word, Jemima, which is "red". Just say "red" and whatever's happening will come to a stop right then. If you just want a time out, or to slow down a little, say "amber", and don't worry, Mel will look after you.'

'I will,' Melody promised.

'Yes,' Penny cut in, 'you'd be the first in the queue to spank her! Come on you two, leave Jemima alone. Can't you see she's scared?'

'I am not!' Jemima retorted. 'I'd quite like to go, actually . . .'

'Oh no you would not!' I cut her off.

'Why not?' she demanded. 'Maybe I'd like my bottom smacked. You do.'

'Not by a load of dirty old men! Look, Jemima, maybe I'll take you to Whispers sometime, and you can see what it's like, or even ... I don't know, maybe I'll let my friend Jade ...'

'Is she the fat one with the enormous tits?'

'I'll tell her that!' Melody laughed. 'Then you'll definitely get it!'

'I'd rather a man,' Jemima said. 'Would you like to spank me, Mr Rathwell?'

Morris had a reputation for staying calm and in control, but at that moment I thought he was going to have an apoplexy. Jemima knew exactly what she was doing as well, smiling sweetly and making her eyes big as she waited for an answer. Melody looked intrigued, and Penny horrified, but her nipples had gone stiff under her bikini top and I couldn't really blame her. That didn't mean I'd given in.

'You're not going, Jemima, and that's final. I'll tell Mum.'

'Will you?' she answered, mockingly. 'I'm sure Mum would love to know exactly what you get up to with AJ.'

'I think your mother has already guessed, Pippa,' Penny put in, 'but she's right, Jemima.'

'Frankly,' Morris stated, 'I think it's Jemima's decision. Here's my card, Jemima. If you'd like to come, give me a ring. I'll even send the Rolls for you.'

He extended his hand, holding out a laminated business card, but I snatched it before Jemima could take hold. She snatched back and I dodged, losing my grip on the edge of the pool and going under. Jemima grappled for my arm and I jerked myself away, the card still in my hand as I took a stroke towards the far side. She came after me, her fingers plucking at my skin, and at my bikini pants. Before I could stop her they were down, with my bare bum sticking up out of the water and, as I grabbed for them, she let go. I was red-faced and furious as I rounded on her,

165

to find her holding the card up out of the water in triumph.

'You little . . .,' I began, only to break off as I realised that even Penny was trying not to laugh.

'Beautiful!' Morris declared. 'And at long last I get to see Pippa's bum. Thank you, Jemima, and if you two ever fancy putting on a little strip wrestling show . . .'

'Shut up, Morris!' I snapped. 'She's not going.'

'Oh yes I am,' Jemima answered.

'I think she is,' Morris agreed.

I looked from Jemima to Morris. Jemima had her stubborn look on and I realised I had lost.

'OK,' I sighed, 'but if she's going, so am I.'

'In that case I'd better come too, I suppose,' Penny added.

'Excellent!' Morris declared, smacking his hands together. 'I think this might be one of our best, Mel, perhaps the very best.'

I drew a heavy sigh as I pulled up my bikini pants.

I'd had my pants pulled down by my little sister in front of Morris Rathwell. It didn't bear thinking about, which meant I couldn't get it out of my head. For the rest of the afternoon it stayed at the forefront of my mind, a constant humiliation on top of all my worries. I was still determined that Jemima wouldn't go to the Rathwells, but she was equally determined to do so and there didn't seem to be very much I could do to stop her. She certainly wasn't going to let me talk her out of it, and wouldn't listen to me or to Penny, even when they'd gone.

In the end I gave up, and tried to make the strength of my feelings plain by not talking to her. It made no difference, except that after a while she began to sulk and went back to Granny's. By then it was time to go home anyway, but Penny promised to drop me over later and we were alone at last, but in no mood for sex. She was nearly as upset as me, but trying to reason away our concerns.

'It's probably for the best,' she was saying. 'Once she finds out what the sort of people who go to Morris's parties are like, she'll soon change her mind. It will probably put her off spanking too.'

'That's true,' I admitted. 'Have you met Mr Mulligan?'

'No.'

'He's a big greasy East End mechanic who likes to make girls show their bottoms in front of his son.'

'He sounds typical. Have you met Mr Judd?'

'No.'

'He likes to bugger us ... sorry, I shouldn't say "us".'

'Don't worry. Mr Todmorden's like that, but worse. He collects girls' anal virginities.'

'I've met him, but he's not as bad as Mr Enos, who's so fat he can only fuck us if we go on top, and he likes to give us enemas. Mr Protheroe's almost as fat, and he likes to make us talk about what he's doing while he spanks us. Then there's Hudson Staebler, who's American and likes to have us behave like dogs, and Mr Spottiswood, who they call the Pantyman because he likes to do things with our knickers, including wear them.'

I grimaced, remembering the pair of knickers I'd left in the basement. Penny was right. Jemima would take one look at Morris's collection of dirty old men and run for the hills. Morris was hardly going to stop her, so I could leave too and that would be the end of the party, no public spankings, no cock sucking. I pushed down a sudden, shameful pang of disappointment.

'What about Morris?' I asked.

'He'll do just about anything,' she said. 'For instance, he has a yoke he likes to make us wear, so our hands are trapped and he can hold on to get a really good push when he fucks us. He has a tiny cock.'

'Well he's not putting it in me!'

'Be careful, he's tricky. He'll try to get you drunk and aroused, then play some dirty game which you'll lose and feel obliged to pay the consequences.'

'I'll refuse.'

'Fair enough. Oh, and watch out for Mel . . . or on second thoughts, if you've been living with AJ she might not seem so bad. At least Mel's not likely to flush your head down the loo.'

'Er . . . yes, sorry about that.'

She answered with a wan smile and we both went quiet, each alone with her own thoughts. Jemima was bound to freak completely, probably as soon as we got to the party, but it still made my stomach crawl to think of the men, all of them hoping to see me spanked, maybe to spank me themselves, and afterwards, to have me attend to their cocks. Some of the ones Penny knew sounded worse than those I'd already met; Judd, Enos, Protheroe, Staebler and Spottiswood, each perverted in his own way, each keen to get his hands on me, and on Jem.

'Bastards,' I said out loud. 'What is it with men? Why do they always want to be so dirty with us?'

'Oh come on,' she answered. 'AJ's no better.'

'Maybe, but . . . you know, wanting to stick their cocks up our bottoms and . . . and things like that.'

I was thinking of what Steve Frost wanted to do to me, but I didn't like to say it out loud. Penny took a moment to answer, and she was looking embarrassed as she spoke.

'That's quite nice, really, as long as they're gentle about putting it in.'

She smiled at me, and I made a face, once more imagining my bumhole spreading to the tip of a man's cock. I knew she liked it already, from some of our more drunken conversations, which had already done quite a lot to contribute to my fantasies, and after all, it does seem rather an appropriate thing to do to a girl's bum after spanking it.

This time it was quite a while before Penny spoke again, and when she did there was a new tone to her voice.

'Do you want to come indoors?'

I nodded, knowing exactly what she meant. She'd turned herself on, and so had I, but neither of us wanted to admit it had been because of the conversation and we stayed silent, simply taking each other's hands as we came into her house. I let her lead me upstairs, to her room, where she kissed me, our mouths opening together for our tongues to touch as we held onto each other. Just the feel of her flesh had my excitement soaring, so smooth and soft, while her hands had moved to the nape of my neck and my bottom, caressing me gently to bring me higher still.

When she slipped down my bikini pants I gave a little wriggle and they dropped to the floor. My top followed and I was naked in her arms, her hand on my bare bottom, stroking, squeezing, then applying a gentle pat. I stuck my hips out, clinging onto her as she began to spank me, ever so gently. This time, I was to be first.

'Over my knee with you, Pippa,' she said as our mouths finally broke apart. 'I'm going to spank your naughty bottom.'

'Yes, auntie,' I told her, hanging my head in submission.

She sat down on the bed and patted her lap. I crawled over, lifting my bottom for her attention. She took me around the waist, still very gently, but not so gently that I wasn't trapped, and I felt deliciously helpless as her hand settled on my bottom. Her fingers pushed down into my crease and my cheeks had been hauled open to show off my anus, giving me a wonderful, delicious rush of humiliation.

'Nice and clean, good girl,' she said, leaning so close I knew she could see every tiny wrinkle of my bumhole and the little star of lines around it, 'but I'm still going to spank you.'

She let my cheeks close and applied a pat, a second, a third, and I was being spanked, already in ecstasy just for the joy of being across her knee in the nude with my bottom lifted for punishment. In no time I was purring with pleasure and wriggling my hips for more, which I got, but only gradually. The smacks were still gentle, just enough to sting, and bring me very slowly on heat as my bottom meat grew warm and sensitive.

'That's nice,' I sighed, lifting my bottom higher still and getting a firmer smack in reward.

'I bet AJ doesn't take so much trouble over you?' she said.

'No,' I admitted, 'but that reminds me. I need to ask her permission.'

'Even for me?'

'I'm supposed to.'

'I suppose you had better.'

Her mobile was on her bedside table, just within my reach, but she still had me around the waist and she was still spanking me, the slaps of her hand on my bum flesh far too loud for me to risk calling AJ and having her realise we'd started without per-

170

mission. I sent a text instead, simply worded, 'May I? With Penny'. The reply was almost immediate, 'URA tart' which I took for a yes.

'She says yes,' I told Penny, as I folded my arms under my chin.

'Good,' she replied, 'although I don't see why you should have to ask her permission when it's me. Since when did an aunt need permission to spank her own niece?'

I giggled. It was a nice image, and there has always been something special about having my own aunt do me. Girls ought to be spanked by their aunts, and just knowing that I got it was often enough to come over, which I intended to do now. Cocking my legs wide to show pussy off, I reached back, only to get a slap on the inside of my thighs.

'Oh no you don't, young lady,' Penny chided. 'I've got a new toy I'd like to show you first.'

'Just stick it up then,' I purred. 'It'll go easily.'

'So I see,' she replied, 'but it doesn't go up, it goes on.'

'On? What, on my bottom? Not a paddle, Penny, bruises would be awkward just now.'

'Not on your bottom, Pippa, on your pussy.'

'You want to spank pussy? OK, but gently, please.'

'Not spank.'

She had shifted her grip as she spoke, but kept me in place over her lap as she rummaged in her bedside table, quickly pulling out a colourful box. Inside was the most bizarre device, a rubber bulb with a tube running from it to a thing like an oxygen mask, only clearly designed to fit over a woman's sex.

'It's a pussy pump,' she explained, 'or a cunt bulger, to use Monty Hartle's less elegant term. He gave it to me.'

'He spanks you, doesn't he?'

'Never you mind who spanks me, young lady, just stick your bottom up again.'

I obeyed, bracing my knees apart on the bed and raising my hips until I was completely available to her. There was a tube of lubricant with the pump and she slapped a little onto pussy, rubbing it in and smearing it around the sides of my lips, over my mound and near my bumhole. That alone was enough to make me want to come again, but when I tried to reach back I got my hand slapped.

'Naughty Pippa,' she chided. 'Be patient.'

She took the pump and I felt it press to my body, cupping pussy like a hand. It felt odd, but quite nice, and I'd realised what it was for, but the sudden sucking sensation still came as a shock. I felt the rubber seal press to my skin, and my mouth had come wide as the most peculiar sensation spread across my sex, as if my flesh was growing.

It was, my pussy lips swelling inside the suction cup as she took out the air, until I was gasping and clawing at the bed for the sensation, and sure I'd burst at any second. My flesh was even touching the plastic, sensitive and slippery with lubricant, and I realised just how much she'd made my lips bulge and how fat pussy was. Not that she stopped, still pumping, until my swollen sex filled the whole cup.

'Ready,' she said. 'Let me take it off.'

I nodded weakly, and gasped as she tugged the cup off my sex with a liquid, sucking noise. Penny giggled.

'Now look at yourself in the mirror,' she ordered.

She gave my bottom a pat and I scrambled off her lap, eager to obey. I was quite a sight, my body, as ever, slender, maybe a bit skinny even, but my pussy bulging out under my belly, fat and glistening and grotesquely sexual.

'It's even ruder from behind,' Penny laughed. 'Go on, bend over.'

I turned around, my humiliation for what she'd done bubbling up with extraordinary power as I bent over. If I'd looked rude from the front, then from behind I looked obscene. My tiny bottom showed as usual, with the pink dimple of my anus maybe just a little fatter, and my slim thighs, only instead of my neat, slightly pouted pussy lips, a fat, blubbery cunt stuck out between.

'Monty says it makes me look like a bonobo chimpanzee on heat,' Penny laughed. 'Now come back here and I'll finish your spanking.'

I managed a nod, shaking badly as I came back, to crawl across her knee and lift my bottom. She began to spank once more, firmer now, and across the crest of my cheeks, so that every slap made my bulging pussy quiver, to keep me firmly in mind of how I looked from the rear, how I would look to her as she punished me, like a chimpanzee on heat.

'Shall I rub you?' she offered. 'Or do you want to do it yourself?'

'I'll do it,' I answered her. 'I want to feel myself.'

She giggled and began to spank harder. I cocked up my bottom and slid my hand back, to touch the bulbous mass of my pussy. It felt as obscene as it looked, fat and puffy, slippery with lubricant and my own juice, and so sensitive. I began to explore myself, thinking of the sight I made from behind and how I was, spanked nude across my auntie's lap as I masturbated my swollen pussy.

'Harder,' I urged, 'and tell me how I look.'

'I told you,' she said, 'like a bonobo chimpanzee on heat, with your little red bum and your fat, puffy cunt. Oh you should see yourself now, Pippa, you bad, dirty girl! Imagine letting me spank you. Imagine letting me pump your cunt up.'

'I'm coming,' I gasped. 'Spank me harder . . . as hard as you can, and tell me how I look . . . tell me what a little tart I am, auntie . . . please, auntie . . .'

'Little tart is about right,' she said as her hand began to piston up and down on my now blazing cheeks, 'a dirty little tart who deserves a good spanking, on her botty and on her cunt too, and a fucking too, Pippa, you deserve to have your fat chimpanzee's cunt fucked, and I'd help. I'd hold you for him, Pippa, a dirty old man, so he could fuck you. If one came in he'd be straight up you, Pippa, and I'd hold you for him. I'd hold you down while he fucked your fat, blubbery cunt.'

'Oh you bitch, Penny!'

She laughed at me, knowing full well what she'd put in my head, and that I was starting to come. It must have been obvious, with my bumhole squeezing and my bloated pussy in contraction, and there was nothing whatsoever I could do about it. The awful image was locked firmly in my head as I writhed and squirmed across her knee, my rear view fixed in my mind's eye, little pink bottom cheeks bouncing as my auntie spanked me, my bumhole winking lewdly between, my great fat wobbling cunt looking utterly obscene as I rubbed myself off, and quite ready to be mounted and stuffed full of cock.

I rode my orgasm for what seemed like an age, still holding the image of myself mounted and fucked while Penny held me down. It was one of the best, and my body was still twitching long after it had died down, with little spasms running through the muscles of my legs and belly. She'd stopped spanking, and held me in her arms, cuddled tight to soothe me for the feelings she knew would be raging in my head, which helped to reduce my guilt and shame, but it was still unfair of her.

'That was mean!' I told her when I'd got myself back under control.

'I'm sorry,' she said, and kissed me. 'You looked so rude, and I couldn't resist it.'

'Well I hope you're ready for your turn, that's all,' I answered as I stood up.

She smiled sweetly and lay back on the bed. My legs still felt a trifle unsteady, and I took a moment before pulling my bikini on, only to find that my swollen pussy lips wouldn't fit under the front, but bulged out to either side, a sight if anything more obscene and ridiculous than when I'd been bare. Penny was giggling.

'I hope the swelling goes down quickly?' I asked.

'In about a week,' she replied casually, and then burst into open laughter at the expression on my face. 'No, seriously, it doesn't take long at all.'

'You have had it,' I told her. 'Kneel on the bed. Face to the wall.'

She was smiling as she obeyed, turning to present me with her bottom, the full white cheeks spilling out to either side of her bright-red bikini pants. The material was pulled taut over her pussy, very wet and not with swimming-pool water. She was puffy too, although nothing like as puffy as me even though my swelling was already beginning to go down. When she was so obviously turned on, and quite capable of lapping up every humiliation I could throw at her, it was hard to know how to get my revenge, but that wasn't going to stop me trying.

'Let's have these down then, shall we, auntie?' I told her, reaching out to take hold of her bikini pants.

I pulled them down, baring the full, pale spread of her bottom, with her pinkish brown bumhole showing at the centre of a little nest of hair and her well-furred pussy open and moist at the centre.

'You're a slut,' I told her, and laid a firm slap across one plump cheek. 'You call me a tart, but you're worse.'

Again I slapped her, hard enough to make her gasp and leave a pink handprint on her pale bottom flesh. I was only getting started, but it was fun to spank her, and I could at least try to get to her as well. Sitting down on the bed, I quickly pulled her bikini top up to flop out her tits and put my arm around her waist, holding her in place as I once more began to spank her bottom.

'How does it feel, being spanked by me?' I asked her. 'How does it feel, Auntie Penny.'

'Lovely,' she sighed.

'You utter slut!'

'Yes, I know. Can I masturbate, please?'

'No, not yet, not until I've made you feel the way I did.'

'I need to come, Pippa. You've turned me on so much.'

'Shut up.'

I continued spanking her, making her cheeks bounce and wobble, her skin redden and her pussy grow ever more juicy. It was tempting to pump her up and she liked having a rear like a turned-on chimpanzee, but it was her pump and she'd probably just get off on the idea. It was no good sticking something up her bottom either, which she loved, so I continued to torment her as best I could.

'Girls ought to be spanked by their aunts,' I said, echoing my earlier thought, 'but for an aunt to get spanked by her niece, now that is a real disgrace. You should be ashamed of yourself.'

She let out an excited sob and her hand began to steal back towards her sex, but I slapped it away. Obviously she had no shame at all, or rather she had plenty, but it just turned her on all the more. I kept spanking, until she'd begun to gasp and sob and wiggle her bottom in her need. Her hand kept sneaking towards her pussy, and I kept slapping it away, but was on the point of giving up when I realised one thing that might just get to her.

'I know who should spank you,' I told her. 'Great Aunt Geraldine. How would that feel, Penny?'

'Pippa, that's not fair,' she answered, and I laughed to hear the trace of panic in her voice.

'Oh yes it is!' I crowed. 'And it's what you're going to think about when you come.'

'No, Pippa, please . . .'

She sounded truly desperate, but I knew she wouldn't be able to stop herself, for all that she was trying. I grabbed her hand and pressed it to her sex, then went back to spanking her.

'I think I'll tell her what you're like,' I said. 'Then she'd spank you. I bet she'd spank you, over her knee and panties down, Penny. Just imagine it, bent over Great Aunt Geraldine's knee with those big white panties your wear taken right down . . . to show off your bumhole and show off your cunt. How you'd kick! How you'd howl! And how I'd laugh, because it would be in front of me, Auntie Penny, in front of me and the whole family, with your panties down and your fat white bottom bouncing as she spanked you. Oh you little slut!'

She was masturbating, furiously, her fingers clutching and slapping at the wet, puffy flesh of her sex, her bumhole and cunt opening in lewd, firm contractions. I spanked harder still, stinging my own hand but too delighted to care and loving every moment of it as she came over the thought of being spanked across her own aunt's knee.

Seven

I ended up staying the night at Penny's, quite a bit of it spent teasing each other for what we'd come over. We also discussed Jemima, with a shared bottle of wine helping to suppress our moral qualms about interfering with her life. As we couldn't stop her going to the party, the sensible choice was to make sure she got thoroughly put off, but by the time we went to bed we were both drunk enough to admit that after the way she'd behaved it wouldn't be too terrible if she did actually end up getting her bottom smacked.

The next day I felt refreshed and ready for anything, even Mr Prufrock. Now that I was going to the party anyway there was no longer quite such a hurry, but I wanted to be able to pay Melody on the day, both to wipe the smile off her face and to make sure she didn't attempt to take unfair advantage of me. I had even worked out how to get around the problem of the key, which meant enlisting Clive's help, and I didn't dare risk being seen talking to him at work.

He was at lunch in Champagne Charlie's, but I ignored him completely and flirted with Steve and Mark, until by the end both of them were distinctly hot under the collar and obviously hoping for more.

I avoided them for the afternoon by going down to the cellar and making sure they saw me descend the stairs, which I knew would fit in when I was caught with Mr Prufrock.

Once I was stripped down and working bare bottom among the stacks, I took a moment to text Clive, suggesting we meet after work, then AJ to say that I had to stay late and would catch up with her at Whispers. It all seemed to be working out, and despite a little guilt for AJ, there was no denying I was enjoying my little conspiracy. I even decided the time had come to suck Mr Prufrock's cock, and put the question to him as I sat on his knee in my normal rude pose, my bare bum in his hand and his cock in mine.

'Would you mind if I did something rather dirty?' I asked, putting a deliberate giggle into my voice.

'What did you have in mind, my dear?' he asked.

'I'll show you,' I said, and rose from his lap.

I was smiling as I got down on my knees in front of him, and if it was a little forced, then there was genuine anticipation too. His cock was already as hard as I'd ever got it, a fat pillar of heavy meat, and it was impossible not to enjoy the sheer humiliation of having put myself in a situation where I was obliged to take him in my mouth. He realised what I was going to do, inevitably, and gave a pleased sigh as I made myself comfortable.

'Ah, ha,' he said, 'so you wish to entertain me in your mouth. What a good little girl you are.'

As I opened wide I wanted to tell him that I wasn't a good girl at all, but a dirty little tart, only he loved to think of me as rude but innocent. A moment later I couldn't tell him anything, because I was sucking his cock, which filled my mouth to capacity. I tried to take him deep, but as his knob touched the back of my throat I immediately began to gag and was forced to pull back, licking at his shaft as he stared down at me in amusement and pleasure.

I continued to lick, holding his cock up and wanking him at the same time as I judged the angle anybody coming in at the door would get on my dirty little floor show. Technically it was perfect, a full view of Mr Prufrock, my bare bum and the junction between his cock and my mouth. Nobody who saw could be in any doubt whatsoever that I was giving a blow-job. The thought of being caught as I was had begun to bring out feelings of shame, but he wasn't getting any harder, so I began to lick the underside of his foreskin, which Clive had told me felt nice, only to have him give his dirty little chuckle and speak up.

'That's no way to suck a cock, popsy. What do you think it is, a lollipop?'

'Sorry,' I said, 'but you're so big you make me gag if I try to take you all in.'

'Sometimes a lady has to put up with a little discomfort in order to please her gentleman,' he told me. 'So in we go, Pippa, right in your mouth.'

I did try, but the moment I took him deep my throat tightened in revulsion and I was forced to pull back, sucking on the bulbous tip instead and rubbing my tongue under his foreskin. Now he'd begun to swell again, and for a moment he was content, only to take me by the hair and push himself deep once more, gently but firmly. The moment I felt his knob start to press into my throat I began to gag, but he wasn't having any of it, holding himself in until I was pop-eyed and breathless. When he did release me I was nearly sick, with my mouth full of spittle which I had to swallow hurriedly before it went down my front.

'Please,' I gasped. 'That's not very nice, Mr Prufrock.'

'I thought you wanted to do it?' he asked, not unkindly.

'I . . . I like you in my mouth,' I managed, 'and licking you, but . . .'

'Girls who suck cock should suck cock properly,' he said, 'and that means taking it in your throat. Imagine if I was some strapping young lad, with a big hard erection. Do you think he'd put up with any nonsense?'

I shook my head.

'No,' he said reprovingly, 'he wouldn't, would he, so it's best to learn from an older man who's prepared to be patient with you. Now try again.'

He seemed to be enjoying toying with me almost as much as he was enjoying having me suck his cock, but I tried again anyway, and again began to gag as soon as the head of his cock touched the back of my throat. Once more he held me down, longer this time, until my eyes had begun to water and when he did let me go I had to swallow hurriedly to stop myself throwing up on his cock and down my tits.

'Enough,' I gasped. 'I'm sorry . . . I would like to, really, but I can't.'

'We'll have another lesson tomorrow then,' he said happily. 'For now, come back on my lap, and you can rub me with your panties.'

I nodded and got up, retrieving my knickers from where I'd hung them on the peg and wrapping them around his cock as I sat my bare bottom down on his knee once more. He gave a contented sigh and began to fondle me, stroking my bottom meat and teasing between my cheeks as his cock moved in my panties, the head poking up and down under the cotton where it usually covered my bum. Soon he was going to masturbate me, and the sense of erotic humiliation was rising with the urge to push my bottom out and let him touch my pussy. To make it worse, my mouth still tasted of cock, and I was looking forward to a good climax when his telephone rang.

The same thing had happened a few times before, but he had always been content to let me wank him and to continue fondling my bum while he talked to the caller. This time he spoke only a couple of sentences before putting the phone down and giving me a purposeful smack under my cheeks.

'We had better make ourselves decent, my dear,' he said. 'Mr Montague is coming down.'

I hurriedly replaced my knickers and pulled my skirt on over them, allowing him to open the door moments before old Mr Montague appeared on the stairs. He spoke briefly to Mr Prufrock, then addressed me.

'I trust your talents aren't being wasted down here, Pippa?'

'Not at all,' I assured him. 'Mr Prufrock has taught me a great deal.'

'No doubt,' he said, 'but I'm sure you can be spared for the time being at least. I am attending court for the summary of the Calstock Securities fraud trial tomorrow, which I feel sure would be of interest to you.'

'Thank you, yes,' I answered, sincerely enough.

'Splendid,' he said, and disappeared in among the archives.

There was nothing for it but to go back to my filing, and Mr Montague stayed with us until it was almost time for me to meet Clive. I managed to get away punctually, and enjoyed myself for a few minutes eluding an entirely imaginary pursuit before starting towards St Katharine. It was also fun to imagine the spanking Mr Montague would have given me if he'd caught me wanking Mr Prufrock in my knickers, which showed just how horny the whole experience had left me, and as I pressed on Clive's bell I was chiding myself for being such a slut.

He came down to let me in, glancing around nervously as I passed him.

'I made sure nobody followed me,' I assured him.

'Come upstairs,' he said, and didn't speak again until we were safely in his flat.

'You've done brilliantly, Pippa. The odds on Steve are down to evens, with Mark himself on 4–1 and Den and Andy 25–1 with no takers. He's put me down to 100–1.'

'But Mr Prufrock's still 500–1?'

'Yes. Everyone knows you're working with him, obviously, but it hasn't made any difference. Nobody could believe you'd be that dirty.'

I made a face.

'Sorry,' he said quickly, 'I didn't . . .'

'Don't worry, that's all right. The only problem is the door, and I think I know how to get round it. First, is there a spare key?'

'I don't know. If so, Maggie would have it.'

'Never mind that then. He always keeps the key in his jacket pocket, even when the door's locked, but he sometimes takes his jacket off, especially if he's getting a bit flustered over me. You can come down and ask for some obscure document, which would give me a chance to pinch the key and get a spare cut, just as long as you can distract him for long enough. Then all you need to do is unlock the door, very quietly, after I've sent the text to say I'll be playing with him, and then find your excuse to have somebody else come down. What do you think?'

'It's a bit complicated.'

'It just takes good timing, and there's a place you can get keys cut in Tower Hill station.'

'We can try, and it might work, as long as I'm not seen opening the door, or heard coming down the stairs.'

'You'll just have to be careful. Come on, Clive, say you'll try?'

He gave me an embarrassed grin, nodding, then was silent for a while before he spoke again.

'Do you have time for a drink? A glass of cold Sauvignon, perhaps?'

'Yes, thanks.'

He fetched the wine and sat down, leaving me sipping my own as I looked out across St Katharine Dock. The plan was a bit fiddly, but I couldn't see any alternative. I remembered about Mr Montague, and turned to tell Clive, to catch him staring at my bottom. He immediately went bright red, but I gave him a reassuring smile.

'Look all you like,' I told him. 'Everybody else seems to.'

His look of embarrassment faded to a nervous grin, and after a moment he spoke again, struggling to get the words out.

'Pippa, I know ... I know we agreed about last time, and I respect that, but there is one thing I would very much like to have done; just a little thing for you, but it would mean the world to me.'

'What's that?'

He took a long time to reply, looking more embarrassed than ever and shifty too, but when he did speak, his words came in a rush.

'Would you ... would you show me your bottom. You have the most beautiful bottom in the world, Pippa, like a little round apple, so small and so sweet, but so wonderfully chubby, the way your hips swell and your lower back curves out, and ... and the way your pretty little cheeks tuck under, and ...'

bum.'

He went quiet, his round face sunrise-re...
waited for my response, the desperation show...
his eyes. I'd dropped my knickers for Mr Mulligan,
...t Clive? At least he'd been nice to me. I smiled

'Oh, you little ang...

Anyone would have thought you...

certain death, not just offered a flash of my bum, and I
was smiling to myself as I rucked up my skirt and
tucked the tails of my jacket and blouse up so he had a
full show of my knickers. I'd put on patterned ones,
white with pink and blue polka dots, which Mr
Prufrock preferred to plain white, although I didn't see
the fuss when he expected me straight out of them every
morning. They were a little tight, hugging my bum and
showing a little meat around each leg hole, which had
Clive wide-eyed with desire. I couldn't help but laugh
for his expression, and pulled them up tighter still,
deliberately showing off, then put my thumbs in the
waistband, looking back over my shoulder as I spoke.

'Shall I take them down, Clive?'

He returned a weak nod and made a quick
adjustment to his cock beneath his trousers, then
went red as I returned a smile.

'Shall I take my knickers down?' I teased. 'Shall I,
Clive? Would you like to see my bare apple bottom?'

'Yes,' he answered, gulping. 'Please, Pippa ...
please.'

'OK,' I told him, 'in a moment.'

Instead of baring myself I pulled my knickers tight
up, spilling my cheeks out to either side. I saw him

wallow, and again as I stuck my bum out and gave
him a little wiggle to make my meat shake. The way
he was looking at me was close to worship, ma
me want to laugh and encouraging me to sh
the same time, while just having my kni
was bringing back all my arousal & and began to
'Here goes,' I told him, '
coming right up.'
I'd put my thumb ...posing myself inch by
push, deliberat... bum stuck well out in the full
inch and ...at once my knickers were properly down
knowl
my anus and pussy would be on show as well as my
cheeks. Clive looked ready to faint, and I saw his eyes
pop as my bumhole came on view, then his tongue
flick out to moisten his lips as I completed my little
strip, turning my knickers down around my thighs to
leave every last intimate detail available to his gaze.

'Is that what you wanted?' I asked.

'God yes,' he answered. 'You are so lovely Pippa.
Would you . . . would you mind if I touched myself
. . . no, of course, that's a stupid thing to . . .'

'Sh!' I interrupted. 'You do what you feel you have
to, Clive.'

'And you'll stay like that?'

'If you're quick.'

He was tearing at his fly immediately, wrenching his
cock free, already stiff. As soon as I saw it I wanted
him in my mouth, an instinctive, dirty reaction I'd
have denied even being capable of just days before.
Not that I had much time, because he was masturbating furiously, with his eyes locked to my bare bum.

'Let me,' I said quickly.

'Oh God, would you?' he asked. 'Do you mind?'

'Oh come on, Clive, of course I don't mind. If I do
it for Mr Prufrock I can do it for you!'

I'd come close, and sat down on his l.... the feel of his trousers against my bare b.... keep me reminded that I was the one with no k.... as I took his cock in hand and began to tug.... sighed in pleasure and relaxed back into the sofa, so that I had to guide his hand to my bottom myself. At last he got the message, and began to feel, squeezing my cheeks as I wanked him, and with an expression of utter bliss on his face.

'You little angel,' he repeated.

'More like a little devil, I think you'll find,' I told him. 'If you like my bum so much, how about this?'

I'd moved as I spoke, with a delicious, daring thrill as I deliberately sat my bare bottom down on his cock. He felt hard, and extraordinarily hot, with his shaft wedged between my cheeks and pussy pressed to his balls. I'd only meant to be dirty, but it felt so good I wanted to come like that, or worse, take his cock inside me and find out how it really felt.

A few quick motions and my blouse was open and my bra up, leaving my breasts bare to my hands as I wriggled my bum on his cock in a rude little lap dance. He was gasping with passion and trying to rub himself between my cheeks, using my bum slit to wank in, a thought so dirty I could no longer hold back. I snatched for his cock, meaning to stuff it up my hole and put an end to my virginity then and there, only to realise my bum was wet and slippery.

He'd spunked in my slit, his shaft now slippery and hotter than ever. I could feel my bumhole rubbing on his veiny cock flesh, and his balls were against pussy, and in my hand. He gasped in what might have been pleasure or might have been pain, but I didn't care. I had his scrotum crushed to my sex, the wrinkly skin and the fat, hard balls within bumping on my clit, on the edge of orgasm, then there as I thought over and

...er of how he'd made me drop my knickers to show him my bum and spunked in my slit.

It was gone eight by the time I arrived at Whispers, after cleaning myself up and being fed pasta with pesto sauce by Clive. He was well pleased with himself, while I had no regrets despite coming within an ace of losing my virginity to him. There was no sorry little conversation afterwards either, not this time. He asked if I'd do the same for him again some time and told him I would. After all, I was doing it for Mr Prufrock anyway, and Clive was not only a lot nicer, but could get a decent erection.

Inevitably I felt guilty about AJ, and I was thinking about her in the cab Clive had kindly paid for. I knew there'd be no compromise in her mind, but I didn't want to give up what I'd found, so I decided to compartmentalise my life: loving sex with women, dirty sex with men, spanking as circumstances dictated. There was also the problem of telling her I was going to Morris's party, because she was bound to find out in the end.

It seemed best to get it over quickly, and she was propping up one end of the bar without anyone we knew near by, so I took my chance, kissing her and immediately making my confession.

'I have a problem, AJ. Morris has persuaded my little sister to come to his party on Saturday. I don't think she'll stay very long, once she sees the sort of man who'll be there, but I couldn't let her go alone. So I'm going. Sorry.'

I expected an explosion of anger, and probably to be dragged into the loos by my hair, where I'd have my head held down in the lavatory bowl, pissed on and flushed. To my surprise, she simply pursed her lips in annoyance, then nodded.

'Typical fucking Morris,' she said. 'OK, you go, and stick around long enough to find out who fucked me over. Get Big Mel pissed or something.'

'She'll probably . . .'

'I know what she'll do. Take it. You're tough enough to handle her.'

I wasn't at all sure about that, but I nodded in turn, and kissed her again.

'Thanks, AJ.'

'That's cool. Just don't get fucked, that's all.'

'I won't. I promise.'

I meant it, despite having come within a moment of taking Clive's cock inside me just hours before. Morris's guests were a very different matter, especially as they were paying. I might enjoy thinking of myself as a tart, but I was quite definitely not losing my virginity as a prostitute. A free ticket to play with Melody was another matter, as she was both frightening and attractive, the perfect combination for me in a female partner.

'So what did you get up to with Miss Muffet?' AJ asked as Gina pushed a drink in front of me.

'She used a pussy pump on me,' I admitted, 'and spanked me while I was all swollen up.'

'Sounds fun,' Gina said. 'I've seen those, but I've never tried it.'

'It feels weird,' I told her, 'but nice, and it looks . . . it looks obscene, but so sexy, like my whole body is centred on my pussy.'

'I'd better invest in one,' AJ put in.

'Yes, please,' I urged. 'I'd like that.'

She took hold of the front of my blouse and pulled me close, kissing me hard on the lips, so that I was flushed and trembling when she let go. Gina gave a knowing grin and moved away to serve another customer, only to turn back as AJ slipped a hand into my blouse.

'If you're going to do that, AJ, please take her in the back.'

'Sure,' AJ answered, and she had taken my wrist.

I was in ecstasy even as she led me around the bar to the back room. Everybody was watching, about thirty girls, and every one of them knew I was about to be spanked and put on my knees. Several of them crowded after us, taking their places around the room as AJ calmly placed a chair at the very centre and sat down. I was taken over her lap, my skirt lifted in a casual, matter-of-fact fashion and my knickers pulled down with even less fuss. She had me bare, and it didn't matter, because I was hers to do with as she pleased.

What happened was entirely up to her, but this evening she was feeling kind. Hooking one leather-clad leg around my calf, she spread me open, stretching my knickers taut between my legs and leaving my bare pussy pressed to her thigh. She began to spank, hard from the very first, so that I immediately lost control to the pain, kicking and bucking across her knee to show off my bumhole and rub myself on her leg.

She held me down, ignoring my yelps and pleas for mercy, because she knew what was best for me. Soon my bottom had begun to warm and the pain faded to be replaced by pure, sexual heat. My squirming became slower and more rhythmic, and with my modesty already gone I was soon rubbing my pussy on her leg with ever greater urgency as the girls clapped and cheered to see me so well punished and so excited.

I came in no time, and was pushed down to the floor, to squat panting and dishevelled as AJ stood and calmly pushed her leathers down from her hips. My vision was hazy with tears and the aftermath of my ecstasy as I crawled close, first to be made to lick up my own juices from the leather of her trousers, then put to her cunt. I was licking immediately, and if I was a novice when it came to cock-sucking I was a practised little tart when I had a mouth full of pussy.

She used me well, showing off to the girls by making me lick her anal star and stick the tip of my tongue in up her bumhole in full view. I did it more than willingly, revelling in my own humiliation and the taste of her bottom, willing to accept whatever she chose to do, no matter how dirty. A lick and a kiss was enough, and I had quickly been put back on her sex, where I was held firmly in place by my hair until she'd taken her orgasm in my face.

I made the best of Tuesday, concentrating on work for once after a night of good sex with AJ. The summation of the fraud trial was extremely useful, especially with Mr Montague to point out the important or interesting features as we walked back down Fleet Street together. I'd expected him to call a cab, which everybody at Montague, Montague, Todmorden and Montague seemed to do as a matter of course, but it turned out he wanted a bit of privacy.

'I'm very much looking forward to Morris's party this Saturday,' he said as we reached the quieter streets near St Pauls. 'It will be your first, I believe?'

'Yes,' I admitted.

'Morris, as you may know, is famous for his amusing little games, and while I am not acquainted with the details of the one he is planning this weekend, I do know it is called Ladies' Choice, and that the title reflects the essence of play. Would it be presumptuous of me to hope that you might consider me for your own selection?'

'Not at all,' I told him, which was perfectly true given the other men I knew would be there, and then had second thoughts, 'although I hope you won't be offended if I . . . if I choose another woman first, you know, just to warm me up.'

'To the contrary,' he replied, 'I can imagine no more satisfying spectacle.'

He meant watching me spanked by another woman, and I felt my tummy go tight at the thought. If I was supposed to play up to Melody, and chose her, it seemed likely she would start by spanking me in front of the everybody, men included. What happened after that was up to me, but I knew I'd have been lying to myself if I tried to pretend I might not end up finally getting a spanking from a man. Of all the people I knew would be there, Mr Montague was by far the best one to do it, stern and yet gentlemanly and fair, without any of the filthy habits which characterised the others, or at least, not to the best of my knowledge.

'There is also the matter of Maggie's punishment,' he went on as soon as a group of tourists had passed, 'which I imagine you will enjoy?'

'Very much,' I replied, earnestly.

'She can be something of a martinet,' he chuckled, 'and you won't be the only one to enjoy her downfall, I can assure you. Lucius has been waiting his chance for quite a while, while there is nothing Morris and his guests enjoy more than to see a dominant woman receive a sound spanking. Seeing her obliged to make her choice will also be rewarding.'

'Isn't she likely to choose you?'

'Oh good heavens no, I think she'd rather have it done by Morris himself! Normally, I expect she would choose another woman, but every girl there will be out for revenge. She can be very cruel, and

Melody in particular would dearly love to make her suffer in turn.'

'So would I,' I told him, remembering the humiliation of being made to feel I should still be in nappies and the sensation of the stamp handle up my bottom.

'While the men,' he continued, 'will know how to deal with her anyway, and may even find themselves offered some interesting encouragement by girls out for revenge. There is always your little sister, of course. Yes, she will choose Jemima in the hope of a weak and inexpert spanking.'

I was going to ask how he knew Jemima would be coming, but it would have been a stupid question. Morris could easily have taken some sneaky photos of her on his mobile while we were swimming, so half the perverts in London probably had pictures of her in her bikini and an offer of the chance to spank her if they came to the party.

'I doubt Jemima will be there very long,' I told him.

'No?' he queried.

'No,' I said firmly.

On Wednesday I was going to be back in the basement, and I knew it was my last chance to win the bet if I wanted to be able to present Melody with a cheque. Even if everything went to plan it was bound to take Clive a while to extract the money from Mark, and ideally I wanted the funds awaiting clearance in my own account by the Friday afternoon.

Inevitably I was nervous, but it's peculiar what routine can make one accept as normal, because it seemed perfectly natural to be taking my knickers down the moment Mr Prufrock had locked the door.

'That's my popsy,' he said happily, his eyes glued to me as always, 'off they come now and let's have that little bottom bare.'

First, I needed to get him sufficiently flustered to take off his jacket, so I threw my discarded knickers at him. I'd chosen the most girlish pair I could find, white with pink checks and a bow at the front. They landed on his thigh, just inches from his crotch, and he gave an appreciative gurgle as he used them to squeeze his cock through his trousers.

I finished my little striptease, removing my skirt and this time my jacket as well, to leave me completely exposed at the front and with just the tail of my blouse to cover my bottom behind.

'It's very hot today,' I remarked. 'I think I'll go like this, if you don't mind?'

'Not at all,' he said, but failed to remove his own jacket. 'In fact it's probably just as well, as you missed yesterday and you'll need to catch up.'

What he meant was that he wanted to squeeze an extra day's humiliation and display out of me, but that was all to the good. I went back to what I'd been doing on Monday, which involved a lot of lifting bundles of files, so I was soon putting on as rude a show of pussy and bumhole as he could possibly have wanted. He kept rubbing his crotch with my panties too, but still he wouldn't take off his jacket.

I was getting turned on, but he seemed unusually calm, spending nearly an hour just watching me work before he called me over to give him his show. Our plan was already running late, but there was nothing for it but to comply.

'A little running on the spot today, I think,' he said. 'Turn around.'

I hesitated only a moment before accepting the new humiliation, turning my back to him as I began to jog up and down, only for him to give a grunt of discontent.

'No,' he said, 'you're too firm for that. Do some jumps instead.'

Again I obeyed, putting my legs together and jumping on the spot to make my bottom meat wobble.

'Faster,' he urged, 'let's see those little cheeks jiggle, shall we?'

He gave a dirty little snigger as I obeyed, and after watching for a while he spoke again.

'Take off your blouse. I want to see those titties jump.'

It was the first time he'd had me strip naked, making me feel more vulnerable than ever as I peeled off with trembling fingers. His eyes never once left my body, and as soon as I was down to my stockings and shoes I began to jump again, now facing him with my breasts bouncing on my chest.

'Excellent!' he said after a moment. 'In fact, I think I'll have you in the nude today. Come along.'

I was grimacing as I took off my shoes and stockings to leave myself completely naked. Things were not going to plan at all.

'Try touching your toes,' he suggested, 'with your back to me, of course.'

It hardly needed saying. I turned around once more and bent at the waist to touch my fingertips to my toes, showing off every detail of my rear view as I did it. He gave a chuckle of appreciation and settled back as I began to repeat the exercise.

'Very sweet,' he said after what seemed like forever. 'Do you know, Pippa, you even have a pretty bottom hole, and a very pretty fanny. Now then, a few handstands and it's time for your little treat.'

'Handstands?' I queried.

'I suppose you should be in a skirt with no knickers underneath, for best effect,' he replied, 'but I'm sure you'll look just as pretty doing it in the nude.'

I made a face, and with considerable difficulty managed to pull off a handstand in the gap between the stacks, showing my open pussy as I did it. He already had me sweaty and covered in dust, but I was made to do it five more times before he finally held his hand up in satisfaction.

'Good girl,' he said, 'and you're quite right, it is a trifle close.'

Finally he was going to take his jacket off, only I was stark naked and running with sweat, in no condition to go and get a key cut, while once he'd masturbated me our chance would be lost for the day. There was nothing for it but to find an excuse to get dressed again, text Clive, and pray Mr Prufrock didn't put his jacket back on. The excuse at least was easy.

'I bet you'd like to continue your cock-sucking lesson, wouldn't you?' he was saying as he put his jacket on the peg.

'Yes,' I said, 'but I really need to pee first.'

'That needn't worry us too much, I don't think,' he said.

'I think it ought to,' I said, squeezing my thighs together, 'or I think I'm going to wet myself.'

'Not on the floor, young lady,' he said sternly. 'Here, come and do it down the drain, and I'll watch. That will be exciting.'

I made to object, but he had already begun to waddle off between the stacks, and I could only follow. At the far end a dusty brick arch opened into a gloomy area beneath grubby squares of glass set into the street above. I'd never bothered to look in there before, but sure enough, there was a drain at the centre. I made a face as I looked down at it, wondering if I should claim to want to do something more, but quickly deciding that he was quite capable of wanting to watch that as well.

'Don't be shy,' he said, standing back to ensure himself a prime view of pussy as I urinated, 'it's only natural.'

'Maybe,' I tried, 'but I'm not sure I can do it while you're watching.'

'Try and see,' he suggested.

I drew a heavy sigh, telling myself that he'd seen me nude, stuck his finger up my bum and masturbated me to orgasm, so peeing in front of him shouldn't have been that terrible. It was still deeply humiliating as I squatted down over the drain, as low as I dared so it wouldn't squirt all over the floor, squeezed, and let go. I wasn't really urgent at all, and only a little squirt came out at first, but it quickly built to a trickle, splashing on the iron grate and wetting my bum cheeks and thighs, so that I was forced to lift myself up a little more.

Mr Prufrock watched the whole display with deep interest, and gave a satisfied click of his tongue as I wiggled to shake the last few drops free from my pussy lips. I stood up, blushing a little and trying to think of another excuse, only to start back in surprise. He had begun to peel down his zip.

'I must say,' he said, 'your little show has had a considerable effect on me.'

He had taken out his cock, which was as fully erect as I'd seen it, even when he'd been in my mouth. I nodded, wondering if it was the smell of me, or whether he was just hopelessly perverse. In any case, I had the answer.

'Maybe you'd like me to do it again?' I suggested. 'You could bring a chair over, to watch properly, and I'm sure I could do a lot more if I had some water to drink. I'll even do it backwards, if you like, so you can see my bum, or I could suck you while I did it? Maybe you could even come?'

At that he nodded, and I knew I'd won.

'I'll just need to buy some water,' I told him, 'but I can go to the shop under the bridge and I'll be back in no time.'

'Yes, why not?' he said. 'You're a very thoughtful girl, Pippa.'

I smiled and kissed his forehead, then scampered quickly back to where I'd left my clothes, which gave me a chance to text Clive. Mr Prufrock was soon back, but I was still doing up my blouse when the knock came on the door, which gave me the perfect opportunity to nip behind one of the stacks so I wasn't seen, and then retrieve the key once he'd returned it to his jacket pocket.

As I ran up the stairs I felt elated. Complicated or not, my plan was working, and although there were plenty more things that could go wrong I felt full of confidence. I raced for the key-cutting booth in Tower Hill station, only to find that they had no blanks for the ancient key. The locksmith was sure he could do it anyway, and I was left hopping from foot to foot in anxiety while he rummaged for bits of metal, ground and cut, finally producing an adequate copy of the key.

I ran back as fast as I could, realised I'd forgotten the water, dashed to the shop under the bridge and once more to Montague, Montague, Todmorden and Montague, only to discover I needn't have hurried at all. Clive and Mr Prufrock were still busy deep in the archives, huddled over a box of ancient, dusty files just a few feet from the drain I'd peed down. I returned the original key to Mr Prufrock's jacket, hid the water so I wouldn't have to admit that particular dirty detail to Clive, and successfully passed on the copy.

Everything was ready, and was sure to work just so long as I could get my timing right. I'd have to drink my water, then wait until I was urgent, which would give Clive plenty of time, and as Mr Prufrock and I would be at the back of the stacks it would be easy

198

for him to unlock the door without being detected. He'd then have to find an excuse for one of the other Blockhouse boys to come down to the archives, and I'd have to take my time over Mr Prufrock's cock, but that was easy. I was so excited that even the hideous embarrassment of being caught sucking off a dirty old man didn't seem completely unbearable.

Clive pretended to abandon his search as hopeless and it was my turn once more. I'd bought two litres of water, which I pulled out from behind his desk as Mr Prufrock locked the door. As I began to drink he was already rubbing his hands together in anticipation.

'Oh you dirty, dirty little thing!' he said. 'Knickers off ready then . . . or no, on second thoughts, take everything else off and leave your knickers on. I think it would be rather fun to watch you pee in them.'

I nearly choked on the water I was drinking.

'But Mr Prufrock, they're the only pair I've got with me.'

'You've gone home bare under your skirt before now,' he pointed out.

'I know, but . . .'

'Come, come, Pippa. What did we say about young ladies and little favours?'

'Yes, but wetting my knickers! Please, Mr Prufrock . . .'

He wagged a finger at me.

'Come along, Pippa, if you want your little treat.'

I threw my hands up in the air. He genuinely seemed to think that he was doing me a favour by masturbating me and not the other way around; either that or he was a brilliant actor and assumed that both of us were playing our roles in a perverted game. If the latter, then I was playing a deeper game than he suspected, and the important thing was to bring it to a successful conclusion.

'OK,' I said, 'if it will help you, I'll do it in my knickers.'

'Good girl,' he breathed. 'Now drink up, and off with your clothes.'

I took another swallow of water, then began to strip, trying not to look too sulky as I peeled off my clothes. It was a hot day and I'd been running around like a mad woman, so I already needed a shower. Once I'd wet myself it would be worse, because the pee was sure to soak in up over my bottom and pussy.

'Back to work,' he said as I hung my clothes up, 'and keep drinking.'

He handed me the water bottle, which I accepted, taking the occasional swig as I went back to my filing. I felt hot and sticky, particularly down my panties, because I was soaking wet and as ready for penetration as I'd ever been. Even the thought of his fingers loitering over my bottom and easing into my holes was exciting, but that was the one thing I wasn't likely to get, not once we'd been caught.

I began to wonder what would happen afterwards, and the consequences if it became public knowledge. It was very likely I'd end up having to explain everything to Mr Montague in order to prevent Mr Prufrock getting the sack, or worse. I'd certainly have to admit I'd been willing, or the police might be called in, which would be disastrous.

Suddenly the entire scheme seemed insane, and utterly unfair of me, but I told myself that whatever the consequences, Mr Prufrock had only brought it on himself with his behaviour. It was true, but it didn't seem right, not when he'd given me so much pleasure, and looking back, there was no denying the excitement I'd got out of our arrangement. Maggie was right, I was a slut, and not just for other girls.

I'd soon finished the first litre of water and started on the second, all the while still agonising over what I was doing. Only two things kept me from abandoning the entire thing – the thought of how badly I needed the money I would win, and because to give up meant that I genuinely was Mr Prufrock's pet tart.

With the second bottle half empty my tummy was bulging so badly I looked as if I was pregnant, while my bladder had begun to ache. I was also heavily aroused, with a multitude of dirty thoughts coursing through my head and that same delicious sense of erotic helplessness I get when I'm being held firmly across a bigger woman's knees. Now was the point of no return, because once I'd sent Clive his text that would be that.

Still I hesitated, but the ache in my bladder was beginning to grow to pain and I was having to wriggle my toes to stop myself from doing it all in my panties by accident instead of on purpose. At last I gave in, telling Mr Prufrock I needed to send a message to ask AJ to bring some clean panties and instead typing in the 'OK' Clive and I had agreed on as a signal. The moment it had gone I spoke up.

'I don't think I can hold on much longer, Mr Prufrock. We'd better go into the back.'

'Oh no,' he said, 'I want you to hold on as long as possible, until you have a real accident.'

'I think I will, soon,' I told him, fighting back the urge to call him a filthy, sadistic bastard.

He was that, and more, grinning as I winced with pain and my hand went to my tummy.

'Please just let me do it,' I urged. 'I thought you wanted to see it come out?'

'I've seen you pee,' he insisted, 'now I want to watch you have a genuine accident.'

'Come into the back anyway,' I suggested. 'You said not to do it on the floor.'

'Ah, but I have plans,' he said, and winked. 'You're going to mop it up, still in your wet panties.'

I made a face, thinking how I'd look, crawling on the floor with nothing on but a pair of pee-soaked knickers, the sodden material clinging to my bum cheeks and pussy, mopping up my own puddle. It would be soon too. The pain had begun to come in waves, to leave me holding my tummy and treading up and down, before fading, only to rise once more.

'Please come in the back,' I begged. 'Please? My tummy hurts . . .'

'Then let go,' he suggested.

I was gasping as the pain hit its peak. It was hopeless, I really couldn't hold it, but somehow I couldn't just let go either. After a moment the pain receded again, only to come back, stronger than ever, leaving me sobbing badly with my poor tummy clutched in both hands. Once again the pain faded, but no more than a little while an altogether different sensation had begun to creep up on me too, and I knew that with the next peak I'd have to let go, or risk doing something infinitely worse than wetting my panties.

'I can't . . . I just can't!' I sobbed, and my nerve had gone completely.

Panic overwhelmed me at the thought of what I was about to do. I snatched at my clothes and dashed for the door, praying Clive had managed to unlock it. He had, and I was through, hurling myself up the stairs and into the Ladies with a desperate hope that nobody would be in the back corridor, or the loos. They weren't, and I made the stall, a moment too late, a sense of utter hopelessness swamping me even as I lifted the seat and the next instant was pissing in my panties.

I slumped down on the lavatory, sobbing in exhaustion and despair as it all came out, hissing and bubbling into my panties, soaking up over pussy and between the cheeks of my bum. My back was to the cistern, my eyes closed, and as my pee dribbled through the seat of my knickers into the bowl below I could feel the tension draining out of my body. I knew I was going to do it, my resistance gone along with every last spark of modesty or decency or self-restraint.

My bumhole had started to open and I didn't even try to stop myself, or bother to push my knickers down. I just let it come, one fat piece squeezing out between my cheeks and into my panty pouch, cutting off as my bumhole closed, only for a second to follow, bigger and heavier still. My panties began to sag, swelling under my bottom as they filled, to pull my wet gusset against my cunt, with my pee still bubbling out through the cotton and dribbling from the bulge now hanging beneath me.

I'd done it in my panties, not just pee but everything, and I didn't want to stop. My bumhole had begun to come open again and I just let it, groaning aloud as a third log joined the two already hanging in my knickers. I could feel more inside, and now pushed on purpose, squeezing it out until my load was so fat and so heavy it had begun to pull my knickers down at the back.

At last I'd finished, my bumhole closing on the final piece, which stayed wedged between my cheeks, and for a long moment I just lay back, sobbing and shivering in reaction to my plight. I was well and truly soiled, my pretty pink and white panties bulging heavy with my own dirt, my bottom cheeks filthy, and utterly ashamed of myself too, but I had to come.

My hand slipped down my panties, between the pee-soaked cotton and my flesh, over the low bulge of my pussy mound and between my lips. As I began to rub I tried to do more, squeezing to make my hole open and bring back that exquisite sensation of utter hopelessness, knowing I was going to do it and that there was nothing whatsoever I could do to stop it, only this time I wasn't going to soil myself, I was going to masturbate.

I could no more hold back the urge than I'd been able to hold back my mess. My legs came wide and I began to wriggle my bum, enjoying the heavy, soggy feeling in my panties where they hung down over the bowl. I found my clit, circling her and flicking at her as my feelings rose, higher and higher still, until I was having to bite my lip to stop myself from screaming, right on the very edge, and over as I went into a shuddering, gasping orgasm that left me limp and shaking.

The scheme had failed miserably, and entirely thanks to Mr Prufrock's filthy expectations. As soon as I came down from my orgasm I cleaned up and dressed, in a state of utter panic for fear of somebody coming in. I nipped out at the back to dispose of my soiled panties in the bins belonging to a nearby Indian restaurant, and returned, just in time to meet Mark himself at the top of the stairs leading down to the basement.

I simply couldn't face a replay on the Thursday. Also, I was worried that Mr Prufrock might have realised something was going on because of the door being open when he'd locked it, but when I saw him on the Friday he didn't mention it, and was even apologetic for pushing me too far. Claire was searching through the archives at the time, and I wouldn't have been able to do anything had I felt capable.

AJ was having a butch only party at the Pumps that night, which almost certainly meant tormenting some femme just as they had done with me. I had to get home eventually, but if she was out having fun I didn't see why I shouldn't be too. Clive and I needed to rethink our tactics as well, so when he sent me a text suggesting dinner at his flat I accepted without hesitation.

I knew my knickers would be coming down, and probably his cock going in my mouth, but found myself facing the prospect with as much excitement as shame. He was a good cook too, and put together a delicious and exotic stir fry while I sat back and sipped wine. A second bottle helped to wash down the dinner, and by the end I was feeling both drunk and horny, so that when he finally found the courage to ask what had gone wrong on Wednesday I was giggling as I replied.

'The dirty old bastard wanted me to wet myself, that's what. He'd already made me pee in front of him, and then he expected me to do it in my knickers while he watched.'

'That's appalling!' Clive answered, but his eyes told a different story.

I burst out laughing.

'What's so funny?' he asked.

'You,' I said. 'You're really sweet, Clive, because you mean it about Mr Prufrock being appalling, but you would love to watch me pee, wouldn't you?'

He'd gone scarlet, and began to babble half-coherent denials, making me laugh all the more. It was a fun idea too, because he'd be so shocked and so turned on all at once, while to do it in front of him would help me to exorcise some of the images I'd had running through my head ever since my accident.

I stood up, swallowed the rest of my glass of wine and beckoned him with one finger. He just stared at first, but when I began to walk towards the bathroom with a very deliberate wiggle of my hips he followed quickly enough. I beckoned again as I reached the door, looking back over my shoulder and crooking my finger. He wanted to say something, but he didn't seem capable of forming words, his mouth opening and closing like a goldfish, a reaction that only encouraged me.

The loo was a big, white porcelain affair standing out from the middle of one wall as if it were a throne. I'd meant to sit down, but I knew how excited he got over my bum and decided on a much ruder pose. Straddling the loo, I rucked up my office skirt, again looking back over my shoulder as I showed him my knickers.

'In my panties?' I offered. 'Or bare?'

His goldfish imitation only grew more pronounced, and I shrugged.

'Both?' I asked, and he nodded.

I was giggling as I stuck my bottom out and braced my legs either side of the loo, making my cheeks as round as possible in my panties, with the gusset pulled taut to pussy and on full show. Clive moved a little to improve his view and I steadied myself on the wall, feeling deliciously naughty as I forced myself to relax. A little squeeze and it had begun to come, soaking into my panties and through, to bubble out from the cotton in a rude little fountain.

'Oh my God,' Clive sighed, 'you've really done it, oh Pippa, you little angel.'

'Do angels piss their panties?' I answered him. 'I don't think so, and they definitely don't let boys watch.'

My panties were getting extremely wet, with the pee trickling down the front to run from my pussy mound and patter into the lavatory bowl beneath me. Some of it had begun to soak up over my bottom too, gluing my knickers to my skin as it spread slowly across my cheeks. It felt warm and wet and lovely, so good I'd have happily put my fingers back and brought myself off through my wet knickers, but I had promised more.

'Watch this,' I told him, and squeezed hard to cut off the flow of pee.

Reaching back, I eased my knickers down, nice and slowly to give him a good show of my bare wet bum, until they were stretched taut, soggy and dripping between my open thighs.

'Can you see everything?' I asked.

He nodded, and I let go, pee squirting from my pussy, only not into the toilet as I'd intended, but all over the floor. I just started giggling, and didn't even try to hold back, delighting in my own dirty behaviour. There was plenty of it too, making a big, pale gold puddle on the tiles before the stream began to die, the last of it dripping into my already sodden knickers before I gave myself a little wiggle to shake the last drops free.

'That was good,' I sighed, 'and don't worry about your floor. I'll mop it up.'

'No, really . . . ,' he began.

'I want to,' I interrupted, 'and I want to do it with my own knickers, while you watch. You can play with your cock too, if you like?'

He did, and he had it out before I'd even stood up. I wanted to do it in the nude, and didn't dare risk soiling my office suit anyway, so I stripped off, stark naked, before I got down on my knees and began to mop up my puddle. Clive watched me work, tugging at his rapidly expanding cock, and he was erect before I was half done.

It wasn't easy, because my knickers were already sodden, and I had to wring them out over the loo again and again. Not that I cared, because it was utterly, exquisitely humiliating, and it was making me ever more horny, and ever more eager to be put to the big cock now being masturbated over my naked body as I crawled in my own piss.

He looked fit to burst by the time I was done, and I was creamy and so ready that if he'd just taken me on the floor I'd have surrendered without any fight at all. Being Clive, he didn't, but stood there uncertainly as I used a little water and loo paper to clean up the last of my puddle and wipe myself. Finished, I knelt up and opened my mouth, inviting him to stick his cock in, which he did.

I let my thighs come wide as I sucked, my hand between them, masturbating lazily as I enjoyed the taste and feel of his erection. Again I knew I could come, and easily, but I wanted more. I suppose every woman knows when the time has come, and mine was now, even if it was a world away from how I'd imagined it. Slipping his cock from my mouth and into my hand, I looked up at Clive.

'I want you to fuck me,' I told him. 'Right now.'

He swallowed and nodded. I was going to get it, a lovely big cock right up my pussy, and I wanted to make it as memorable as possible, and as dirty. Scrambling around, I braced myself against the lavatory bowl and let my knees slip wide, showing off my naked, virgin pussy to the man about to penetrate me for the very first time. I'd split my hymen long ago, an inevitable consequence of riding, but no man had ever had his cock inside me. Now it was going to happen. Clive got down, his cock in his hand, brandishing it at my open cunt as he spoke.

'Are you sure, Pippa?'

'Just fuck me! I don't want to be a virgin any more.'

I pulled my back in, making myself as available as I possibly could as he shuffled forward, my cheeks spread wide to show off my bumhole and the slippery wet target I was so eager for him to hit. His cock touched, round and firm and meaty, spreading my little hole, pushing inside, and up, filling me until he seemed to be inside right up to the top of my head, and I was being fucked.

For the first time in my life I had a man's cock inside me, and it felt wonderful, pumping in and out of my hole to set me gasping, and I wanted more, far more, to be fucked until I screamed and fucked until I came and fucked until I fainted. My hand was already back, rubbing at my juicy, cock-filled cunt, my fingers slipping against my slimy flesh and bumping on the fat shaft in my hole. I was coming immediately, my pussy squeezing on Clive's cock as I gasped and shook in my ecstasy, utterly given over to pleasure and more than happy to have him spunk up inside me.

Only as my orgasm faded did the risk I was taking sink in, and I quickly pushed him back. His cock slipped free and I slumped panting over the lavatory bowl, babbling my thanks as he began to wank over my upturned bottom. I smiled and held my dirty pose despite my already aching knees, happy to take his spunk on my cheeks in return for what he'd given me.

He grinned back and moved a little closer, to rub his cock on my bottom, and between my cheeks. I stuck my hips up higher still, making a cock-slide of my bottom crease and giggling as began to rub in it, only to squeak as his helmet touched my anus. He grunted, and I thought he'd come over my bumhole, a thought that sent a shiver right through me.

'I would love to sodomise you,' he sighed, 'you've such a beautiful bottom, and I've never . . . never ever . . .'

His words broke to a sob and again I thought he'd spunked up over my anus, but again he pulled back, rubbing himself in my slit once more. My ring had begun to twitch for what he'd said, the dirty thoughts were crowding in, imagining the same cock I'd just had put in my virgin pussy also stuffed up my bottom. It was filthy, gloriously filthy, and there was no denying I wanted it, and that soon enough I'd get it anyway.

What if I got carried away and let Lucius Todmorden have me at Morris's party? He'd bugger me without a second thought, and then I'd be just one more in a long line of girls who'd had their bottoms fucked by him, and some of them as virgins. With Clive it would be his first time as well as mine, a far better, far more dignified surrender, if allowing a man to insert his penis in your rectum can ever be considered even remotely dignified. Clive would be patient with me too, and didn't mind playing with my bumhole in front of me.

'You can if you like,' I sighed, 'but let me get myself open first. Have you got any lubricant?'

I was blushing as I said it, for having to ask to lubricate my own bottom so he could insert his penis, but that only added to the thrill. He had jumped up as I spoke, and began to rummage urgently in the wall cupboard above his sink, quickly pulling out a tube of mint-flavoured toothpaste.

'Not toothpaste, it stings,' I told him.

He nodded and pulled out a slim silver canister, shaving foam, with the words 'For Sensitive Skin' written below the brand name.

'I don't know,' I admitted. 'You could try.'

I reached back, to tickle my bumhole and rub a little pussy juice in, which felt nice and helped me to get my head around what I was about to do. He sank down once more, clutching his cock as he pressed the nozzle between my cheeks, and squeezed. My mouth came wide in shock as the chilly foam squirted in up my bumhole, and I quickly began to rub it in. As I popped the very tip of my finger into my now slippery anus I was wondering if the tiny hole could possibly accommodate his cock, but what came out was sometimes just as thick, and I knew that Clive would stop if he began to hurt me.

'More?' he asked, and I nodded.

Extracting my finger, I held my cheeks wide for him, showing off my slippery bumhole. I felt the nozzle touch and cream squeeze out up my bottom for a second time. A second squeeze and he'd laid a fat blob onto my anal star, a bit like the top of a meringue, which gave me plenty to play with. It stung a little as I pushed my finger back up, but it was really no more than a pleasant warmth.

He was watching me intently, and nursing his erection as I pushed my finger deep, right up into the hot, mushy cavity of my rectum. It felt good, and my hole was beginning to loosen, so I pushed a second finger in, holding myself open to make my ring stretch and slacken. Clive reached out with the spray can again, holding it to my now open hole and squirting it up inside me, to leave me feeling loose and urgent.

'Try it,' I said, 'but gently.'

I pulled my fingers free, allowing my bumhole to close slowly and to squeeze out a fat worm of shaving foam onto pussy. Clive's cock touched, in my slit, and lower, pressing to my slippery little hole. A long sigh escaped my throat as I gave myself up for buggering, my ring already taut on his cock head as he pushed. It didn't hurt, my well-lubricated anus opening really quite easily as I pushed out to take him, just as AJ had taught me when I accepted dildos in the same dirty passage.

'I'm nearly in, Pippa,' he grunted. 'I'm nearly up your bottom.'

'Do it,' I told him.

Again he pushed, and again my ring spread to the pressure, wider this time, until my mouth had come open in sympathy. He was up though, his helmet wedged in my open hole, and even if he gave up now, or came in me, I was no longer an anal virgin. One more good shove and he was in me properly, my bumhole taut around the neck of his cock, and he'd begun to wank into my rectum.

'No ... deeper,' I gasped. 'Put it right in, all the way ... bugger me properly.'

'Say if it hurts,' he puffed, spreading my cheeks between his thumbs and began to jam himself further up.

I felt my bumhole push in and forced myself to relax, allowing another inch of cock to be stuffed up my bottom. He pulled out a little and pushed again, lubricating his shaft with the foam and my own slime. I knew he could see everything, the full bare spread of my bottom, my empty, dripping pussy and the taut pink ring of my buggered anus, bringing my feelings of humiliation up to an unbearable peak.

Not that it mattered how I felt. He was in me and he was going up, all the way up, getting faster now, and sticking a little more cock shaft up me with every thrust. I felt as if my eyes were going to pop out of my head as he worked himself slowly deeper, until at last I felt the wrinkly sack of his scrotum press to my empty cunt and I knew he was in me up to his balls.

I reached back, because I had to come again, but he'd begun to pump in my rectum, bringing me to the very edge of control. My fingers found pussy and I tried to frig, touching my empty hole and the junction of his cock and my straining bum ring, snatching at his balls to rub them on my clit. He got harder, and I just couldn't do it anymore, my hand slipping away as I gave in to my buggering.

He began to grunt and pant, now pumping so hard his belly was slapping against my meat, knocking the breath from my body and jamming me against the lavatory. I clung on, out of my mind with ecstasy, so high I didn't even care when the toilet lid fell on my head. My head was in the bowl, inches from the water stained yellow with my own piss and the loo paper I'd used to mop up my puddle.

'I'm coming,' he gasped, and rammed himself deep one last time.

His fingers locked hard in the flesh of my hips as he gave me his full load deep in my rectum, and with the same hard thrust my face had been pushed down the loo and into the mess of pissy water and half-dissolved paper. I came up gasping, my face dripping piddle, my hair full of bits of loo paper, only to have my head jammed in again by a last, unexpected shove, this time with my mouth wide open.

A second later Clive was stammering apologies, but I didn't want them. I wanted his cock up my bum and my head down the loo while I came, and I was going to. He'd began to pull out, but I snatched for his balls, ignoring his gasp of pain as I slapped them to my cunt. My face went back in the water, blowing bubbles in my piss, and as I found my clit I was snatching at the handle, to deliberately flush my own head down the lavatory as my orgasm exploded in a tearing, wrenching ecstasy that lasted until my vision went red and my muscles were so slack I could no longer keep my hand pressed to my greedy cunt.

Eight

Whatever else happened at Morris's party, I was not going to have my anal virginity taken by Lucius Todmorden.

Jemima was determined to be collected in Morris's Rolls Royce, as he had promised, but I wasn't having it turn up outside our house, and Penny was equally reluctant in case Granny saw and wondered what was going on. In the end we agreed to meet at The Fox on the Reading Road, which was far enough away to feel safe. I'd been dithering over what to wear all day, and it was not an easy choice. Morris expected me to look sexy, but I didn't want all the dirty old men homing in on me, while I did want to be attractive for Melody.

I needed to speak to Penny, to ask her to take the hopefully shell-shocked Jemima home so that I could play with Melody, so I went over first thing. She also gave me some advice on what to wear, which was to make myself up as an animal girl. Melody apparently had a thing for pony-girls, which Penny was into herself, and she had a beautiful tail, which plugged in up the wearer's bottom with a spine between her cheeks so that the hair hung down realistically. There was an elaborate leather harness that went with it, and I was intrigued, but couldn't handle the embarrassment of men seeing me with a plug up my bottom, while I was also concerned it might tempt them to bugger me.

The other choice was very simple, to be a piggy, with a pink-rubber snout and a curly tail above my bum, both of which could be stuck on with gum arabic. Otherwise I would be stark naked, which would have been quite appealing but for two things. The first was that I'd feel horribly uncomfortable effectively in the nude with men around, and perhaps even more importantly, Jemima would never let me live it down.

In the end Penny persuaded me to put the piggy-girl stuff in my bag and go as I was, in tight blue jeans and a skinny top, which apparently the majority of men preferred to exotic costumes. She was doing the same, which made sense if she wasn't going to stay long, so after a quick shower and a little playful spanking on each other's wet bottoms, we were ready.

I was already getting nervous as we drove over to the pub, and things got rapidly worse. Jemima was already there, and dressed, exactly as she had been most days for several years, in her school uniform, except that she had made one or two alterations. The jacket and blouse were as usual, as were her long white socks and even the scholar's tie fastened neatly around her collar. Her skirt was not as usual, but had been cut down so far that as she sat sipping bottled orange juice through a straw the full, long length of her legs was on display, and even a tiny white triangle where her panties showed.

'You can't go like that!' I hissed as I sat down beside her.

'Why not?' she asked. 'I look all right, don't I?'

'All right!? They'll eat you alive!'

She just giggled, and I threw my hands up in despair. Obviously she needed to be confronted with the likes of Lucius Todmorden and Mr Protheroe.

'Anyway, your knickers are showing,' I went on, hoping to embarrass her, but she merely made the tiniest adjustment to her skirt and went back to her orange juice.

Penny had gone to the bar, but before she could get the attention of the barman I saw Morris's gold Rolls Royce pull up in the car park.

'Shall we just go?' she suggested.

'We may as well,' I agreed, eager to get Jemima out of the pub before any of our highly respectable neighbours came in and got treated to a flash of her knickers.

We went outside, with Jemima still sucking orange juice through her straw, until she saw the car and ran over to inspect it, crying out with delight. The driver was Harmony, Melody's twin sister, but much the gentler of the two. She was in a tight, bottle-green chauffeur's uniform, complete with peaked cap and a skirt so short that she was quite obviously sitting bare bottom.

'Climb in,' she offered, grinning.

The three of us got into the back, Jemima excitedly examining the TV and miniature fridge as Penny made the introductions. Harmony was always friendly, and very good at making people feel relaxed, which was exactly what I didn't want. Melody would have probably had Jemima terrified before we even got to the party. As it was, she and Harmony barely shut up for a minute all the way to London.

Morris's house was a huge mansion in the most expensive part of Highgate, with a high wall built around the garden and tall gates to keep out both intruders and the gaze of curious passers-by. He had always boasted that it was safe to walk naked anywhere on his property, and aside from the risk of the occasional helicopter, it was true.

Jemima was awestruck, gazing about her in rapture as we got out of the car, and pretty excited too, giggling as Harmony swung her legs out of the car and gave a brief flash of bare black pussy. There was no sign of Morris, but we were greeted by Annabelle, Melody's personal slave and plaything, whom I'd met once or twice when she was let off her leash to go to clubs. Now she was on it, literally, with a tight black leather collar encircling her neck, from which hung what was obviously a real dog lead rather than a piece of custom-made SM kit. Otherwise she was nude but for high heels, stockings and a tiny black corset that left her breasts bare and her bottom only half covered by a puff of lace. She was completely exposed at the front, with the tattoo marking her as Melody's property clearly visible on her pussy mound.

That really had Jemima staring, and looking shocked, so my hopes began to rise as we were conducted indoors. Morris was in the huge hallway, along with a lot of other people and a buffet table laid out with glasses and bottles of champagne in buckets full of ice. Melody was there, and cast me a cool look, but she was speaking to an enormously fat man I took for Mr Enos. Annabelle fetched us drinks, and Morris began to perform introductions.

Mr Montague and Mr Todmorden were there, both smiling and nodding to me, then leaning together to share a whispered remark as they glanced at Jemima. Maggie was with them, looking less than happy in an abbreviated sailor suit that left her bare bottom cheeks peeping out from under the rim, and also Helen, dressed the same except that she had been allowed to wear panties.

There was another girl, calling herself Toy, in a pretty evening gown of green silk set off by an elaborate peacock-feather mask, which made nine women in all. There were also nine men, which seemed to imply a girl each, and I found myself very glad I'd accepted Mr Montague's invitation, as while he was one of the oldest, he was also the most attractive.

Mr Mulligan was there on the opposite side of the room, admiring the turn of Annabelle's bottom as she bent to serve drinks to Hudson Staebler, a huge man in a white-leather suit complete with cowboy hat, which he'd neglected to take off. There was also Mr Protheroe, a fleshy, balding man with a red face, no neck, and massive, flabby buttocks spilling over the edge of his chair.

He'd been talking to Mr Judd, who was fifty or so, and very average, a bit flabby maybe, and with his hair slicked back around a bald spot. Standing alone and eyeing the girls in turn was Mr Spottiswood, a small, compact man, thin on top and really quite ordinary except for a pair of bright, beady eyes that seemed to bore right through my clothes. He had what appeared to be a pair of girl's panties hanging half out of one pocket.

I'd known more or less what to expect, but was still taken aback. Never had I seen such a collection of obviously dirty old men assembled in one place, and they weren't just there for the conversation. They expected to spank our bottoms, and probably more, a lot more. I glanced towards Jemima, expecting to find her looking as horrified as I felt, just in time to see the little tart drop a curtsey to the big American, Staebler, then twirl around to make her school skirt rise and show her knickers.

She was giggling too, and quite obviously enjoying herself, but there was nothing I could do save console myself that she obviously hadn't realised what she was letting herself in for. Every pair of male eyes in the place had turned to watch her little display. Melody was looking too, making me wonder if a good spanking followed by having her head sat on for a lick of the black girl's pussy and bumhole wouldn't teach Jemima a valuable lesson.

Obviously I couldn't let anything of the sort happen to her, even if it meant taking the same myself, but with the way she was behaving the thought was certainly tempting. Even as I pictured Jemima's expression as Melody's ample black bottom was lowered onto her face, Morris had started towards me, bringing Mr Spottiswood with him. I forced a smile and took a badly needed swallow of champagne.

'Ah, Pippa,' Morris addressed me, 'I'm delighted you've come. This is Ken. I thought I'd put the two of you together. Ken, this is Pippa, who is an absolute delight as you can see for yourself.'

'What colour panties are you wearing, darling?' Mr Spottiswood asked without further conversation, bringing the colour to my cheeks as I hastened to answer.

'White,' I told him, 'but Mr Rathwell ... Morris, how do you mean put the two of us together? I thought it was Ladies' Choice tonight?'

'Just for the time being,' Morris assured me. 'We'll play later, don't worry.'

I drew a sigh of relief, very glad indeed that I wasn't going to be stuck with Mr Spottiswood all evening, although Mr Enos or Mr Protheroe might have been worse, or maybe not, if my companion's conversation was anything to go by.

'I adore white panties,' he was saying. 'I spanked the most delightful little thing a few weeks ago. June, she was called, fat little thing with big round titties and a bum like a peach. She was in school uniform, with a pair of white panties perhaps a couple of sizes too small, so that her cheeks bulged out around the leg holes, giving me plenty of bare flesh to smack as well as her panty seat. I pulled them down in the end, of course, because you have to, don't you? But I do like to leave the panties up for a while, and then whip them down just when the girl thinks she's got away without going bare bottom. I did that with June, and of course it's always that much more embarrassing when the girl has a fat bottom, don't you think?'

I nodded vaguely. He'd been making gestures with his hands as he spoke, to indicate the shape of the girl's bottom and how he'd exposed and spanked her, with me listening in growing alarm. When it came to sheer smut, Mr Spottiswood could have given Mr Prufrock lessons. He wasn't finished either.

'I mean, it's bad enough for a girl to be bared without the man who's going to spank her seeing how overweight she is. Not that June's panties hid much, but she was so big I had to pull her cheeks apart to make sure she knew she had no secrets left from me. I like to do that. It shows a girl who's boss when she knows I've seen her cunt and bottom hole. Now a skinny little thing like you, I expect you'd be flashing it all from the start, wouldn't you, fanny adams and brown eye too?'

I tried to say something, but all that came out was a little whimper, and as he went on I was wondering if he'd have seen my cunt and bottom hole before the end of the evening. It was an awful thought, but as usual, pussy seemed to disagree, and I was already getting sticky down my panties.

Morris finally saved me by calling us all into a different room, in which the centre had been cleared but for a single straight-backed chair stood in the middle of a large and expensive-looking rug. A couple of sofas and various other chairs had been set around the room, clearly for the audience, while the central one was obviously for the girls to be spanked over.

I'd managed to detach myself from Mr Spottiswood, and sat down next to Jemima on the sofa. She was bright-eyed with excitement, and hadn't even bothered to adjust her skirt, so that she was showing a triangle of white panty material again.

'Pull you skirt down a bit,' I urged.

'Don't be silly,' she replied. 'Annabelle's stark naked, and Harmony's got no knickers. Who was that man you were talking to?'

'Mr Spottiswood. He's obsessed with girls' panties, so watch out for him, as you seem determined to show everybody yours.'

'He looks creepy . . .'

It was the first thing I'd wanted to hear from her all day.

'. . . I prefer Hudson Staebler, he's so big, and I love his accent.'

'He's worse than Mr Spottiswood. He likes to put girls on leads and treat them as dogs.'

To my utter horror she just giggled. Morris had raised his hands for silence, and we went quiet along with everybody else, my stomach slowly tying itself into knots as he began to speak.

'Ladies and Gentleman, if I might have your attention please, now that we've all had a little drink and a chance to get to know one another, it is time to begin. As always there will be a round of spankings first, but with a rather different structure this time. We're going to play a little game called Ladies' Choice. The rules are simple. Each of you beautiful young ladies, my own lovely wife included, must choose somebody to spank her, the punishment to be delivered in front of us all and on the bare, naturally. Spankers may decline in the hope of being chosen by another girl, if they wish, but nobody can go twice until all nine girls are standing against the wall with their red bottoms to the room. Girls may choose other women to spank them, but if so, she must take it with a small plug in her bottom, which must stay in while she does corner time. No girl doing corner time may spank. Is that clear?'

As he spoke he had reached out to indicate the mantelpiece, on which a line of squat butt plugs had been arranged, each with its lubricated wrap, and with a big pot of jelly at the end just in case some poor girl's bumhole proved a bit tight. They were made of clear plastic, which meant that once it was in a girl the interior of her bottom hole would show. My stomach twisted tighter still as I wondered which was worse, being spanked by a man or having a plug inserted in my anus before taking it from another woman, but still with men watching. Both choices seemed equally appalling, but Jemima was looking shocked, which was at least something.

Morris was smiling as he went on.

'Good. First then, I'm told that there is a small matter of office discipline to be sorted out, which means that tonight, rather than dishing it out, our Miss Phelps will be on the receiving end. Maggie?'

I turned to Maggie, as did everybody else. Her face was full of consternation, her eyes darting between us, and for all my pleasure in seeing her get it, I could fully sympathise with the way she felt. I'd be making the same choice myself, soon enough. In fact, the sooner the better, because the worst men were sure to be left until last. I leant back to take another glass of champagne from Annabelle as she passed behind my sofa, hoping to boost my courage.

Maggie was still vacillating when the intercom sounded from the hall. Morris went, looking irritable, but came back well pleased with himself.

'Sophie and June are here,' he announced. 'What an unexpected pleasure.'

Something in his tone of voice told me the pleasure wasn't unexpected at all, but if he had some perverted little scheme in mind it didn't seem to involve me. I knew Sophie, a friend of Penny's whose happy playful attitude to spanking had always inspired me, and June was obviously the girl Mr Spottiswood had been talking about. Both were in school uniform, although not the real thing, with scruffy white blouses half open and tiny red-tartan miniskirts that deliberately left their knickers showing.

'Maggie?' Morris asked when the two girls were settled. 'I believe you were about to chose who is to give you your punishment spanking?'

'Mr Montague,' she replied in an almost inaudible whisper.

He looked surprised, but got to his feet immediately, crossing the room to offer her his hand. She took it and allowed herself to be led to the spanking chair, her head hung in shame and pink-faced with embarrassment. I'd been hoping to get Mr Montague myself, and my enjoyment was mixed with resentment as Maggie was prepared.

It was still exciting, and not just because she'd punished me and helped to make me Mr Prufrock's pet tart. To see another woman spanked is always exciting for me, and because she was older and usually dominant there was an extra thrill from knowing just how humiliated she would be feeling as

Mr Montague turned up the skirt of her sailor suit to show off her naked bottom.

She was quite fleshy for such a slim woman, with soft, full cheeks and smooth pink skin. I could just see her face, still set in consternation for her fate, an emotion that became abruptly stronger as Mr Montague put his hands on her bottom and pulled her cheeks wide. He made a brief inspection of her anus, just as she had inspected mine, nudged her legs slightly apart so that the hairy bulge of her pussy showed from behind, and began to spank.

I was thoroughly enjoying myself as I watched. She took it well, at least managing not to throw a complete tantrum, but the expression on her face was a joy to behold, with her eyes glaring at me, at Lucius, and even at Helen. I gave her a smile and a little wave, which had her glaring harder still until the expression broke to pain at a harder smack. Her bottom was so soft that each smack made her flesh spread out and sent ripples through her cheeks, which was also comic, and had most of the audience grinning or laughing, including Jemima.

'So you think it's funny, do you?' I asked her quietly, trying to stifle my own chuckles. 'Wait until you're the one with her bottom bare and everybody's laughing at you because you look silly and you're in pain.'

She shrugged and spoke.

'That's OK. My bum's not all sloppy like that, and besides, Hudson's promised to take it slowly if I suck him off afterwards.'

'Jemima! You little tart!'

The words had come out by instinct, and I immediately realised I'd called her by the name I like to be called myself. The blood rushed to my cheeks and I sat back again, speechless. I knew she was no innocent, but to offer to suck some dirty old bastard's cock in order to make sure he took care over her first ever spanking was ... was just the sort of thing I'd done, several times now.

Across the room, Mr Montague was delivering a last, blistering salvo to Maggie's now well-reddened bottom. He'd been stern with her, and she was gasping and trembling quite badly, with her make-up spoiled where a few tears had escaped her eyes. She'd been punished, properly, which was highly satisfying.

Her tiny skirt was turned up into its own waistband to leave her bottom showing and she was sent into the corner, to stand with her hands on her head, her nose pressed to the wall and her red cheeks showing behind. A few of the men clapped politely and Mr Montague took a small bow before returning to his seat. Morris took the floor again.

'That is our only punishment spanking of the evening,' he stated, 'so from now on we will draw lots. Harmony?'

Harmony picked up a what looked like a magician's top-hat from the table beside her and walked over to Morris. He dipped his hand in, rummaging for a moment before drawing out a piece of folded pink paper. I felt my tummy tighten again as he opened it, hoping it wouldn't be me but knowing it would be best if it was.

'Penny,' he announced.

She made a face, then leant towards me behind Jemima's back.

'Who's your worst?' she whispered.

'I don't know,' I answered. 'Mr Spottiswood? Mr Protheroe?'

'No conferring,' Morris ordered.

'Sorry,' Penny answered, 'just checking something. Um ... Mr Spottiswood please.'

His podgy face immediately split into a dirty leer. She and I exchanged sympathetic looks as she stepped forward, to stand by the punishment chair as he approached. It was sweet of her to take him out of the line-up of spankers, although I was pretty sure her choice was also an excuse to make sure she got a good dose of humiliation.

'I've never spanked you before, have I?' he asked as he sat down.

'No,' Penny answered.

'Then you're in for a treat,' he said. 'Over you go, and make sure you get your bum well up in the air. I like it that way.'

Penny obeyed, posing herself over his lap with her feet together on the floor to make a plump, cheeky ball of her bottom within her jeans. Mr Spottiswood begun to unfasten her, fumbling at the button and peeling down her zip, all the while with the emotion growing stronger on her face.

She had to lift her hips even more to let him peel her jeans down, and her panties came with them, a thoroughly undignified stripping. He wasn't finished either, but pulled off her shoes and took her jeans off completely, then adjusted her knickers so that her bottom was perfectly encased in smooth white cotton as she got back into the spanking position he had ordered. She'd begun to tremble a little, but he went on with her preparation, laying one hand across her bottom to stroke the seat of her panties and giving her cheeks a little wobble as she spoke.

'Plump little thing, aren't you?' he asked.

Penny just made a face, but got a hard smack for her obstinance.

'Plump little thing, aren't you?' he repeated.

'A little . . . I suppose,' she answered.

'A little?' he chuckled, planting a second smack to set her bottom quivering. 'Hardly that! I think you should cut down on the pies, my dear.'

It was completely unfair, as Penny's bottom may be full, but is firm and shapely too, not overweight at all, really, while he had a nasty little pot belly and was starting to get a double chin. However, she was the one over his knee, and not the other way around.

He gave her another smack, and I realised it was to be a panty spanking and not bare, only to remember his nasty habits. Sure enough, after maybe a dozen swats he stopped and spoke again.

'Oh dear, we seem to have forgotten something, don't we? Girls are spanked with their panties down, aren't they? Even fat girls are spanked with their panties down, especially fat girls.'

Penny let out a little, broken sob. He chuckled and put his thumbs into the waistband of her knickers, speaking as he began to push them down over her full, pink cheeks.

'You should have reminded me, dear, shouldn't you? I suppose you didn't want to show everyone how fat your bottom is, eh? Well you're going to. You're going to show it all, and for an extra little punishment, I think you should wear your panties in your mouth while I spank you, and perhaps a little tail.'

He'd exposed her, the wide, pale spread of her bum now on show, stripped and ready, her body naked from the waist down but for a pair of short white socks. I thought of all the times I'd spanked her, and kissed her better, even licked her bottom, which sent a powerful shiver through me. He carried out his threat, pulling off her knickers and forcing her to take them in her mouth, so that a little scrap of white cotton was hanging out between her lips as he turned his attention back to her bottom.

'You're firm, I'll say that for you,' he remarked, squeezing one cheek. 'Well scrubbed too, but I wonder: do you wipe properly?'

His hands had closed on her cheeks as he said it, and I saw Penny wince as her bottom was hauled wide, showing off the thick growth of hair over her pussy and around her bumhole, which was twitching in response to the sudden exposure and what must have been overwhelming shame. I was very glad I'd soaped between her cheeks when we'd showered.

'Pristine, apparently,' he remarked, and he'd put his finger to her bumhole, tickling the little knot of pinkish brown flesh and laughing as her ring began to open and close, 'and well trained too! I suspect Mr Willy's been up the chocolate mine. You should shave though. We spankers prefer a nice nude cunt, while I'm sure you get bits of loo paper caught in all that bum hair.'

Penny was sobbing badly, with little shivers running through her body and the first tears trickling from her eyes. She made no effort to get up though, and I knew exactly what was going through her head, and also that it was far stronger than I could possibly have coped with, not from him, let alone in front of an audience.

'One last little detail,' he said, letting go of her bottom.

She looked back, no doubt wondering what further humiliation he could possibly inflict on her after having her panties stuffed in her mouth and her bumhole inspected in public. He'd put his hand in his jacket pocket, and I saw her expression change to puzzlement as he drew out the girls knickers I'd seen earlier, a tarty scarlet pair, and another in black. Only as her cheeks were once more hauled rudely apart did I realise what he was going to do with them, and my mouth came open in shock and sympathy as I watched.

The red panties were inserted into her pussy, well up, then drawn out again, now wet and sticky with juice, which he wiped on her bumhole to open her enough to let him poke them in with a finger. Lifting the red pair, he inserted the black in turn, pushed well up her cunt, and she was left with the two pairs of tarty knickers hanging out of her twin holes as he finally set to work on her bottom.

After what he'd done to her, just having her bottom slapped must have been a relief, at least for a while. He did it really hard, putting his whole arm into every slap and hitting her thighs as well as her bum cheeks. She was kicking immediately, and wiggling her bum around in a pathetic and useless effort to dodge the smacks, and I was sure that if her knickers hadn't been in her mouth she'd have been squealing like a pig.

Everybody thought it was hilarious, laughing and clapping, complimenting Mr Spottiswood on his technique and remarking on how much he'd added by stuffing all three of her holes with panties. I was very grateful indeed it wasn't me, and felt genuinely sorry for her, but I was getting ever more turned on, both by the fuss she was making and the view of her rear end with her cheeks wobbling to the smacks and the red and black knickers jerking and bouncing in her holes. Jemima just thought it was hilarious.

'You wait,' I told her as the spanking finally stopped and Penny slumped exhausted across Mr Spottiswood's knee. 'Just you wait.'

'I told you,' she answered. 'Hudson's promised to be gentle with me. But wasn't it funny watching Aunt Penny spanked like that?'

I didn't answer, and she gave me a pert look as Penny was sent into the corner with a final smack to her now blazing red bottom. Our eyes made contact as she crossed the room, and I managed to mouth my thanks before she'd joined Maggie against the wall with her hands on her head and the tears still trickling slowly down her face.

'An excellent spanking there, Ken,' Morris said as he stepped forward once more, 'and so, without delay, we have . . .'

He dipped his hand into the top hat.

'. . . Helen.'

She chose Lucius Todmorden, and was duly turned over his knee, her sailor skirt lifted, her knickers pulled down and her sweetly formed bottom spanked to a rosy pink. He was far nicer to her than Mr Spottiswood had been to Penny, but she was a bit of a baby about it and cried, still snivelling as she joined the others against the wall. With three red bums now decorating his living room, Morris went to the hat once more, selecting Harmony.

Her choice was Morris himself, and he added an extra humiliation by opening the top of her chauffeur's uniform and pulling her breasts out, so that they bounced and jiggled as her bottom was smacked. Melody watched with undisguised approval as her sister was punished, even ducking down to tease Harmony's nipples while Morris inserted a finger at the other end.

With Harmony sent into the corner Morris picked again. June's name came out of the hat and she chose Mr Judd, who tried to outdo both Morris and Mr Spottiswood for sheer dirtiness, taking her big, coffee-coloured tits out of her blouse, and gagging her with her school knickers while she was spanked. It didn't work, because she just lapped it all up, wiggling her bottom and mumbling encouragement through her panty gag. His response was to beat her with one of her own shoes, which finally got some reaction out of her, and she was looking distinctly sorry for herself as she went to the wall.

Toy followed, and choose Mr Mulligan. He hesitated, glancing at me, and I remembered how I'd promised him first go, but Toy was already at the chair, kneeling on it with her pretty evening gown turned up onto her back to show off the French knickers she had on underneath. He gave me what was presumably supposed to be an apologetic look and went to her, turning down her knickers and dishing out what would have been a quite elegant spanking if he hadn't kept stopping to pull her pussy open and show off the pink inside her hole.

Annabelle was chosen next, and selected Melody, but to my surprise she was refused and forced to chose again. With Mr Enos, Mr Protheroe and Hudson Staebler left, there was really only one choice. She went for Staebler, and I heard Jemima click her tongue in annoyance. I threw her a worried glance, because a very nasty suspicion indeed had begun to grow in my head, worse even than having to take a spanking from either of the two dirty old men still in the game.

Hudson Staebler made a thorough job of Annabelle, leaving her snivelling badly and clutching her little red bottom as she joined the line of punished girls standing against the wall. I tried to catch Morris's eye as he went back to the hat, but he ignored me. Sophie's name came out.

She was spanked by Mr Protheroe, another one who liked to humiliate his victims. He made her talk her way through the punishment, asking him to pull her knickers down, open her cheeks and even for a tickle of her bumhole. Like June she took it well, openly enjoying her degradation, even when he tried to break her composure by fucking her with one of the butt plugs.

That left three of us, and Melody looked as unhappy as I felt, eyeing the enormously fat Mr Enos even before her name had been drawn from the hat. She knew she'd be going over his knee, and so did I. Sure enough, her name was picked, and over she went. He was actually really nice to her, comparatively, only taking down her knickers to the top of her thighs and spending a lot of time stroking and patting her bottom before getting down to the proper spanking. Despite that she obviously found the experience utterly humiliating, and she was pouting badly by the end.

Morris stepped up again, now grinning right across his face, and rubbing his hands in unconcealed joy as he looked down on Jemima and me. All my suspicions were confirmed, the entire game a set-up so that he could arrange for a fresh sister-to-sister spanking in front of his dirty old men, and presumably he thought that when all the others had taken their punishment, including his own, very dominant wife, neither of us would have the guts to refuse. He was wrong.

'You're a cheat, Morris,' I said as I stood up. 'Sophie and June arrived late, but you already had their names in the hat, and I want to know why Melody turned down Annabelle. You set this whole thing up, didn't you, so you could all watch Jemima and me spank each other, you bunch of perverts.'

'Absolutely not!' Morris answered, but he was having trouble hiding his grin. 'It was completely fair. You saw me draw the names out of the hat myself.'

'I'm not stupid, Morris,' I answered him, picking up the hat. 'It's one of those magician's hats, isn't it, with a false piece so you can hide things.'

There were two pieces of paper in the hat, obviously mine and Jemima's, but that wasn't stopping me. I punched my fist into the hat, as hard as I could, and again, bursting the crown and ripping the seam of the silk lining.

'That was actually quite an expensive topper,' Morris stated, 'from Gieves and Hawkes.'

'Not any more!' I told him, jerking at the torn silk to discover the secret compartment.

There wasn't one.

'You're paying for that,' Melody remarked, turning around, 'and don't forget you already owe me for my bike.'

'Shut up!' I snapped. 'You've been spanked, haven't you? Keep your nose against the wall and pull your knickers down properly.'

Her mouth came wide in astonishment and fury, but I wasn't finished.

'I don't know how you did it, Morris, but you did, didn't you, and if you think I'm going to spank my baby sister in front of this crew of lecherous old bastards you've got another thought coming, and also . . .'

'Pippa!' Jemima spoke up from behind me. 'You're spoiling the fun, and I'm not a baby.'

'He's trying to trick us into spanking each other, Jemima,' I exclaimed, 'knickers down and with plugs up our bums! Jesus, Morris, you're a . . .'

'Oh come on, Pip,' Jemima urged. 'I'll be gentle with you if you're gentle with me, and I'm sure Morris will let us off the plug thingies if . . . I don't know, we give them a little striptease or something.'

'Now there's a girl with sense,' Morris cut in, 'a nice sisterly striptease after the spankings, maybe a little feel of each other's titties, and you needn't plug each other.'

'Shut up!' I yelled at him. 'Jemima, for goodness sake . . .'

'That sounds OK,' she interrupted, 'and anyway, it's not like it will be the first time we've got dirty together, except for the spanking.'

I could not believe I'd heard her correctly at first, but I had, and so had everybody else. An excited buzz ran around the room, both among the men and the long row of spanked girls against the wall, whispering together and looking at Jemima and I as my face flared to a blazing heat, my cheeks redder than any bottom in the room. It was the one secret I'd never told anybody, not even Penny, and she'd blurted it out to a room full of lechers and sadists, kinky girls and dirty old men, including my employers and our own aunt.

For a long moment I couldn't even speak, my mouth locked open and my every muscle frozen, until a red spark seemed to ignite in my head. I looked down at Jemima, thinking of all I'd done to try to protect her, and the way she'd reacted; teasing me, laughing at me, getting off over my smacked bum, pulling down my bikini pants in front of Morris and Melody, and now this. It was the final straw.

'Right you filthy little brat!' I shouted, snatching at her wrist. 'You want to be spanked? You're going to get spanked! You're going to get spanked until you howl, you little slut! Come here.'

She'd begun to struggle, suddenly frightened, but I had a good grip on her wrist and I was still stronger than her. As I lurched backwards she came with me, onto the rug, now babbling protests and pleas as I dragged her across to the spanking chair and sat down. She was fighting as hard as she could, now desperate to stop what she'd been willing to take just moments before, but I wasn't going to give in. I managed to get her arm twisted up behind her back and wrenched her off balance as I sat down hard on the chair.

'Get over, you!' I screamed, and I'd done it, hauling her into place across my knee with her arm locked tight in the small of her back.

Her long legs were kicking in every direction, her free arm flailing wildly in her efforts to scratch me, her hair tossing, and she was screaming too, begging me to get off her and threatening to tell Mum almost in the same breath. I just tightened my grip, until her protests gave way to a squeak of pain and she went suddenly limp, panting for breath as she continued to talk.

'I will, Pippa,' she said. 'I'll tell Mum. I'll tell her everything, about what you and AJ do, and how you like to be spanked, and how we play dirty together, and . . .'

'Oh no you won't,' I told her, 'because you're just as bad as me, you little tart . . . slut. Right, let's have your panties down.'

'Pip, no!' she squealed, and she begun to fight again, struggling desperately as I flipped up her abbreviated school skirt to show off the seat of the white knickers she'd been flashing all afternoon.

'It's what you want, isn't it?' I demanded. 'A good spanking in front of the boys? Well you're going to get it, and you're going to get it bare. So . . . down . . . they . . . come.'

She'd gone absolutely wild, screaming abuse and thrashing in my grip, but I had her arm locked up tight and a good grip on her panties. As I spoke I'd pulled them down in three sharp jerks and her bottom was bare to the room, her pussy on plain show as her legs pumped in her desperation to break free. She realised, suddenly pressing her thighs together to hide

235

herself, but it made little difference. I couldn't see her cunt properly, but her cheeks were too slim to conceal her anus, and her pussy hole showed too.

The anger was still burning in my head, and I was determined to see it through and give her a proper spanking. I kept my grip as I adjusted her panties and skirt to make sure I had the full expanse of her bottom to smack. She'd stopped fighting, knowing she couldn't escape and would only succeed in making a show of her cunt, but she was still alternately pleading and threatening to tell Mum.

'I will, Pippa, I'll tell! I don't care if I get told off too, I don't!'

'Act your age, Jemima,' I snapped. 'You wanted a spanking, and now you're going to get it, but first: what was it you thought was so funny when Aunt Penny was spanked? That's it, when that dirty old git asked if she wiped her bottom properly. Well let's see how clean your own bumhole is, shall we? Will that be funny too?'

'No!' she screamed.

She gave a violent lurch, nearly knocking the chair over, but I'd been expecting it and clung on, my spare hand digging between her cheeks to open them wide, spreading out the tight pink dimple of her anus for all to see. The star of tiny lines leading to her anus was ever so slightly brown, and there was a little piece of blue loo paper stuck in the hole itself, at the sight of which all my anger just collapsed.

It came home to me what I was doing, showing off my little sister's bottom hole to a room full of gawping men. I quickly let go of her cheeks, but it was too late to stop. She deserved it, and she'd wanted it, so I began to spank her, struggling with my own feelings as my hand slapped down on her neat little cheeks, my own sister's cheeks.

She'd gone limp, surrendered to the smacking, not even caring for the display of cunt and bumhole she was making from the rear. I knew how she felt. They'd seen it all. What did it matter if they had a good stare? Her panties were down for exactly that reason. What was wrong that she was over her big sister's knee? Who better to punish her for being such an utter brat? Who cared if her bumhole was dirty and her pussy was wet? She was being spanked, and the more she was humiliated the better, because then maybe, just maybe, she would realise it wasn't just an adult game.

I stopped, my hand still on her bottom, now fighting my own guilt for what I'd done. Yet everyone was still watching, and I couldn't show my feelings in front of them. I already felt awful for losing my temper, and I wasn't going to give them the satisfaction of seeing me get in a state too. Determined at least to look as if I was in control, I gave Jemima's bottom a little rub as I spoke.

'There, Jem, now you know what it's like. Do you want some more?'

She glanced back, looking up at me out of eyes wet with tears, and gave a single, tiny nod. I smiled, let go of her arm and went back to spanking her, gently now, peppering her bottom with little pats and dabs, just hard enough to sting. She stayed exactly as she was, her breathing a little harsh as I dealt with her bottom the way an inexperienced girl should be dealt with, gently and patiently.

Nobody said a word as they watched me spank Jemima. I was sure they all knew it was her virgin punishment. Morris would have made very certain of it, and not one of them was prepared to risk breaking the spell. Nor did I, because her sobs had turned to sighs and she'd begun to lift her bottom, now

willingly displayed the pouted, puffy lips of her sex
and the wet heart around her vagina. Her cheeks were
an even, flushed pink, hot to the touch, and her
bumhole had begun to wink in her excitement.

I'd been wrong, she was genuine, as genuine as I
was, not just wanting her bottom smacked, but
craving it. Now she was getting it, hopefully the way
she'd imagined it in her fantasies, spanked bare
across the knee with an audience to witness her
humiliation and pain, and with her sister to deal with
her bottom. I had to make it special, as special as I
could, even to make her come, if she wanted to.

'Shall . . . shall I take you there, Jem?' I asked. 'All
the way?'

Her answer was a whimper, deep in her throat, and
I knew she wanted it. I began to spank harder, and
lower down, applying my smacks to the tuck of her
cheeks to jolt her pussy. She began to wiggle, and
moan, giving herself up to the pleasure of her
punishment with no more thought for her modesty at
all. Her bottom was up, her cheeks open to show off
her slippery brown bumhole, now squeezing and
spreading as her muscles began to contract. She'd set
her feet apart, bracing her legs with her swollen pussy
naked for all to see and her school panties stretched
taut between her slender thighs. Juice was oozing
from her hole, a tiny squirt every time I smacked her
bottom and her moans were growing loud and
urgent.

I slipped my hand between her thighs, cupping her
cunt as I began to spank her with the other one. A
voice in the back of my head was screaming at me,
demanding to know what the hell I thought I was
doing bringing my little sister to orgasm in front of a
load of men, but it was what she wanted and I didn't
stop, rubbing at her clit and spanking her bottom as

she bucked and wriggled over my knee. She began to gasp, then to scream, and suddenly her legs had kicked out, long and straight, her bottom had gone tense under my hand and both her pussy and bumhole had gone into contractions, with shiver after shiver running through her flesh as she came.

The moment it was over she had twisted around on my lap, to cuddle into me, her whole body shaking violently as she let out her emotions onto my chest. I clung on, kissing her, stroking her hair and whispering into her ear, ignoring my own hardly tolerable feelings as I soothed her instead. We stayed like that for a long time, nobody speaking, until at last Jemima pulled away. Morris began to clap, then others, and to congratulate us, in a crescendo of happy noise that broke only when Morris raised his hands for silence.

'Magnificent!' he declared. 'A perfect climax to our little game, and now, perhaps a little more champagne before we . . .'

'Hang on a minute,' Jemima broke in. 'I thought all the girls had to choose somebody to spank them?'

'No,' I said quickly, and went on in rising panic. 'You have to go in the corner now, like the others, and then the game's over. You said the girls doing corner time couldn't be chosen to spank, didn't you, Morris?'

Morris took his chin in his fingers.

'An interesting point,' he said. 'You're both right, so perhaps it would be best if we were to take a vote. Those in favour of Pippa having to take her spanking, please raise your hands.'

I'd closed my eyes, but I needn't have bothered. When I opened them every single hand in the room was up, including Penny's.

'OK,' I sighed, 'I suppose I couldn't put it off for ever, but who to choose?'

'Jade mentioned that you like to be passed around,' Morris suggested.

'She was teasing you!' I answered him. 'I've never even been done in front of a man, never mind by a man!'

I was going to continue, but they'd all begun to talk among themselves, nodding agreement. Finally Morris spoke up.

'I think you're going to be passed around, Pippa.'

'There are nineteen of you!' I protested, but my voice was lost beneath a chorus of agreement with Morris.

I drew a heavy sigh and looked around the room. Everybody was looking at me. All ten girls had bare, smacked bottoms and no sympathy for the fact that mine alone was still white and covered up. From the men I had no chance of mercy at all.

'You will of course be forgiven the hat,' Morris told me.

'And my bike,' Melody added, 'but you're going to have to be plugged.'

'Plugged! Why?'

'Because you're going to be spanked by girls.'

'I . . . I didn't plug Jemima!'

'More fool you. Come on, knickers down and bend over. I'm doing you first.'

'But Melody . . .'

She had started towards me, pulling up her knickers as she came. The rest of the girls in the spanking line up began to come away from the wall and adjust themselves. I was for it, with a vengeance.

'I think I'll have you naked,' Melody said as she reached me. 'Strip.'

I hastened to obey, her command giving me a sharp erotic thrill, but also because if I was in the nude then Mr Spottiswood couldn't stuff my panties

240

in my mouth or up my cunt. Everybody watched as I stripped, making themselves comfortable around the room with most of the men clustered where they'd get a good view of my rear end. Jemima lingered a moment to collect my clothes, squeezed my hand and went to sit on Hudson Staebler's lap. Something close to jealousy caught me as I saw his huge hand close on her bottom, but I had other worries. Morris had passed Melody a butt plug and the large tub of anal jelly.

'Touch your toes,' Melody ordered.

It had begun, humiliation and spanking in front of men, and by men. As I bent down to take hold of my ankles I was trying to tell myself it was one of my deepest desires, something I'd fantasised over a thousand times when I masturbated, but that did nothing to lessen the trembling of my body or the agonising shame as bumhole and pussy came on show from behind.

'I like the way her tits quiver,' one man remarked. 'She's really got the shakes.'

'Yeah, and look at that cute little arsehole,' another answered. 'I think it's winking at us.'

'I do like to see a cleanly shaved cunt,' a third put in.

I couldn't see who was speaking, because my eyes were tight shut, but every word stung. Melody's hand touched my bottom, two fingers settling between my cheeks to spread my anus. I felt the nozzle of the jelly tub touch, just above my hole, and gasped as a thick worm of cold, slippery lubricant was laid over my anal ring. A second followed, across the first, to make an X with my bumhole at the exact centre.

'You know what to do, don't you?' Melody asked. 'I suppose AJ's had plenty of things up you?'

Even as I nodded, the tip of the butt plug touched my hole. I pushed, allowing my ring to spread on the hardness of the plug and thinking of how the bright pink interior of my passage would be showing to my audience as I opened up. Melody pulled the plug clear, smearing jelly over my slowly closing bumhole before pressing once more. Again I pushed, and this time the plug went in all the way, my bumhole straining to take it and closing on the neck with a soft, squashy sound.

I was plugged. Now I was to be spanked. Melody wiped her hands on my back and returned the jelly tub to the mantelpiece, then sat down on the spanking chair. She patted her lap and I came to her, waddling a little for the plug in my bumhole. I didn't fight at all, but draped myself across her knees in meek submission.

Her arm came around my waist, and I was well and truly trapped, my bum available for spanking and about to get it whether I liked it or not. She was far too strong for me, and would hold me easily however much I kicked and squealed and begged, hold me and spank me. I was utterly helpless, and that made it so much easier to give in, even with my cunt flaunted to the room and my plugged bumhole on plain show.

'Two minutes only, darling,' Morris told Melody. 'Some people are getting a little urgent.'

I glanced around to find Jemima with Hudson Staebler's cock in her hand, wanking him as they enjoyed the view of me spread bare over Melody's lap. At least two other men had their cocks out, but as Melody's hand smacked down on my bare flesh the number of dirty old men wanking over my bum became instantly less important. It hurt like anything; hard, no-nonsense spanks delivered right across my meat, each one jamming the plug in up my hole.

My single, feeble attempt to protest broke to a scream and I was fighting despite myself, my legs kicking in every direction and my fists thumping on the floor in a pathetic spanking tantrum. She just clung on tighter, spanking me with the full force of her arm and ignoring both my struggles and my pitiful, pig-like squealing. I was crying in moments, from the appalling frustration of being held helpless and spanked as much as from the pain, but she didn't even slow down, taking her full two minutes before stopping to let me tumble to the floor.

I sprawled on my back, cunt spread to the room, taken completely by surprise. My bottom seemed to be on fire, my vision hazy with tears, and before I'd had a chance to begin to recover Morris himself was hauling me to my feet. Over I went, bum in the air, for my first ever spanking from a man, Morris Rathwell himself, the biggest, greediest pervert of them all, who'd spanked more girls than he could remember. I was the next in line, just one more little tart to have her bum smacked, and no more import-ant than any other.

That was what hurt, as I kicked and wriggled across his knee with the tears running down my face at one end and a mixture of lubricant jelly and cunt juice running down my thighs at the other. My first, and it had to be Morris, and worse, I suspected he'd known full well I'd end up over his knee from the moment he met me. Now I was nude and spanked with a plug up my bum, in utter disgrace with an audience of men, women and my own baby sister to witness my humiliation.

By the time Morris was finished with me I was dizzy and faint, hardly able to stand up as Harmony ordered me across her lap. I got it anyway, and again, from Annabelle, and from Mr Enos, from Sophie and from Mr Judd, until they'd all begun to blend into one and it seemed as if my smacked bottom was the centre of my whole world. Some took me further than others – Penny, squirting jelly all over my burning cheeks and rubbing it in before she began to spank me; Mr Spottiswood, who retrieved my knickers and stuffed them up my cunt; Mr Protheroe, who extracted the plug from my anus and let everyone have a good stare up my gaping, slippery bumhole before putting it back in; Toy, who transferred my panties from my cunt to my mouth and stuck a second plug up me instead, for a brief fucking, before it was once more extracted. She was second last, and left me spread-eagled on the floor, almost out of my senses, and yet I knew who was left.

'One last time, Pippa,' Morris announced, 'but rather a special one, I suspect. Come along, Jemima, time to spank your big sister.'

I wasn't even sure where Jemima was, but I heard her voice.

'Should I, do you think?'

'Of course,' Morris answered.

'She spanked you, didn't she?' Melody put in.

'I know, but . . . are you OK, Pip?'

She sounded worried, and no surprise. I must have looked a sight, with my naked body slick with sweat and my face wet with tears, my bum like a shiny red cherry from spanking and jelly. Forcing myself to roll over, I spat my panties out and nodded, my vision swimming slowly into focus. She was standing up in front of Hudson Staebler. Her panties were around her ankles, her school blouse was open to show her tits, and he had a full erection sticking up from his fly.

'I . . . I suppose I'd better do it then,' she said.

I pulled myself up to my knees, waiting as she came across and took her place on the spanking chair, as breezy and fresh as ever, smiling as she patted her lap for me to come across. She was going to spank me, my own baby sister, and if I thought I'd had emotion slapped out of me, I was wrong. A huge bubble of shame had begun to grow in my throat as I crawled close, and as my belly pressed to her bare legs and I lifted my bottom I was thinking of how she'd always followed my lead, how she'd always looked up to me, how she'd always copied me. Now I was over her knee in the nude, and she was about to copy me one more time, by smacking my bare bottom in front of an audience, just as I'd smacked hers. She giggled as her hand settled across my cheeks.

'Can I, Pip?' she asked.

'Yes,' I managed.

'Yes what?' she replied.

'Yes you may ... you can spank me.'

'No, Pippa, I want the magic word.'

I heard Morris chuckle.

'Yes, please!' I answered. 'Please spank me, Jemima.'

'No, Pippa,' she said again. 'I want you to say it properly. How about "please spank my naughty bottom, Jemima"?'

I looked up, to glare at Hudson Staebler, who'd obviously been coaching her. He smiled and waggled his erection at me.

'Come on,' Jemima urged. 'Say it.'

'OK, if I have to ... please ... please spank my naughty bottom, Jemima, you little cow.'

'Hey! That's no way to speak to me when you're over my knee.'

She'd planted a single slap on my bottom as she spoke, but that meant everything. It was done, my bottom smacked by my little sister, and as I spoke again I could barely get the words out for the sulky, resentful feelings inside me.

'Please, Jem, just do it if you're going to.'

'No. I want you to say it properly, and just for calling me a cow you have to say . . . to say "please, Jemima, I want my naughty bottom spanked, and . . . and I think big sisters ought to be spanked by little sisters, a lot".'

'Jem, please, I already feel utterly humiliated!'

'Just say it, Pip. Oh, and apologise for how you did me.'

'Jem . . .'

'Just say it.'

She had that stubborn tone in her voice, and I knew she'd hold me over her lap all evening if I didn't give in.

'OK,' I told her, my voice cracking to a sob as I spoke. 'I . . . I'm sorry I spanked you in a temper, and . . . and I think big sisters ought to be spanked by their little sisters . . . especially me, so please, Jemima, spank my naughty bottom. OK?'

'That's better,' she said, and began to spank me.

It wasn't hard, but I was over my little sister's knee, my bare bottom flaunted to the world with a big fat plug in my anus and my cunt dripping juice down my legs. Before she'd even got to work properly I was fighting an awful desire just to spread my legs apart and rub pussy off on her thigh, and as the smacks got harder and each one started to jam the plug in up my bumhole I knew I couldn't hold it back any more.

'Sorry, Jem, I have to,' I gasped. 'I know I'm a slut, but I have to . . .'

I broke off, my thighs coming wide, around her leg.

'Pippa!'

A great wave of shame hit me at the sound of her voice, but it was too late. I was rubbing myself on her leg, my cunt splayed on my own sister's bare flesh, the plug pumping in my bumhole to my frantic bucking, and the spanks had only stopped for a moment.

'You bad girl!' she laughed. 'You bad, bad, bad girl, Pippa!'

Again her voice filled me with shame, but she was spanking me, and hard, raining smacks on my bottom as I rubbed myself towards an orgasm of orgasms, and all the while calling me a bad girl and saying my name over and over again. She was right. I was bad, a filthy little tart, and she was right about the spanking too, because I did need my naughty bottom smacked, and by her, because there could be nothing quite so perfectly humiliating for a girl as taking a spanking from her baby sister.

I was screaming as I came, and bucking my bottom up and down on her leg in the most filthy, lewd display possible, with everything showing and no doubt at all that I'd made myself come deliberately, masturbating on Jemima's leg like the dirty, debauched little tart I am. Not even the clapping and cheers from the audience penetrated my senses until I was nearly finished, and that only for an instant before my vision turned red and the whole room seemed to cave in around me.

The next hour or so passed in a blur. I'd only been out for a few seconds, but I had everybody crowding around me trying to help or giving advice. Soon I was propped up on the sofa with a glass of brandy, cuddled up to Penny with a ring of people standing around me. With the spankings over, the men were doing their best to persuade the girls to go upstairs, generally successfully.

I'd seen Sophie lead Mr Enos from the room by his hand, which seemed a most bizarre choice, and Toy had gone with Mr Mulligan, presumably for a bit of rough sex. Helen hadn't even been allowed the privacy of a bedroom, and was down on her knees with her still-flushed bottom stuck out behind, sucking Mr Montague's cock. Jemima was close by, talking to Hudson Staebler and with her blouse done up again, although at some point she'd lost her knickers. Morris was with me too, and I had to know if I'd really been tricked.

'Did you cheat?'

'Yes,' he admitted, 'of course, but please don't think I am insulting your intelligence. The idea was to give you an excuse to spank your sister, which she undoubtedly deserved. I'm not sure I've ever met such a brat. Lovely girl, of course, but an utter brat.'

I shrugged, unable to deny what he was saying. He gave a wry grin. I stood up and went over to the nearest of several mirrors, turning to admire the state of my bottom. Even sitting on the sofa I'd felt tender, and it was no surprise. My cheeks were both rich red, with bruising in places, and it was going to be a while before I could sit down comfortably.

The plug was still in up my bottom, which looked and felt extremely rude. I was giggling to myself as I turned away, and wondering what I should do with the rest of the evening. It felt good to be in the nude, and I remembered the snout and tail in my bag, which I was sure would add a certain something.

Penny helped me put them on, transforming me into a skinny little pig, with my upturned snout and the curly pink tail bobbing over my smacked cheeks. Everyone seemed to like it, and I soon found myself getting attention from the men, one of whom, I knew, was going to take me upstairs. Mr Spottiswood asked first, and I turned him down, but he wouldn't go away, and so when Lucius Todmorden asked, I accepted.

He took my hand and led me from the room, he fully dressed in dinner jacket and black tie, me stark naked save for my snout and tail with the plug showing between my wiggling bum cheeks as I walked. I'd already decided to let him have me, and the way he liked best. In one of Morris's bedrooms I was made to kneel on all-fours and suck his cock while he admired my rear view in one of the mirrors.

When he was hard his cock went up me for my second ever fucking, again on all-fours and in front of the mirror so I could watch as I was penetrated, as my bottom squashed to the thrusts of his belly, as my tits jiggled and bounced beneath me. I looked good, a little fucked pig taking her gentleman from the rear, but I kept my hands firmly off pussy, because I knew full well that he wasn't finished with me.

Soon he'd begun to move the plug in my bottom and ask me how it felt. I said it was nice and that he could put his cock in if he liked, and that was that, seduced to sodomy in two sentences – but then I am a little tart. He withdrew and pulled the plug out, leaving my anus agape, had me suck my own juice from his cock for good measure, and buggered me.

I was creamy and well stretched by the plug, my bumhole giving easily to the pressure, and for the second time in my life I had a man's cock in my rectum. As he began wedging himself deep inside me I was thinking that it was something I could get used to, especially if it was done after a good spanking. Soon I'd slipped my hand back, masturbating over both the feel of his cock as it worked in my bum and the thought of being spanked and sodomised.

'Good idea,' he grunted as I began to masturbate. 'You make yourself come.'

My fingers were already busy, and I just nodded, enjoying the feel of his cock pumping in my bumhole as I snatched at pussy and let my mind run on the joy of a good buggering. I thought of how rude I looked in the mirror, with my little round pig's bum stuck in the air and his cock up my bottom hole. I thought of the first time, with my head down the toilet as Clive spunked up in my rectum. I thought of the men I'd let inside me in the future, and how I'd get them to spank me and then bugger me, and worse.

There was worse, something else I wanted to do too, had to do, one more filthy detail the boys had fixed in my head. He was deep in me, pumping towards orgasm in my now aching bumhole, faster and faster, and as my pleasure rose my embarrassment for what I wanted gave way to need, the words finally tumbling from my lips.

'Not up my bum, Lucius . . . not up my bum. Do it in my mouth . . . spunk in my mouth, Lucius . . . I want to suck your dirty cock! Please!'

'Never refuse a lady,' he grunted, and pulled out.

Even as I said it I hadn't known if I could really do it, but now it was too late, his cock pushing at my face as I scrambled around on the bed. My mouth came wide, in it went and I was doing it, my head filling with the taste of my own bottom as I snatched and slapped my dirty, greedy little cunt, with jelly and froth blowing from my open bumhole as my muscles went into contraction.

We came together, his spunk filling my mouth and exploding from around my lips as my own orgasm tore through me, and running thick and sticky down over my tits as he pulled out to sit me up and finish off in my face. I was still coming, my mouth wide to show off the pool of spunk on my tongue, my breasts filthy with mess as I rubbed it over them, my face spattered with blobs and streamers of sticky white, over my cheeks and in my eyes, hanging from my chin and my piggy snout too. At the very end he stuck his cock back in my mouth and I took it as deep as I could, still tasting myself as my orgasm gradually faded away.

I was in the most appalling state, and as soon as I could I ran for the loo, still blowing bubbles out of my bumhole. The bathroom was empty, luckily, and I was soon towelling myself after a shower as Lucius washed his penis. He put it away before he spoke.

'May I ask,' he enquired. 'If that was your first time? In your bottom, I mean.'

'No, not the first,' I told him, and I saw his face fall ever so slightly. 'I would have let you, I think, but no. Clive Carew got there first.'

'Clive?' he asked, in open astonishment.

I managed a shame-faced grin.

'And, um . . .,' he continued. 'May I enquire if young Clive was the first employee of Montague, Montague, Todmorden and Montague to whom you gave the privilege of your body.'

'Yes,' I answered, an instant before the implications of what he was saying sank in. 'You . . . you know about the bet, don't you? About Mark James keeping a book on who'd have me first?'

'As do you, evidently,' Lucius replied. 'Mark knows that I am no prude, although that is all he knows, and told me himself in the hope of making a profit, which he has now done.'

'He has?'

'So it seems, as I had placed an *ante-post* bet on myself and hedged a trifle on old Montague. I knew you liked being spanked, you see, and so presumed to suppose either he or I might have the privilege and so be first. I was wrong, at least as regards being first, but no matter. After the privilege of your exquisite bottom, the loss is small, even though you were not virgin.'

I smiled, trying to put a brave face on it. The bet would now be over, and I would come away with nothing, unless a sore bumhole counted. I'd lost my virginity and been sodomised by the office fat boy, sucked cock for probably the filthiest old pervert in London, prostituted myself in all but name, been spanked, pissed on, wanked over and humiliated in a hundred ways, and all for nothing.

At least I could report to AJ that Trilby was the one who'd told Morris what had happened at the Pumps. I'd recognised her while I was over her knee, from her voice and because she'd used almost exactly the same words to me when she stuck the second butt plug up as when she'd fucked me with her strap-on. It had only really sunk in later, but there was no doubt at all, Trilby and Toy were one and the same. She'd been a bitch to me too, so I had no regrets, and she'd only get what I had anyway, more or less.

Nothing too awful had happened to Jemima, if you didn't count the spanking I'd given her, which was also good. She'd latched onto Hudson Staebler from the first, and stayed with him all evening. He'd had her, including making her suck his cock in front of everybody, but he was the only one. He was also American and only in the UK on a visit, so there weren't even going to be any long-term repercussions.

There was a lot of embarrassment between us for what we'd done together, but that didn't last long, and I knew that it was more than likely that I'd be spanking her again, and that she would be spanking me. Otherwise, it was impossible to deny that I'd enjoyed the party, although what I'd done raised more questions about my sexuality than it solved. Only the bet was an unmitigated disaster, and I was kicking myself for letting Lucius Todmorden know about Clive. At least that meant there would be no more playing dirty with Mr Prufrock, although even that came with a trace of regret.

I'd let Mr Montague spank me at some time in the early hours of Sunday morning when the party was beginning to wind down, and on Monday he asked if I'd like to work with him for a while. I accepted, and sent a text to Clive asking him to take me out to lunch at Champagne Charlie's, as there was no point in hiding what we'd been up to any more. They all knew, because I'd been getting funny looks all morning, adding to my ill-feeling as I entered the wine bar. Clive was already there, with a bottle of one of their best champagnes in an ice bucket. He was grinning.

'What are you so cheerful about?' I asked.

In answer he took a slim piece of paper out of his jacket pocket and laid it on the table in front of me. It was a cheque, for a quite astonishing amount of money, and made out to me.

'I trust you will forgive me,' he said, 'but in the circumstances I felt it wise to hedge our bets a little by putting a small sum on myself. We have done rather well, what with this morning's odds on the post at 200–1, doubled for your generosity with your delightful derrière.'

nexus

The leading publisher of fetish and adult fiction

TELL US WHAT YOU THINK!

Readers' ideas and opinions matter to us so please take a few minutes to fill in the questionnaire below.

1. Sex: Are you male ☐ female ☐ a couple ☐?

2. Age: Under 21 ☐ 21–30 ☐ 31–40 ☐ 41–50 ☐ 51–60 ☐ over 60 ☐

3. Where do you buy your Nexus books from?

☐ A chain book shop. If so, which one(s)?

_____

☐ An independent book shop. If so, which one(s)?

_____

☐ A used book shop/charity shop
☐ Online book store. If so, which one(s)?

_____

4. How did you find out about Nexus books?

☐ Browsing in a book shop
☐ A review in a magazine
☐ Online
☐ Recommendation
☐ Other _____

5. In terms of settings, which do you prefer? (Tick as many as you like.)

☐ Down to earth and as realistic as possible
☐ Historical settings. If so, which period do you prefer?

_____

☐ Fantasy settings – barbarian worlds
☐ Completely escapist/surreal fantasy
☐ Institutional or secret academy

- ☐ Futuristic/sci fi
- ☐ Escapist but still believable
- ☐ Any settings you dislike?

_____

- ☐ Where would you like to see an adult novel set?

_____

6. In terms of storylines, would you prefer:

- ☐ Simple stories that concentrate on adult interests?
- ☐ More plot and character-driven stories with less explicit adult activity?
- ☐ We value your ideas, so give us your opinion of this book:

_____

_____

_____

7. In terms of your adult interests, what do you like to read about? (Tick as many as you like.)

- ☐ Traditional corporal punishment (CP)
- ☐ Modern corporal punishment
- ☐ Spanking
- ☐ Restraint/bondage
- ☐ Rope bondage
- ☐ Latex/rubber
- ☐ Leather
- ☐ Female domination and male submission
- ☐ Female domination and female submission
- ☐ Male domination and female submission
- ☐ Willing captivity
- ☐ Uniforms
- ☐ Lingerie/underwear/hosiery/footwear (boots and high heels)
- ☐ Sex rituals
- ☐ Vanilla sex
- ☐ Swinging
- ☐ Cross-dressing/TV
- ☐ Enforced feminisation

☐ Others – tell us what you don't see enough of in adult fiction:

_____

_____

_____

8. Would you prefer books with a more specialised approach to your interests, i.e. a novel specifically about uniforms? If so, which subject(s) would you like to read a Nexus novel about?

_____

_____

_____

9. Would you like to read true stories in Nexus books? For instance, the true story of a submissive woman, or a male slave? Tell us which true revelations you would most like to read about:

_____

_____

_____

10. What do you like best about Nexus books?

_____

_____

11. What do you like least about Nexus books?

_____

_____

12. Which are your favourite titles?

_____

_____

13. Who are your favourite authors?

_____

_____

14. Which covers do you prefer? Those featuring:
(Tick as many as you like.)

- ☐ Fetish outfits
- ☐ More nudity
- ☐ Two models
- ☐ Unusual models or settings
- ☐ Classic erotic photography
- ☐ More contemporary images and poses
- ☐ A blank/non-erotic cover
- ☐ What would your ideal cover look like?

_____

15. Describe your ideal Nexus novel in the space provided:

_____

_____

_____

_____

16. Which celebrity would feature in one of your Nexus-style fantasies? We'll post the best suggestions on our website – anonymously!

_____

THANKS FOR YOUR TIME

Now simply write the title of this book in the space below and cut out the questionnaire pages. Post to: Nexus, Marketing Dept., Thames Wharf Studios, Rainville Rd, London W6 9HA

Book title: _____

NEXUS NEW BOOKS

To be published in January 2008

BLUSHING AT BOTH ENDS
Philip Kemp

Funny, full of surprises and always arousing, this is a brilliant collection of stories about innocent young women drawn into scenarios that result in the sensual pleasures of spanking. It features girls who feel compelled to manipulate and engineer situations in which older authority figures punish them, over their laps, desks, or chairs.

£6.99   ISBN 978 0 352 34107 5

NEXUS CONFESSIONS: VOLUME 2
Various

Swinging, dogging, group sex, cross-dressing, spanking, female domination, corporal punishment, and extreme fetishes . . . Nexus Confessions explores the length and breadth of erotic obsession, real experience and sexual fantasy. This is an encyclopaedic collection of the bizarre, the extreme and the utterly inappropriate – the daring and shocking experiences of ordinary men and women driven by their extraordinary desires. Collected by the world's leading publisher of fetish fiction, this is the second in a series of six volumes of true stories and shameful confessions, never before told or published.

£6.99   ISBN 978 0 352 34103 7

If you would like more information about Nexus titles, please visit our website at www.nexus-books.com, or send a large stamped addressed envelope to:
Nexus, Thames Wharf Studios,
Rainville Road, London W6 9HA

NEXUS BOOKLIST

Information is correct at time of printing. To avoid disappointment, check availability before ordering. Go to www.nexus-books.com.

All books are priced at £6.99 unless another price is given.

NEXUS

☐ ABANDONED ALICE	Adriana Arden	ISBN 978 0 352 33969 0
☐ ALICE IN CHAINS	Adriana Arden	ISBN 978 0 352 33908 9
☐ AQUA DOMINATION	William Doughty	ISBN 978 0 352 34020 7
☐ THE ART OF CORRECTION	Tara Black	ISBN 978 0 352 33895 2
☐ THE ART OF SURRENDER	Madeline Bastinado	ISBN 978 0 352 34013 9
☐ BEASTLY BEHAVIOUR	Aishling Morgan	ISBN 978 0 352 34095 5
☐ BEHIND THE CURTAIN	Primula Bond	ISBN 978 0 352 34111 2
☐ BEING A GIRL	Chloë Thurlow	ISBN 978 0 352 34139 6
☐ BELINDA BARES UP	Yolanda Celbridge	ISBN 978 0 352 33926 3
☐ BIDDING TO SIN	Rosita Varón	ISBN 978 0 352 34063 4
☐ THE BOOK OF PUNISHMENT	Cat Scarlett	ISBN 978 0 352 33975 1
☐ BRUSH STROKES	Penny Birch	ISBN 978 0 352 34072 6
☐ BUTTER WOULDN'T MELT	Penny Birch	ISBN 978 0 352 34120 4
☐ CALLED TO THE WILD	Angel Blake	ISBN 978 0 352 34067 2
☐ CAPTIVES OF CHEYNER CLOSE	Adriana Arden	ISBN 978 0 352 34028 3
☐ CARNAL POSSESSION	Yvonne Strickland	ISBN 978 0 352 34062 7
☐ CITY MAID	Amelia Evangeline	ISBN 978 0 352 34096 2
☐ COLLEGE GIRLS	Cat Scarlett	ISBN 978 0 352 33942 3
☐ CONCEIT AND CONSEQUENCE	Aishling Morgan	ISBN 978 0 352 33965 2
☐ CORRECTIVE THERAPY	Jacqueline Masterson	ISBN 978 0 352 33917 1
☐ CORRUPTION	Virginia Crowley	ISBN 978 0 352 34073 3
☐ CRUEL SHADOW	Aishling Morgan	ISBN 978 0 352 33886 0
☐ DARK MISCHIEF	Lady Alice McCloud	ISBN 978 0 352 33998 0

- - - - - - ✂ -

Please send me the books I have ticked above.

Name   ....

Address   ....

               ....

               ....

               .... Post code ....

Send to: **Virgin Books Cash Sales, Thames Wharf Studios, Rainville Road, London W6 9HA**

US customers: for prices and details of how to order books for delivery by mail, call 888-330-8477.

Please enclose a cheque or postal order, made payable to **Nexus Books Ltd**, to the value of the books you have ordered plus postage and packing costs as follows:

UK and BFPO – £1.00 for the first book, 50p for each subsequent book.

Overseas (including Republic of Ireland) – £2.00 for the first book, £1.00 for each subsequent book.

If you would prefer to pay by VISA, ACCESS/MASTERCARD, AMEX, DINERS CLUB or SWITCH, please write your card number and expiry date here:

....

Please allow up to 28 days for delivery.

Signature ....

Our privacy policy

We will not disclose information you supply us to any other parties. We will not disclose any information which identifies you personally to any person without your express consent.

From time to time we may send out information about Nexus books and special offers. Please tick here if you do *not* wish to receive Nexus information.   ☐

- - - - - - ✂ -